Four

JOHN GLASS

First published in Great Britain in 2019

Instant Apostle
The Barn
1 Watford House Lane
Watford
Herts
WD17 1BJ

'A fantastic novel with wonderful characters you will love, but, more importantly, a clear reminder of the unstoppable power of the Word of God.'
Gavin Calver, Director of Mission, Evangelical Alliance; Chair, Spring Harvest

'A moving story and gripping read that highlights the awful atrocity of human trafficking in our generation.'
Ben Cooley, CEO, Hope for Justice

British Library Cataloguing-in-Publication Data

A catalogue record for this book is available from the British Library.

This book and all other Instant Apostle books are available from Instant Apostle:

Website: www.instantapostle.com

E-mail: info@instantapostle.com

ISBN 978-1-912726-06-6

Printed in Great Britain.

Dedicated to

Ben Cooley, founder of Hopeforjustice.org

Andy and Zoe Clark-Coates, founders of sayinggoodbye.org

6th May 1996
Cotswolds

The man slid back the covers, swung his legs out of bed and slowly drew himself into a standing position. Slipping his feet into his slippers, he turned to glance at the clock on his bedside table. It registered a fraction past 7.30am.

Having showered and shaved, he went downstairs and switched on the machine and prepared the first coffee of the day – inwardly warming to the sound of the grinding of the beans followed by the welcoming sight of the stream of dark brown liquid that made its way into the long glass he had placed in front of it.

He was just about to reach for the cupboard to retrieve the bottle of hazelnut flavouring that he always added, when the telephone rang. Moving across to retrieve the handset from its vertical cradle on the kitchen wall, he addressed the mouthpiece with, 'Hello, Albert here.'

He instantly recognised the voice at the other end as his godson, Phillip.

'Hi, Uncle! I'm just phoning to check if it's still OK to drop in at around eleven.'

Albert's wife had died just over a year before. They had not had children, and the number of people that had called him 'Uncle' over the years had grown – though none of them were biologically related to him. He thought the world of them all, but Phillip and his wife, Penny, were particularly special. He had lost count of the times he had asked them to just call him Albert, but it made no difference. People always smiled when he gave the reason that it 'made him sound old'; he was, after all, seventy-four. He assumed it was a respect thing.

Annexed to Phillip and Penny's property in a village five miles from Cumbernauld was a small flat. They knew their favourite 'uncle' was incredibly fit for his age, but had noticed that not only was he struggling with maintaining the house and garden where he currently lived, but was also becoming increasingly forgetful.

Albert's doctor had said that there was nothing much to worry about, as there were no signs of any debilitating disease such as dementia.

'When people walk into a room,' he had said, 'and wonder why they have come in, that's nothing to worry about. When folk forget where they put their car keys, they need not be overly concerned about that either. However,' the doctor had continued, 'when people leave their keys in the fridge and then try to open their car door with a frozen yoghurt …'

Everybody had laughed in unison and the GP had ended the conversation by saying, 'And I can assure you, Mr Porter, you are nowhere near anything like that condition, believe me.'

Phillip and Penny had asked Albert and his wife on several occasions to move up and live in the flat, but they had always politely declined. However, now that Annie had passed away, Albert had taken their offer more seriously. So his house had been put on the market and a sale had been agreed. The new people were moving in in just ten days' time.

'If eleven is still OK,' continued Phillip, 'we can get stuck into the packing. I know the removers will box most of your stuff but, knowing you, there will be some things that you will want to handle yourself.'

'Eleven will be great. I can't believe you have come 300 miles just to help me sort out my things.'

'It's not a problem, Uncle Albert, I assure you. I have a business appointment in Oxford tomorrow, and spending some time with you today means I will really only have about fifty miles or so to travel after we have finished.'

Phillip was right. All the heavy lifting, and most of the packing, was taken out of Albert's hands, but the issue was not what would be going with him; it was sorting out all the things that he had decided not to take.

Annie had been a hoarder – not in the obsessive sense of those people you see on TV who can't throw anything away – but to the point that she would keep birthday cards and letters going back years. Albert was totally the opposite but, even so, there would be clothes and other odds and ends that would need to go to the charity shop. Some of the furniture that he would not be taking had been given to a young couple he knew, and the rest had been passed on to a family of asylum seekers who he had bumped into recently when he had been out shopping. The biggest problem that he and Phillip would have to sort out was all the books he had accumulated throughout his long ministry. People didn't buy books like they used to. They simply downloaded them. He wished he could have done that kind of thing when he was young. It would certainly have saved a lot of space.

Albert normally read the morning paper as soon as the breakfast dishes had been cleared away. He was a creature of habit, though today he was a little behind schedule. But there was still an hour or so before his visitor was due to arrive.

He read right through until he got to the sports pages and learned that the FA had announced that Glenn Hoddle, the current Chelsea manager, was going to succeed Terry Venables as manager of England after next month's European Championships, which England would be hosting for the very first time.

Phillip always arrived on time. You could set your watch by him and, true to form, the bell rang just a minute or so after eleven.

'Hello, Uncle Albert,' Phillip said, as he gave him a hug and followed him down the hall.

'I've got the kettle on ready, Phil. Just go through to the kitchen and we'll have a cup of tea and a couple of your favourite biscuits before we get going.'

Phillip sat down as Albert poured the tea into the pot via a tea strainer. 'Could never get used to those teabags. Annie and I never liked them,' he said, as he pushed a plate of dark chocolate digestives towards his guest.

'How have you been, Uncle?' asked Phillip, as he accepted the proffered cup.

'Right as rain, though I don't know what I would have done without you coming today. It's not just the sorting out down here.

The biggest problem will be the loft. Obviously that will have to be cleared before the new people move in.'

By four in the afternoon the lion's share of the work had been finished. Phillip had ensured that Albert's contribution had been limited to standing next to him as he had pulled the books from the shelves, indicating which should be kept, given away or discarded.

At about one o'clock Phillip had encouraged his uncle to sort out a light lunch while he set about moving everything from the loft into the garage. Most of the things he had brought down were of no monetary value, and he thought that some of the stuff must even have been there since the days of the previous owner.

'Is it alright if I have a quick shower before I get on my way, Uncle? Oh, and by the way, I phoned one of my friends while I was sorting things out. He lives just a few miles away and has assured me that he will be more than happy to drop round in a couple of days and empty what's left in the garage and take it to the skip if you want him to. He promises to phone well in advance to let you know when he's coming. That's of course if you decide to contact him.'

'That's very thoughtful of you, Phil. Of course you can have a shower. You'll find a clean towel in the airing cupboard.'

'Oh, Uncle, there is just one thing. I found something that you need to look at and decide what you want to do with it. Just hang on a minute. I've left it at the bottom of the stairs.'

A couple of moments later Phillip returned with a small cardboard box and, removing the lid, revealed four heavily worn leather books.

Phillip noticed Albert's eyes slightly moisten as he glanced over the contents.

'You know, I haven't seen these for ages. I really didn't know where they had got to. Annie must have put them in there nearly ten years ago, knowing how important they were to me. She never mentioned that she had kept them or, if she did, I must have forgotten. They are the Bibles, Phil, that have been with me throughout my entire ministry.'

Reaching for the most worn of them, and slowly lifting it from the box as something precious and of great value, he added, 'I got this one for my birthday. My parents gave it to me when I was just a boy. This next one …' he continued, laying the first aside and selecting another, 'was given to me by a youth group in the church on the occasion of my going off to theological college. The rest were bought as each of the previous ones wore out.' Albert paused reflectively for a moment and then, sweeping his hand over them as if to include them all collectively in his next comment, said, 'It's hard to believe, but I suppose they must cover a period of nearly seventy years between the lot of them. My current one is getting a bit worn too, but I have no doubt it will see me out.'

Albert stood at the front door and waved as Phillip set off for Oxford.

The first thing he did on returning to his favourite chair was to put the box on his knee and slowly examine each of the Bibles again in turn. Selecting one of them, he caressed the leather lovingly and, lifting another, riffled with his thumb along the Bible's edge, as if by doing so he was releasing a myriad of memories from their almost translucent pages.

But what was he going to do with them? They were not in any condition to be passed on as an heirloom and, if he offered them to a charity shop, they would be unlikely to be even taken into stock. The thought of disposing of them in one of his wheelie bins was unthinkable. It would, he thought, be like burying old friends in bin liners. Putting the lid back on the box, he resolved to think about it over the next day or two. Even though Phillip had done all the physical work, the day had left him feeling tired and he decided that once he had watched the news he would probably get an early night.

Over the years Albert had come to the conclusion that some of the best solutions to things that he had been thinking about on the previous day came in those few brief early morning moments between exiting sleep and becoming fully awake. As he awoke, he knew precisely what he would do with the Bibles.

When he had finished his breakfast, and had washed and dried the few dishes that he had used, Albert lifted the Bibles from the box and placed them in a shopping bag. Closing the front door, he opened the door of his dark blue Renault Clio and placed them on the passenger seat before going around to the other side, climbing in and setting off for town.

Half an hour later he pulled into Kingsditch trading estate on the outskirts of Cheltenham. He pulled the shopping bag towards him, exited the car and set off in the direction of a department store that he knew had a coffee shop on the first floor. He used the escalator, turned left into the coffee shop and secured a seat by placing his bag on it, as he knew he would not be able to carry both the bag and a tray at the same time. He returned to his seat with a pot of tea and a toasted teacake. Fifteen minutes later he placed the cup, teapot and plate back on the tray. Whenever a friend had asked him why he did that, his answer was always the same, 'To save the waitress.'

The next thing he did was to reach down into the bag for one of the Bibles. Albert gently laid it on the seat he had just vacated and, as the escalator only ascended, took the stairs down to the ground floor. Albert repeated the exercise in two other locations around Cheltenham until he had just one Bible left.

As it was such a nice day, he decided to take a run out to one of his favourite villages before returning home. True, it was the best part of twenty-five miles away, but it was there he had decided that the final item would be left.

There were two car parks: one at each end of Broadway High Street. Finding the first full, Albert parked at the second. He then made his way to his last location. Though the bag was a lot lighter than it had been when he had set out, all the walking had made him weary, so he was happy to select one of the two benches that faced the simple memorial that the locals called the Broadway cross. There was something appropriate, he thought, about bringing a Bible to a cross. He reached into the bag for the last time and, as his hand wrapped around it, paused momentarily before lifting it out. The thought had crossed his mind that he might be committing some minor public offence by leaving – or some might even say discarding – his property in a public place. He smiled at the very idea. He was hardly dropping litter, and one book on a bench fell some way short of fly-tipping. He placed the final Bible on the seat at his side, folded the carrier bag into a neat square and, putting it in his pocket, set off in the direction of his car.

As Albert retraced his steps along the High Street he cast his mind back to two things he had done that morning before he had set out. The first was to pray over the small bundle, asking God to direct the right people to each Bible. The second was to write something in the blank page at the back of each of the books. It would seem incongruous at first, even cryptic, but he was quite sure, he thought with a smile, that it would not take whoever found these Bibles too long to decipher it.

19th May 2002
Estonia

Celia thumbed down the index of her guidebook until she got to 'St Olaf's Church'.

She had been in Estonia for almost a year now. Her time at university was over and she had promised herself that before she embarked on a career, she would spend some time travelling. Convincing her parents about it had been less than easy – especially her mother – given that Celia had said she wanted to travel alone. Initially her best friend had said that she would join her, but a relationship that Lucy had recently entered into had put an abrupt end to that idea.

Her parents had only agreed when their daughter had promised regular phone calls and, when that was not possible, at least a regular email or text.

Tallinn was without doubt her favourite place, with its labyrinth of medieval cobbled streets and open squares around which old men would sit on stone seats and pass the time with their friends in the shade of the tall buildings. That was in the summer, and summer was great, but at that time of year the town had to be shared with the droves of tourists, many of whom were regularly disgorged from the cruise ships that docked alongside one another in the port.

She knew that it was silly to resent the tourists, as she was one herself – though deep down she considered herself in a different category to those who dropped by just for the day or perhaps even a week. She was surprised by how proprietorial she had become about this place, as if in some way it was 'hers'. She really had become captivated by it.

The weather was unpredictable at this time of year but it was certainly warm enough to sit at one of the tables that were always to be found outside the cafés and restaurants, and this one, in what the locals called Raekoja Plats, was among her favourites. She ordered a cappuccino and a pastry. It was 11am and she had had hardly any breakfast, so this mid-morning indulgence created not the slightest crisis of conscience for her.

She moved her guide book to one side to make space as the waiter delivered her drink, and continued to read:

> St Olaf's church, dedicated to the eponymous St Olaf (995–1030), was built in the twelfth century and then rebuilt in the fourteenth. Before Denmark conquered Tallinn in 1219, it is believed to have been the centre for Tallinn's Scandinavian community ...

'It's got an amazing tower, you know ...'

Startled, Celia looked across to the next table, where a man she guessed to be around her own age, twenty-three, was sitting.

'Excuse me, what did you say?' Celia asked.

'I just said it has got an amazing tower.'

'What has?'

'The church – you were reading out loud.'

'I was what?'

Celia knew that she sometimes did read out loud, and had done so since she was a child, especially if she was concentrating. She was embarrassed to the point of mortification.

'I'm sorry. I didn't mean to offend you,' the man offered, though it was clear from the twinkle in his brown eyes that he was not sorry at all.

'My name is Jack, Jack Tr ...'

'I'm not the least bit interested in who you are,' Celia retorted. 'Do you mind just leaving me alone?'

She was about to flounce off – her coffee and croissant untouched – when he took hold of her elbow in an attempt to apologise further.

'Do you mind? Please take your hands ...' she began.

Then Celia stopped as quickly as she had started, took a deep breath, and after a pause said, 'Look, I'm sorry. It really was silly of me. The thing is that when I'm concentrating on something I sometimes do that – read out loud, I mean – I've done so since I was little. I really shouldn't have reacted like that. Sorry … what was your name again?'

'It's Jack, Jack Troughton, and it's my fault entirely. It was wrong of me to have been so intrusive. It's just that I know a bit about the building that you are interested in and …'

'It's OK, Jack. Oh, and my name's Celia,' she said, as she extended her hand. 'Do you live here or are you just visiting, like me?'

'Yes and no. My father is an importer of shipping-related equipment and I work for him. We are based here at the moment but the family moves around quite a lot. He's got contacts in various parts of the world but mostly they are in Europe. How about you?'

'I'm on a gap year, but it's turning out to be a little longer than that, I'm afraid.'

'Why afraid?'

'Well, when I finished uni I naïvely thought I would just walk into a job – at least a job that paralleled with what I had studied – but it didn't turn out like that. I did bits and pieces for a few months, and right now I am taking some time out, getting to know the country better. I love it out here.'

Unbeknown to Celia, Jack sensed an opportunity. He realised he was becoming quite attracted to this beautiful fair-haired woman with her feisty personality. The past few months had been hectic as he and his father had been involved in the restructuring of the business. There had been very little time to relax, let alone to develop relationships. Something told him he did not want to lose either the initiative or the momentum in this conversation.

'I'll tell you what, why don't you let me show you around the church? The view from the top of the tower is amazing. You certainly don't want to miss it while you are here.'

'But it's Sunday, won't there be a service on?' asked Celia.

'Actually, there are two services on during the morning. The first is traditional in style and attracts mainly older people. Then, after that, there is a short break and they have a second, far larger service.

The style is far more contemporary and attracts mostly younger people.'

'So why would we want to go now if the place is full?'

'Don't worry, it'll be fine,' said Jack. 'You'll understand when you get there.'

Celia agreed and they began to wend their way through the picturesque town. Vendors capitalised on the long history of Tallinn by selling street food that the tourists were assured was based on medieval recipes – even going so far as to dress in the clothes that matched their wares. It created a great atmosphere.

'You seem to know quite a lot about the church,' said Celia. 'What can you tell me that might not be in the guidebook?'

'Well, originally it was Catholic in tradition, but after the Reformation became Lutheran and it remained that way for hundreds of years. Eventually, in 1950, it became a Baptist church. That might be in your guidebook, though. However, one thing that I am pretty sure will not be is that the Soviet KGB used the spire as a radio mast and surveillance point between 1944 and 1991.'

'You're joking,' said Celia. 'Why on earth would the church put up with that?'

'They wouldn't have had a choice, I suppose. There would be nothing that they could do about it. Remember, the Soviet regime was atheist. They would be looking for any excuse that was offered to them to shut the place down and expel the congregation.'

By the time they reached St Olaf's, the second service had already ended and they watched as the congregation spilled out into the streets to go home for lunch or stop by the street cafés and blend in with the tourists.

When Celia climbed the few steps from the road into the entrance, she quickly realised why, even if a service had been going on, they could not have interrupted it. To their immediate left inside the sparse interior of the hall were steps to the tower, which were entirely separate to the sanctuary area where the congregation would have been.

Jack paid their entrance fee to the tower and, ushering Celia in front of him, they began the slow climb up the stone spiral staircase.

'I perhaps should have mentioned a couple of things,' said Jack as they began their ascent. 'It's not only a long way up but it's also single file – well, in theory, anyway. It obviously wasn't built for the tourist trade but for individuals making their way up and down. These days it's not just a continuous line of people climbing, but it's also the only route out for people coming back down, so it can be a bit of a crush. I hope you're not claustrophobic.'

Celia was about to say that she was OK when a nun three steps in front of her on the spiral staircase caught her shoe in the hem of her habit as she tried to negotiate a tight turn, and stumbled back onto the person immediately behind her. Everyone quickly regained their equilibrium, but not before Celia had tottered backwards towards Jack who, more sure-footed than the rest, halted the domino effect by catching her in his arms.

'Are you OK?' Jack asked, with genuine concern written all over his face.

'Yes, I'm absolutely fine,' Celia reassured him. 'It's all good.'

'But did you see that nun?' Jack said. 'She never even turned to apologise. Well, I suppose that's Christians for you.'

The minor collision was all over within a matter of seconds, and everyone in the line meandered upwards as before. Except for two people who, though no words had been exchanged, both knew that the smallest of sparks had just been ignited between them.

When they eventually reached the top, Celia came quickly to the conclusion that the climb had been worth every step. They stood side by side and surveyed the landscape that reached out beyond the striking ochre-red rooftops of the town.

After a few minutes of taking in the beauty of the surrounding area, they decided to commence the much easier descent towards the vestibule of the church.

Stepping out into the street, Jack suggested that as it was now lunchtime they should get something to eat. He wasn't particularly hungry but didn't want a reason to have to say goodbye to Celia any time soon.

Being 'spoilt for choice' for somewhere to eat in Tallinn was an understatement but, passing along the street, they took in the smell of fresh baking and simultaneously turned towards the café from which the inviting aroma had arisen.

'OK, so tell me a little more about yourself,' said Jack as they took two seats by the window.

'Well, I was born and brought up in a small Cotswold village a few miles outside Tewkesbury. I have a younger sister, and an older brother. What about you? Do you have any brothers or sisters, or are you an only child?'

'My parents had just me, I'm afraid,' responded Jack. 'I grew up in a loving home but I never really saw my dad as much as I would have liked to. He started the business from scratch and threw his whole life into it. My parents obviously love one another very much, but I think both my mother and I felt that the business always seemed to come first with him. It's not that he was materialistic. It was probably because his parents really struggled financially during their lives, and he just wanted to make sure that we were all well provided for and never had to have those kinds of worries.'

'Well, now that you work for him, is he still as driven a person as he was when you were small?'

'He is, but somehow in a different way. The business has gone well and we certainly don't have any money worries – though I wouldn't say that we are wealthy. I suppose you might say we're "comfortable". While I've worked alongside him I've got to know the operation inside out. I think I'm good at what I do, and I suppose I will carry on the business when he feels he is ready to retire. The problem is that I'm not sure that I really want to.'

'Has he got any inkling about how you feel about the future?' asked Celia.

'Absolutely not. I think he would be devastated if he knew. He's had a few heart scares in the last couple of years that his doctor has told him are not serious in themselves but should certainly be seen as warning signs. The thing is that he just won't slow down. He says that when he starts to do that it will be the beginning of the end for him. He's always going on about people his own age who, once they retire, are dead within a few years. The problem is that if he doesn't listen to the medical advice he's been given, he could become a casualty himself. More than once when I've expressed my concern, all he says is how much a consolation it is to him that I'll be there to take the company on when he feels ready.'

'I see,' said Celia. 'So you are worried that if you opened up, it would cause him increased stress and add to the pressure he already appears to be under?'

'Absolutely. It's about the worst thing I could possibly do, and I wouldn't entertain it for a moment. I'm just going to have to carry on as normal.'

'Excuse me, sir and madam …'

They had both been so engrossed in conversation that they had not noticed the waiter standing there with a pen hovering over a white pad upon which no order had yet been placed.

'I'm sorry,' offered Jack. 'Could you give us a couple more minutes, please?'

'Of course, sir, no problem at all. I'll come back shortly.'

Jack and Celia could not believe that, when the bill was called for, they had been in the café for almost three hours. Over the next few weeks they spent time together at every available opportunity. Jack was in no doubt that he was falling in love, for even when they were not together, Celia was rarely far from his thoughts. For Celia's part, she could not believe how far her feelings for Jack had grown.

Yet one thing made her anxious and, although part of her wanted more than anything for their relationship to flourish further, the issue would never completely leave her thoughts.

6th August 2002
7am, Estonia

'Hello, is that Mr Troughton – Mr Wesley Troughton?' the voice on the phone enquired.

'Yes, but who is this and how did you get hold of my number? Do you realise it's seven in the morning?'

'Yes, sir, I am sorry to call you at such an early hour, but I needed to contact you before you left for your office. I am phoning on behalf of Customs and Excise. We would like you to come to the dock area by 10am as we are planning to conduct an inspection on a number of shipping containers – one of which is registered to your company.'

'To my company? What's the problem?'

'We don't know if there is a problem, sir, and legally we do not need to inform you of our inspection. We have authority to open and examine cargo at our discretion. This is just a courtesy call. You do not have to attend, but we are offering you the option to be present as we open your container, in the event that you should wish to do so.'

'Very well, I will be there,' responded Wesley, 'and I'll probably have my son with me. Is this a random check or have there been some paperwork issues? We try to be as meticulous as we can and do our utmost to operate within all statutory regulations.'

'I am sure you do, sir. However, I am not at liberty to give you any more information at this point. We are simply acting on intelligence received. I do, however, look forward to seeing you at 10am. And by the way, Mr Troughton, it would be helpful if you could bring some personal identification with you so that you can be admitted to the inspection area by the port authority – together with any paperwork that you may have in respect of your expected delivery.'

Jack and his father arrived at the docks a little after 9.30am and were cleared to enter the quay area shortly afterwards. There were eight metal containers on the dockside, some of which had been originally yellow and others brown, but all of which were currently showing signs of wear and discolouration through exposure to continual movement by cranes and the ever-present salt in the atmosphere.

Already, a group of men and women, some in uniform and others in suits and mostly carrying clipboards, surrounded the area. As the two men approached, a woman officer left the group and walked towards them. Addressing the older of the two, she said, 'Are you Mr Wesley Troughton of Shoreside Engineering?'

'Yes, I am,' Wesley replied, and half turning to indicate the presence of Jack, continued, 'and this is my son who works alongside me in the company.'

'Thank you, gentlemen. Would you both please come with me?'

She led them to a small functionally built single-storey building that was a grey-beige in colour and looked only a few times the size of one of the containers that were due to be inspected. The office contained two small filing cabinets, a chair behind a desk, and two black plastic chairs in front of it. Taking up at least a half of one wall was a rectangular space, which Wesley and Jack immediately realised was a one-way window. They had hardly noticed it as they approached, but now inside, saw it maintained a clear view of the quayside on which the containers sat. The woman, in her mid-forties, wore dark grey trousers and a black T-shirt. Apart from the clipboard, the only other noticeable thing was a photo-identification card with her name on it, secured in a plastic wallet that was suspended by a ribbon around her neck.

'Good morning, gentlemen, my name is Pamela Abbott and I am the senior officer on duty today. And you ...' she said, addressing not them but the paperwork on her clipboard, '... are the principal directors of ... Shoreside Engineering, am I right?'

It appeared to be only a rhetorical question, for before Wesley or Jack could respond, she looked over to the A4 folder that Wesley carried and, holding out an arm towards them, continued, 'And is that the consignment details that you have been good enough to bring with you?'

Wesley passed the forms towards her. She took them and held them adjacent to her clipboard, checking them alongside her own documentation.

'So, what we are expecting here, then, are spare parts for cranes, is that correct?'

'Mostly,' Jack concurred, 'though there will also be eleven boxes of electrical components. They serve the computerised side of the business. Look, can't you tell us what all this is about? My father was only offered the most minimal of details on the phone.'

'Certainly, sir. We have received intelligence, a tip-off if you want to call it that, that there are likely to be irregularities in the consignment under the name of your company.' Here she paused to consult her notes and then continued, 'Consignment number BACF97747.'

Wesley moved forward to retrieve his paperwork, which the woman handed over for him to identify and, that done, agreed with her that that was indeed the reference.

'You will realise, gentlemen, that most of the data we use is computer based. We have endeavoured for some time to go paperless, but many people like to work with hard copy, even though these days it's not always entirely necessary.'

'Ms Abbott,' began Wesley Troughton, 'exactly how long is this process likely to take? I mean, are you asking us to stay around while you examine all the containers we saw as we came in?'

'Well, of course I can't say exactly, but, frankly, we won't be looking at the others at all. It's now only yours that we're interested in. In fact, we can start right away if you're ready to go.'

They followed Pamela Abbott outside and stood back as she double-checked the reference on the document against the numbers on the side of the steel structure. She motioned to some men in green overalls to begin unbolting the designated container. As soon as the two metal doors swung open, she signalled for a forklift truck to start the process of bringing out the contents piece by piece. The eleven boxes that ostensibly contained the electrical components came out first, followed by wooden crates of varying dimensions.

'I'm sure that you understand, gentlemen, that this is the easiest part. We can't rely on the labels on the crates any more that we can take at face value the inventory listed in your documents. Every container will have to be scrutinised meticulously.'

'So how long is that going to take?' asked Jack, 'What are you looking for, anyway … drugs?'

'To be honest, sir, we don't really know. We were given intelligence from a source that has proved reliable in the past that the container we are now looking at, and which has been opened by us in your presence for the first time since its arrival in port, is something that we should pay serious attention to. What I suggest is that you make your way back to the office over there and one of our staff will offer you some coffee while you wait, and then we will take it from there.'

It was just under two hours before Pamela Abbott returned. Jack could see that she had a look of consternation on her face and he tried to analyse whether it had been engendered because of what she had found or by disappointment that nothing irregular had materialised during the search that they had made.

'I'm sorry, gentlemen, we have clearly been wasting your time. The eleven boxes of components are precisely as they have been designated and, regarding the heavy pieces of machinery – it did not take too long for us to conclude that they were nothing other than what they were purported to be.'

Jack looked across at his father and, as their eyes connected, it was clear they were both thinking the same thing: 'Do we make a fuss, followed by an official complaint, or are we just relieved that this is all over and should simply insist that everything is delivered to our site as soon as possible and in pristine condition?'

It was Wesley that made the call.

'It has been a waste of a morning, Ms Abbott, but I'm sure that you were just doing your job. All we ask is that the contents of the container are conveyed to our warehouse in due course.'

'Well, thank you for your understanding, Mr Troughton. My staff and I were acting in accordance with due process, but nevertheless I recognise that this has caused you a measure of inconvenience and I am obviously sorry about that. It is evident that we will have to review the credence of our sources more carefully in the future.'

As Wesley and Jack made to leave the office and set out for their car, they heard a loud cracking sound, followed by a noise generated by the running of heavy chains. Then, a silence of only a few of seconds was interrupted by the sound of metal crashing heavily on metal. Father and son simultaneously spun around to find out what had been the source of the jarring cacophony.

They quickly realised that it had come from some containers that were in the process of being unloaded. One of them had broken free from its crane and had catapulted down onto a corner of the container only next but one to their own that had just been examined. Pamela Abbott, who had also witnessed the accident, was running from her office towards the scene. As her eyes darted back and forth, it was evident that she was far more concerned for the safety of her staff than for any damage that had been inflicted on the containers.

Miraculously, no one had been hurt. The Health and Safety regulations that the dock operated under always ensured that there was a controlled area when unloading, but it was impossible to provide for each and every eventuality. It was considered almost unprecedented in this day and age that cargo could break free in such circumstances. But today it certainly had.

The senior officer had moved quickly to control the situation and, signalling to the men who had earlier opened the container for Shoreside Engineering, said, 'You'd better open up the damaged one over there straight away. The primary damage seems to be to the rear right-hand corner so you shouldn't have any problem with the doors. If toxic substances were inside, a notice to that effect would have been displayed – so that at least is not a concern. In any case, such freight wouldn't be coming through our section of the port in the first place. Nevertheless, you'd still better check.'

The Customs officials who had been involved earlier had already been dismissed, and so that just left the workmen and Pamela Abbott to investigate the level of damage.

Wesley and Jack were about to set off towards their car for the second time when they glanced across towards the area where the containers were being unlocked. They watched as the heavy steel doors swung open to reveal what at first seemed nothing more than a dark space. However, moments later they watched in alarm as the workmen involved recoiled, as if in terror, from some terrible sight.

Wesley and Jack watched as one of the men swayed backwards before bending double in order to empty the contents of his stomach onto the ground in front of him. Pamela Abbott seemed to stand motionless for a moment as she peered into the void. Then, she turned and ran back to the cabin, holding her right hand over her mouth in shock. She raced past Wesley and Jack as if they were invisible.

What appeared to be the lifeless bodies of thirteen young women were later conveyed into waiting ambulances. The container, which had now been designated a crime scene, had been photographed, and a forensic team had completed their work. The women, some no more than girls, had originally been found sprawled on filthy mattresses. Later, when the story reached the press, reporters would ask why mattresses had also been fastened to the walls. They would be told that the mattresses had not been installed for the comfort of these latest victims of the sex trade, but to ensure that no alarm could be raised by the banging of fists or shoes on the sides of the captives' steel cell.

The police had arrived at the scene in minutes and, as soon as Pamela Abbott had explained who Wesley and Jack were, the officers, having taken their details, had allowed them to leave. But not before adding that there was a strong possibility that statements would be needed at a later date.

It would later be revealed that the reference on the side of the container that had now become a tomb had actually been BACF87747 and that, by the smallest of human errors, the person who initially provided the tip-off had simply mistaken an '8' for a '9'.

Jack looked at his watch as their car sped towards home. 'Dad,' he said, 'can you believe that its 3pm already? I have to pick up Celia around seven. If you don't mind, I suggest we mention nothing of this to her or Mum tonight.'

His father agreed.

6th August 2002
7pm Estonia

'But darling, you can't stay out there forever ...'

'Of course not, Mum,' said Celia, during one of the phone calls that she knew had been too infrequent over the past few weeks.

'It's not just that Dad and I miss you, or that we don't want you to enjoy yourself, it's just that everything seems so, well, I don't know ... open-ended. You don't seem to have a plan. We don't just worry that you're safe, it's ...'

'I'm perfectly alright. There's nothing to worry about, Mum. Listen, I'm sorry that I haven't been in touch quite as much as we'd agreed, it's just that ...'

Celia wondered if this was the right time to mention Jack. If she did, she knew her mother, who seemed to be forever hinting that she needed to 'find someone', would be picking a wedding outfit before the end of the week. But if she didn't mention Jack then, how could she explain her lack of clarity about how long she was spending out here? She resented her parents' view that the word 'single' was synonymous with the word 'incomplete'. Why couldn't people come to terms with the fact that not everyone wanted, or needed, to be married? Deep down, however, she was well aware that it was not really a case of her parents trying to 'marry her off'. They obviously wanted the best for her, as they saw it. Sometimes, though, she thought that the whole thing was not about her finding a husband but more about them having grandchildren. So many of her mother's friends doted over their children's children. Perhaps it was all about *them* feeling incomplete and not her. But perhaps she was being unfair. The fact was, she knew that the way her feelings for Jack were developing meant that she would soon have to tell him the one thing that could well bring everything to a halt, and if it did, apart from the effect it would have on her, it would disappoint her parents too. Yet at the end of the day this was not about them, it was about her, and so she decided to let them know.

'It's just that what?' her mother asked impatiently.

'Well, there's this guy …'

'This guy?' said her mother rapturously. 'Harold, come to the phone. I'm talking to Celia. She's got a young man. Isn't that wonderful? Listen, I'm putting your dad on.'

'But Mum …'

There was a short silence, interspersed by the sound of a fumbled phone being passed from one hand to another.

'Hello, love, is that you? Did Mum just say that you've found someone?'

'Hi, Dad! Look, this is ridiculous. I've just being seeing someone for a few weeks …'

'A few weeks? It must be serious, then?' said her father, in a tone that was far more a statement than a question.

'Dad, listen, I love you both lots, but I wish you wouldn't do this. Yes, I have met someone, and yes, we have been seeing one another regularly, but it's a bit soon to talk about the future! I haven't even met his parents yet.'

She avoided mentioning that this was to take place that evening. She had concluded that if she mentioned it then it would probably only serve to reinforce the assumption that things were far more serious than they were.

'Does he live in – where is it you are staying at the moment, love – Tanning? What's his name? I suppose he speaks English. What does he do for a living?'

'Dad, Dad, calm down. Its Tallinn, not Tanning, and he is English. All I wanted to do just now was to mention to Mum what was happening in my life. I don't want you both rushing off and coming to conclusions that may never materialise.'

The rest of the call was filled with Celia asking how her parents were and how her siblings, Stephanie and Mark, were doing. By the time the receiver went down, she felt exhausted and wondered if she had made the right decision in talking to them about Jack at all – but she supposed it had probably been for the best. If she was meeting Jack's parents tonight, it would hardly be fair if her own parents were left unaware that she was seeing someone.

The sound of a car drawing up on the gravel drive alerted her to the fact that this would most likely be Jack. She could not pretend that she was anything less than nervous about this evening. Locking the door behind her, she ran down the stairs from her second-floor apartment to save him having to get out of the car and ring the bell.

It was a beautiful summer's evening, with just enough breeze to be comfortable. Her landlords were a lovely couple, and the plants that spilled over the earthenware containers in the courtyard yielded a gorgeous aroma as Jack greeted her with a kiss and held open the passenger door for her.

'How's your day been, Jack?' Celia enquired, expecting the normal, 'It's all good – and what about you?'

'I can't lie,' said Jack. 'It's been grim – very grim, in fact – but I'd rather not talk about it now. I want us to have a great evening.'

'Were there tensions with your parents about me coming for supper tonight?'

'Oh, of course not,' Jack replied reassuringly. 'Far from it, they can't wait to meet you! Frankly, they think it's terrible of me hiding you away from them for so long, given it's nearly three months since we first met.'

'So you were hiding me away from them, then, were you?' Celia said, trying to sound outraged, but knowing that Jack would instinctively realise she was only teasing.

'Hey, listen, you can't put that on me,' said Jack, with a smile. 'At least you're meeting my parents – yours aren't even aware that I exist!'

'Well, they are now,' rejoined Celia. 'I told them on the phone just a few minutes before you picked me up.'

'Wow, landmark decision, then,' said Jack and, as he did so, was totally unaware of the degree to which Celia had concluded that that was exactly what it had also been for her. She was forced to admit to herself that Jack was more special to her than anyone she had ever met before.

The car slowed down as they reached a gated driveway. Celia watched as Jack pressed a button on a small remote control that, within seconds, caused two wide, ornate iron gates to swing inwards, giving the car access to grounds that were a million miles from the cosy Cotswold cottage in which she had been brought up.

'Goodness, this is some place, Jack. Why did you forget to tell me that you lived in a mansion? I really *am* feeling nervous now.'

'Don't be silly! Mum and Dad are going to love you, and I hope you are going to like them too.'

By the time they had exited the car, Jack's parents were already at the door and immediately moved towards Celia with warm smiles to welcome her.

'Mr and Mrs Troughton, it's so lovely to meet you,' said Celia, as she responded to the open arms that Jack's mother stretched out to greet her.

'It's wonderful to meet you too, Celia. Jack has told us so much about you. Please call me Sarah. This is Wesley, my husband.'

'This is some place,' thought Celia to herself.

Jack's parents could not have been more genuinely welcoming. A huge chandelier illuminated the large parquet-floored entrance hall that revealed tall wooden doors to the right and left. The centre of the hall was graced with a thick oriental carpet in pale green and gold, which led the eye to a wide double staircase that accessed the first of the three floors.

The evening was to go better than anyone could have expected. It had not only been Celia that had been apprehensive. Sarah and Wesley Troughton had been anxious too. It was not that they were overly concerned about how Celia would respond to them; they had already gathered from what Jack had said about her that this would not be a problem. It was simply that they had quickly come to realise how much Jack loved her and they wanted everything to go well for the sake of their only son. Now, having met Celia, they could clearly see why Jack had become so attracted to her. She looked lovely but, more importantly, they instinctively felt that this was exactly the kind of person that would make their son happy.

As soon as they were back in the car, Celia said, 'Jack, what awesome people your parents are! They were just so lovely. By the end of the evening it was as if I had known your mother for years. They both did everything possible to put me at ease.'

'I told you there was nothing to worry about, didn't I?' responded Jack. 'And I could tell that they loved you to bits too.'

'Your father is just as I imagined him, but he looked a little preoccupied during the evening. Sometimes it was as if his mind was far away and then, if ever I caught his eye, he would intentionally snap back, as if he were trying to pick up the threads of the conversations that were going on around him. Was he OK?'

'It was probably to do with what I mentioned to you earlier, when I picked you up at the apartment. To be honest, neither of us have had a day like it in our lives. Under any other circumstances tonight's meal would have been cancelled, but we didn't feel we could do that as my parents had been waiting for such a long time to meet you. So we decided we'd just go ahead with it. My mother doesn't know anything about what happened yet, so that's why you wouldn't have picked up any sense of tension from her. Frankly, there's not any reason why she needs to know anything – at least for now.'

'Jack, what on earth happened?' asked Celia anxiously.

10th August 2002
Estonia

It was Saturday before Jack saw Celia again and, given the news coverage in the press, Celia had pretty much pieced most of the story together for herself. The only thing that hadn't initially leaked into the public domain was that all the young women were found to have been branded. At first glance, the investigators had thought they were simply tattoos, but on closer inspection, two things had become clear. The first was that all the marks were identical. The second was that they had been crudely and, most likely, extremely painfully, applied. It had also become obvious that these were little more than marks of ownership. Those whose lives had ended in that suffocating steel container had been dehumanised into merchandise by their captors and branded like cattle. A serpent inside a pentangle had depersonalised them to the level of a commodity. The investigators were surprised at the branding aspect as, although some traffickers liked to inflict their trademark, it was unusual, as it carried the risk of the girls being traced back to them.

Jack and his father had made the required statements and, as far the police were concerned, that had been the end of the matter. From their perspective, they had been no more than witnesses to the breakage of a crane.

'Celia, do you know what I would like us to do tomorrow?' asked Jack, as they sat in the shade of the terrace at the home he shared with his parents.

'No, what's that?' answered Celia, leaning towards him.

'I'd like us to have coffee tomorrow morning in the same café where we first met.'

'That would be wonderful. But would it be possible to make it lunchtime rather than mid-morning?'

In the three months that Jack had known Celia, he had grown to love her more than he could have imagined he could love anyone. They were so much alike in some ways and so totally opposite in others and, as far as he was concerned, that was a perfect mix.

There was just one thing, however, that he could never get his head around. Why was it that Celia never met him on a Sunday morning? He had never asked her about it, just assuming that she enjoyed a lie-in and that this was territory that should not be encroached on by anybody – not even him. But her refusal to meet earlier didn't really make sense, the more he thought about it. Hadn't their first meeting been on a Sunday morning? He remembered the occasion perfectly. Though he considered it strange, if that was what she wanted on the following day, it was going to be fine with him.

'OK, then,' said Jack. 'Let's make it 12.30.'

'That's perfect, but on one condition,' Celia said with a smile. 'We're not going up the tower again. Remember, the last time we went was in May and that was crowded enough. In August it will be impossible.'

At the appointed time they met outside the café and, after they had embraced and kissed, went inside. The place rarely reserved tables, as the tourists ensured a constant stream of customers, and any table left unclaimed was considered revenue lost. But Jack had been persuasive and had secured a place in an alcove towards the back of the café – not just for the sake of privacy, but because it was certain to be much cooler. This was not only the height of summer, but also about the hottest time of the day.

The food was ordered and delivered and Celia noticed that Jack appeared somewhat nervous. But perhaps she was wrong and he was just preoccupied.

'Still thinking about the tragedy at the docks?' she enquired.

'To be honest, I can't seem to get the event out of my mind, but I wasn't particularly thinking about that just now. Celia, I am going to get right to the point. I'm not the most romantic person in the world. I could have said this under a starlit sky, looking across a shimmering sea, but ...'

Celia had imagined that this moment might come at some point, but was startled that it was taking place quite so soon. She was totally in love with him, and she knew that he was also in love with her, but she could not let him continue. She should have raised the issue she had been putting off almost since the moment they met, but she had been afraid to do so. Now it could not be postponed any longer. She raised her hand towards him as he spoke, like a traffic policewoman halting a vehicle that was travelling towards her.

'No, Celia, don't stop me. I know it's only been three months, but I also know that it's been long enough for me to be totally certain that I want to spend the rest of my life with you. You know that I love you and I think you feel the same way about me too ...'

The last ten words that Jack uttered tailed off into silence causing what was a statement to change shape into a question that searched longingly for an answer.

Celia hesitated uncertainly before she spoke, and then with a halting voice said, 'Jack, you know that I love you. In fact, you can never know how deep my feelings go, but it's just that ...' She paused, not knowing how, or even whether, to continue. 'It's just that ... it's just that it can't work.'

'What do you mean, it can't work? Why wouldn't it work? It's a relationship made in heaven,' countered Jack.

'Made in *heaven*?' responded Celia, with emphasis on the last word. 'Really, Jack, made in heaven? You see, Jack, that's the whole point.'

'What *point*? What did I say?'

'Do you remember yesterday when I said that I would rather us meet at lunchtime than mid-morning?'

'Of course I do,' said Jack. 'You don't like up getting early on a Sunday, do you? So what's wrong with that, and why would that have anything to do with what we're talking about now?'

'It's got everything to do with it, Jack,' Celia said softly, leaning a little towards him and sliding her hand over his. 'It's got everything to do with it because I don't use my Sunday mornings for a lie-in. I use them for going to church. I'm a Christian, Jack, and my faith means more to me than anything else in the world.'

'What do you mean, more than anything? Does that "anything" include me as well?' responded Jack, with more uncertainty in his voice than animosity. 'I thought you said you loved me, and anyway, you don't go to church every Sunday morning – that's nonsense.'

It seemed to Jack that what had been intended as the most important moment in his life was now deteriorating into a complete train wreck of a conversation.

'We actually met in this very place on a Sunday morning,' said Jack, pressing his point home.

'It's not nonsense at all. On that morning I had intended to go to church, but I woke up with a frightful headache. I took a couple of tablets, but they didn't seem to work so, as it was late, I decided to miss breakfast and church and go for a stroll to clear my head – and later that morning, we met.'

'Well, what's the big deal about you being a Christian, anyway? You can believe what you want. You can be a Muslim, Hindu – you can be a Jedi knight as far as I'm concerned. It doesn't mean that I have to buy into it. And anyway, why would you worry about telling me? You've just heard me say that I'm not bothered about how you, or anyone else for that matter, makes their personal choices. And apart from that, all roads lead to the same place in the end, don't they? Surely, religious affiliations or none are just a matter of how we were brought up.'

'Listen, Jack,' interrupted Celia. 'I don't want us to have an argument. I just wanted to be with you today and have a quiet lunch. If you think about it, you are proving my point perfectly. Look how easily an issue like this can cause tension – even a rift – between us. Can't you see how impossible it is? If we are acting like this now, imagine what it would be like if this became a factor in any future marriage. All relationships have their own inevitable stresses and strains, without the issue of incompatible beliefs. We would be just asking for trouble. You don't seem to realise how much my faith means to me, Jack. It's not a lifestyle choice like a hobby someone takes up or the kind of car they choose. It's huge to me. And as far as "Why would I worry about telling you" – do you remember when we were climbing the spiral staircase and that nun tripped and began to tumble backwards?'

'Of course I do,' said Jack. 'That was when I caught you as you fell.'

'And do you remember what you said afterwards about her when she didn't apologise? I mean, she was probably so embarrassed she didn't know what to say. You said, "I suppose that's Christians for you." It was then that I realised that, for whatever reasons, you had issues in that area. We had just met and I didn't feel the need to challenge what you were saying or even ask why you should say something like that. You have to realise that at that point there was no reason for me to think that we would ever see one another again beyond that day. It was only when things began to get serious that I began to realise that this would have to be addressed at some point and, for better or worse, that moment seems to be now. Anyway, what's your problem with Christianity? Why would you even have said something like that?'

'I don't know,' retorted Jack. 'It's probably because we once had this guy working for us who told us he went to church and there were, frankly, times when we were less than happy with the way he related to our clients – especially on the phone. He would be kind of surly and defensive if a customer had the slightest issue with our products or service. One day Dad brought him into the office when I was there. A good client had just told Dad that he was thinking of moving his business elsewhere and cited the attitude of this chap as the main reason. When Dad confronted him, the man's attitude became aggressive and he said that he didn't care how much money the client's business was worth, but he was not going to be challenged by people like him. There clearly was no sense of remorse, let alone an apology – just defensiveness. Then, when the cycle was repeated a few weeks later, we had to let him go. So that's it. That's your churchgoers for you.'

'Well, to begin with,' said Celia, 'the act of just going to church doesn't make you a Christian any more than sleeping in a garage makes you a car. But even if he was a Christian, Christians don't claim to be perfect. By definition we are disciples, or learners, if you like. If you go into a supermarket, and an assistant is rude to you, you don't make a vow never to buy food again from supermarkets.

Neither do you conclude that because one member of the organisation is rude then everyone else must be rude as well. That's just not rational, Jack. Why would you apply those criteria just to Christians?'

Jack held up his two hands as if fending off an assault. 'OK, OK, OK. Listen, I brought you here to propose to you and now it's all turned into this. I'm sorry if I offended you, and perhaps in some way I get your point, but …'

'I'm not offended, Jack. All I'm trying to say is that my faith is central to my life. I know that's not true for you, and that's fine, but if we are to have a future together it's important that you not only know me but also are aware of the things that I see as priorities. I haven't always been a Christian, in fact I don't know anyone in my family who would say they are one. My parents certainly wouldn't. They're awesome people and I love them and they love me, but they don't share my beliefs and don't have a great deal of interest in what I do. Their attitude has always been that whatever makes me happy makes them happy.'

'Well, there you go then,' interrupted Jack. 'If they are such awesome people, why would they want to become Christians? There isn't any need. My parents are the same. They do a whole lot of good stuff, not just within the family but also for people they don't even know. Shoreside supports several charities, for instance. What more can they do than that?'

'It's not about the good that we do. You can't earn your way into God's good books, Jack.' Celia reached across to pick up an empty water glass, and then lifting it, said, 'Imagine someone was to offer you this glass filled with cyanide. Would you drink it?'

'Of course I wouldn't. What point are you trying to make?'

'Just hear me out a minute. What happens if I offer you the glass filled with 99 per cent spring water and 1 per cent cyanide – where are we now?'

'Of course not, you know I wouldn't drink it, and neither would you.'

'But why not?' responded Celia. 'It's 99 per cent pure.'

'You know why not, you're being ridiculous. The 99 per cent pure water doesn't make the cyanide acceptable because the 1 per cent poison means that the water remains both toxic and deadly.'

'Precisely,' said Celia. 'You've got it in one. That's what I am trying to explain. Even if we were 99 per cent pure – and nobody is, because we all fall short of perfection by a much higher margin – we would still not be acceptable to God, who is perfect.'

'You can't be serious,' retorted Jack, 'and you accuse me of not being rational! If what you said is true, then no one could ever become a Christian. That argument makes no sense at all.'

'It would make no sense at all if it was all left to us,' said Celia, 'but thankfully it isn't all left to us. There's a reason why the cross is the symbol of Christianity. God the Father knew that no one could be acceptable to Him, so he sent His Son, Jesus, into the world. When He died on the cross, He carried the punishment that we deserved. This means that, if we trust in what He has done for us, then God the Father accepts His son's death as a payment for the judgement that we should have had to endure.'

'If you ask me, Celia, there are some huge jumps there even before you start.'

'I agree,' said Celia, 'there are, and those jumps are what some people call "steps of faith".'

'So when did this all happen for you?' asked Jack. 'If you didn't get this stuff from your parents, where did it come from? Were you brainwashed at some church or something?'

'If you really want to know, it happened while I was out shopping.'

'For goodness' sake – what on earth are you talking about now?'

'It's just as I said, I was out shopping in the Montpellier area of Cheltenham. I had in mind to walk towards the centre of town and reach the Promenade, which is like the main street. But I hadn't realised how heavy the bags I was carrying were and I was looking for somewhere to rest and take a break. I was near a hotel, and just in front is a huge, square grassy area planted with flowerbeds. It looks gorgeous in the summer. It's called Imperial Gardens. I noticed that around the perimeter were a number of benches facing into the centre of the square, so I opted for the nearest, sat down and kicked off my high heels for a moment. I still remember the relief. It was bliss. I really should have worn more sensible shoes.'

'When was this?' interjected Jack.

'It wasn't all that long ago. I think I was about seventeen at the time. Anyway, I was sitting there, just taking in the view, when I noticed this old book that I assumed someone must have been reading and left on the bench. To begin with I paid no attention to it, but after a few minutes or so I glanced around to see if perhaps it had been left there by someone who was reserving their seat while examining the flowerbeds. But there was no one lingering around – just a few people heading for the Prom. I couldn't link anyone to it. I was curious, so I reached for it. As I picked it up, with its heavily worn black cover, I noticed the two words in faded gold letters that identified it as a Bible. I opened it at the first page and saw there was an inscription on what had once been a white page. In blue ink, written with a fountain pen, were the words "To Albert, on your tenth birthday from your loving mother and father, December 1932".

'I felt for a moment that I was somehow intruding so I closed the Bible up and moved it back to its space on the bench. I looked around again, but the area was deserted now. It began to rain, so I quickly slipped my feet back into my shoes and headed towards the nearest shops for shelter. I had hardly gone more than a few steps when I thought of the Bible sitting there and getting soaked. My first instinct was to think how ridiculous it was that I should be at all concerned. It had, after all, reached the end of its useful life as a book. I turned to rush on to get out of the rain, but it was no use – I just couldn't leave it there. I went back to the bench, picked it up, threw it in my shopping bag and headed off.

'The first thing I did when I eventually reached home was to take a shower and put on some dry clothes. Of course, later when I unpacked my shopping, there was the old Bible looking up at me from the bottom of the carrier bag. Sitting down with a cup of coffee, I decided to look at it more closely. I noticed that some parts had been underlined and sometimes notes had been written in the margins. But the words were mostly illegible – some of the biro was faded, or smudged.

'I flicked through to the end and came across a blank page at the back where someone far more recently had written some kind of cryptic phrase. It was like something you'd find in a crossword clue. Underneath the words was the capital letter J followed by a string of numbers and dashes which made no sense to me at all. It obviously wasn't a phone number.

'That night, after I'd got into bed, I took up the old Bible again. Then I noticed something I hadn't seen before. At the top of the spine was a dark blue ribbon that acted as a kind of marker and which had been placed about three-quarters of the way through. When I opened it up it was positioned four books into the New Testament. It was at what I later learned was the Gospel of John. Over the next few days I read through John's Gospel and, by the time I had reached the end, my life had changed. It was remarkable, it was like instead of me reading the book, the book had been reading me.'

'It's an interesting story,' responded Jack. 'But for me it frankly poses more questions than it answers.

'Listen, Celia. There were actually two reasons why I wanted us to meet today. The first was to propose – and we both know how well that has gone. And the second was to let you know that I have to leave for the UK in two weeks' time and I'll be staying in Manchester for a couple of months. We love it out here but Dad and I both think that we need to move our base to the UK. We've talked about it as a family and, while Mum will really miss living in this part of the world, she knows it's the best thing to do. Dad's not getting any younger, and soon everything will be in my hands. We're going to hold on to the house so that my parents can retire out here when the time comes, if they want to. Even though Mum loves it, I'm not sure that if anything happened to Dad she would want to stay.'

'How is it you never told me anything about this before, Jack?' Celia asked, in a voice betraying more surprise than hurt.

'To be honest, the family has been thinking about all this for some time. Today was to be about consolidating what was happening in our relationship so that at least we both would know where we stood during the time that I'd have to be away. You know how I feel about you, but I'm beginning to think, after this conversation, that it might be a good idea for us to step back a bit from everything. The reason I'm going to Manchester is to look for a potential site for our new premises and assess the logistical implications of the move. I know Manchester seems strange for our type of business, but we serve ports throughout Europe, and not only is Manchester served by a good motorway network, but property is far more reasonable in the north than it is in the south. So, getting back to what I was saying, I suggest we put things on ice and then perhaps review things again by the time I get back.'

'Well, Jack, if that's how you feel, then that's what we'll do. The only reason I haven't returned home is because of what was happening between the two of us. So your new plans perhaps indicate that my time here is drawing to a close as well. Apart from all that, I really need to start looking for a job.'

The bill settled, they left the café, and Jack dropped Celia back at her apartment.

2nd October 2002
Manchester

Manchester on a wet and windy autumn night was no worse than any other northern city, except for the fact that, in Jack's case, the inclement weather was just one further addition to an already bleak few weeks. Negotiations had not gone anything like as well as he had anticipated – but that was not the only reason he was not sleeping properly at night. He was missing Celia far more than he had anticipated. They had agreed to 'put things on ice', but the reality was that, far from the time apart being a cooling-off period, his feelings for her had, if anything, become even more intense.

There had been absolutely no contact. Both of them had agreed that that was how it should be. He assumed that she was probably now back home and, though he had never had any reason to know her new address, he at least had her email and mobile number. He had lost count of the times when, sending a business-related email or a text to a friend, he had wanted to send her a message just to say that he was thinking about her. He wished now that he had never suggested the arrangement in the first place. How could he propose one moment and within an hour sever the relationship, even if it was only for a few weeks? And what would he do if, at the end of the time they had set, she had decided that this wasn't going to work – or even had met someone else?

Of course, he knew precisely why he had acted as he did. He was angry that she could ever think of choosing her personal convictions over him. His pride had been hurt and, if he was honest, he had used the 'taking time out' arrangement as a weapon to get back at her. On top of this, he was troubled by some of the things that she had said in the café about how she had decided to

44

become a Christian. It was far easier for him to analyse how he was feeling about missing her than it was to decode his emotions around issues that had to do with her faith. It was not that he was anti-Christian; it was simply that he had never considered faith to have any particular relevance. For him, 'church' was about what some people did on a Sunday, while other people chose to wash their car. He frankly did not care one way or another. If people wanted to believe, then that was up to them, but this kind of stuff was not for him. So here he was – in a strange pub on a foul night – away from family, away from Celia and away from his friends.

He was just about to order a second glass of whisky when the door swung open and through it came a man about his own age, about six foot four, who was asking, 'Anybody here drive a Mercedes Coupé?'

For a moment Jack looked around to see if anyone was going to respond, and then he remembered that that was the hire car he was using while he was in Manchester. Signalling to the man, who by now had reached the bar, Jack asked, 'What colour are you talking about? Is it black? What's the problem?'

'It is black, mate, and, if it's yours, your sunroof is open. Though why anyone would have a sunroof open on a day like this escapes me. Anyway, if I were you, I'd do something about it pretty quick. It's tipping down.'

Grunting some inaudible appreciative response, Jack slid off his stool and sprinted to the door. When he reached the car, he discovered that the interior was totally soaked, and he knew that if this was anything more than superficial, he would certainly lose any deposit he had left with the hire company. This was not the first time he had had a problem with the key fob, but it was the first time it had happened when it was raining and blowing a gale.

Having sorted the problem, at least for the present, he made a dash back to the bar and, when he had closed the door behind him against the wind and rain, extended his hand to the man who had alerted him to the problem.

'Thanks for that, mate. Can I buy you a drink?'

'No, it's fine. I've just ordered a slimline tonic.' He added, by way of explanation, 'I'm driving!'

Of course, Jack was driving too, and was glad he hadn't ordered that second whisky.

'Seriously, I really appreciate you taking the trouble to let me know,' he said, as the extended hand was taken and shaken. 'I'm Jack Troughton.'

'And I'm Damian Clarke,' the man replied, as he turned away from the bar and pointed at a nearby table, inviting Jack to join him.

After indicating to the barman that he would have a tonic water too, Jack moved across and sat down in the seat opposite.

'You don't sound like a northerner,' Damian said. 'It's pretty hard to place where your accent comes from.'

'I suppose that's because I've moved around a lot. Right now, I live with my parents abroad, but we are hoping to move the company to new offices in Manchester. So the reason I'm over here is to look for possible locations. I take it that you were brought up around here, then?'

'Born and bred,' Damian replied. 'I grew up in a suburb in the south of the city. We still live not a million miles away from the place where I grew up.'

'You said "we". Does that mean that you're married?'

'Yes, got married to Sue just last year at our home church.'

'Home church?' said Jack, incredulously. 'I know about home teams but I've never heard about anyone having a home church.'

'Sorry,' said Damian, smiling. 'That must sound a bit strange. It just means that we've both attended the same place for a few years now and have come to regard it as our spiritual home.'

'Oh, Chri …' Jack began, and stopped himself just in time.

Damian drew his head and broad shoulders back in mock alarm, and smiling, said, 'Wow, Jack, why such an extreme reaction?'

'You don't want to know – you really don't,' replied Jack.

'I actually do,' Damian said. 'You just can't leave that hanging in the air. After all, I'm the man who saved your car from turning into a swamp, remember? You might owe me just a slight explanation.'

Over the next thirty minutes, Jack told Damian everything. He found himself more than a little surprised that he was opening up in such a way to someone he had only just met. It was especially strange in that he was unused to sharing his feelings at this level, even with people he had known for years. Everything came out, beginning with how he had met Celia, right through to the last conversation he had had with her in the café in Tallinn; including how she'd found a Bible and become a Christian.

'Listen, Jack, why don't you come to church with Sue and me on Sunday? You've already told me that you've been alone here in Manchester for a couple of weeks now, so don't start telling me you've got something on, because I just won't believe you.'

'No, it's out of the question,' responded Jack, parrying the invitation as if recoiling from a thrust.

'Look, just hang on a minute,' said Damian. 'Think about it. You say you are in love with … was it Celia? This is a prime opportunity to get at least an inkling of why being a Christian means so much to her – and, think about it, she won't even know. What have you got to lose, anyway?'

Jack thought for a moment. Damian was right, and he would not be believed if he said he was otherwise engaged. Of course, he could just say no. After all, who was this bloke who had just walked into his life? Yes, he had been kind enough to alert him about his car, but that did not mean he could commandeer his entire schedule for the weekend. On the other hand, the questions that Celia had raised in the café on the last occasion they had been together were still preying on his mind. So he could hardly believe the evidence of his own ears when he heard himself saying, 'OK, Damian, I'll come with you. What time does the service start?'

6th October 2002
Manchester

Jack had arranged to be at the front entrance of the hotel lobby, and when Damian's car pulled up he noticed that Damian's wife, Sue, was in the back seat. As it came to a standstill, Sue indicated that Jack should sit in the front and, after Damian had briefly introduced them, they set off.

Within just a few minutes they had pulled into the car park of a large contemporary-styled church building. Jack expressed surprise when they were directed by an attendant into an overflow car park, as the first area was already full. 'How many people attend this place? I thought church attendance was on the decline?'

'We normally go to the first service,' Sue responded, 'but we thought that that might be a little early for you. Over the day, the number of people who will have gone through the doors would not be far off 1,400, I suppose.'

Entering the reception area, the three of them were warmly welcomed by several people who seemed to be there for that purpose. Moving towards the main sanctuary area, Jack noticed that Damian and Sue were being embraced by people he assumed were their church friends.

There was much about the service that followed that Jack found unusual, and there were also some things that he considered confusing. He did not expect the music, led by what was referred to as a Praise Band, to be either so contemporary or so competent. They were as good as any secular group of musicians he had heard, and it struck him as odd that they did not appear to be 'performing'. It was as if they were as much part of the worship as the congregation.

Damian was later to refer to the sermon as 'the message' and Jack was surprised when he looked at his watch to find that it had been more than thirty minutes in length. It had been clear, relevant and occasionally laced with humour. He did, however, find some elements of it a little disconcerting, in that it addressed some of the issues that he had been mulling over since his conversation with Celia.

Damian and Sue had invited Jack back to their home for lunch, and the afternoon stretched into evening, with Jack either asking questions about the morning service or raising objections to the possible existence of an all-powerful God in such an unjust and cruel world.

It was approaching 10.30pm before Jack had exhausted the majority of the questions that he had had on his mind. He did not feel entirely convinced by all the answers that Damian and Sue had given him but, in fairness, he thought some of those issues may have to do with what Celia had referred to as 'steps of faith'. Something that at this point he felt unable to make.

'Just one thing before I get back to the hotel,' said Jack. 'The thing that confused me most this morning was how it all made me feel.'

'How do you mean?' Sue enquired.

'Well, it's hard for me to admit it, but when everyone was singing – worshipping – I found myself on the edge of tears. At some points I felt this kind of tingling sensation over me. It was weird. I mean, even at those times recently that I realised that things may not work out with Celia, and even though I felt totally gutted, tears were not on the agenda with me. I don't want to sound overly macho or anything, but I can't remember the last time I cried. I'm just not wired up like that.'

There was a pause and Damian and Sue looked across at one another.

Jack continued, 'It's just that I became aware of something that I had neither encountered nor experienced before. I suppose it could be that my issues with Celia were catching up with me, but I don't think so. It was more than that. Something else was going on, and you know what? I can even feel the same thing happening again right now as I'm talking about it with you.'

Then, in a voice that indicated he was trying to compose himself and move away from a conversation in which he was feeling increasingly uncomfortable, he said, 'Look, guys, thank you both for a great day, but listen, I really need to get back to the hotel. I've got an early start tomorrow and I'm sure you both need to get some rest too. I can get a cab back to the hotel, Damian. No need to drag you back out.'

'Come on, Jack, it's no trouble at all,' Damian countered, as he ushered Jack towards the door.

When Jack reached his room, he showered and settled into bed, but found it very difficult to drop off to sleep.

16th December 2002
Cotswolds

It had been hard for Celia not to make contact with Jack during the many weeks they had been separated. She missed him, and although her feelings were the same as before he left, she knew that the relationship could not work out if they didn't share the same basic world view.

She had been back home in the Cotswolds now for six weeks and, though her parents were thrilled to have her back with them, hardly a day went by when they did not ask whether she had heard from Jack and if she intended to get back with him. She had endeavoured to explain her dilemma to them, but they refused to countenance any thought that the position she was taking should be allowed to pose a problem.

'There are lots of couples who have different political views, Celia, and they seem to have happy enough marriages,' her mother had said.

'But Mum, it goes deeper than that, you don't understand.'

'I understand that you are throwing a relationship aside on something that I can't see as anything more than a whim. I know we haven't met this young man, but you seem to love him and apparently he loves you. What you are doing simply doesn't make any sense at all.'

'But Mum, it was Jack who suggested we take time out, and I have to agree with him.'

'Well, I hope it works out. I really do. Your father and I ...'

'Mum, I am aware that you and Dad want me to get married and I know you want to have grandchildren! There's nothing wrong with that, but when it all comes down to it, this is about my happiness and Jack's happiness – not yours.'

As soon as the words had come out of her mouth she regretted them; not because they were untrue, but because they sounded so harsh. On the other hand, she had become tired of skirting around the issue. 'How can a person be brutally honest without being brutal?' she asked herself. The last thing she wanted to do was to hurt her mother, but she would not spend all her time walking on eggshells, pretending this was 'all about her and Jack', when it clearly wasn't.

Later that day, Celia decided to go for a coffee at one of her favourite places, a country restaurant on the outskirts of Tewkesbury. It had comfortable leather armchairs and quiet corners, and she needed both of those just now.

She was just turning into the car park when her phone rang. Steering into a vacant space, she drew her phone from the centre console. She would normally have looked at the caller ID first but, with the time it took to complete the manoeuvre, she put it straight to her ear, anxious that she might miss the call. When she recognised the voice and heard the words, 'Celia, is that you?' her heart skipped a beat.

'Yes, Jack, it's me. Are you OK? Where are you phoning from?'

'I'm still in Manchester. I finished my work here a couple of days early. I heard from my parents that you were back in the UK. It was nice of you to drop round and say goodbye to them. Thank you – they really appreciated it. Look, are you free tomorrow? It would only take me a few hours to drive to your area. We need to talk.'

'I'm glad things are good with you, Jack, and I'd love to see you, though I'm not sure what's changed in the time we've been apart. But what time were you thinking of?'

'I was thinking lunch. Where would you suggest?'

'As it happens, I'm in my car outside somewhere that would be easy for you to find. It's just ten minutes from junction 9 of the M5. I'll text you the address and postcode as soon as this call ends.'

Jack was not a little anxious as he stepped out of the car and greeted Celia at the restaurant the following day. It was evident that they both were hesitant and guarded, and their initial embrace reflected that. It was as if they were in a kind of emotional no man's land – a place somewhere between separation and commitment. At any moment, either one of them could run to the security of their personal territory.

It was Jack who was the first to speak.

'I've really missed you, Celia.'

'Me too,' she said, as they linked arms and strolled towards the door.

In the summer the covered terrace was the first place to aim for when selecting a place to sit. But it was mid-December, so they headed inside to an alcove table across from a crackling log fire.

'When are you due back in Estonia?' enquired Celia.

'In a couple of days. I have a flight booked for the weekend.'

'So, how has your trip been? Have you managed to secure premises for your business yet?'

'I've looked at a number of options, and of course have been on the phone to my dad throughout the process. When I get back, the two of us will talk it all through and then he'll probably come over with me when we're ready to finalise everything. There's still some way to go. I suppose it's fair to say we're working on a shortlist.'

'Three months is a long time to be away from home when you had such a big role in the company. How has your dad been able to cope?'

'It's not really been much of a problem. A lot of my work can be done via email, as you know. How have you been?'

'Well, my parents are glad to have me back home with them, of course. To be honest, they were a bit unsure about me travelling in the first place, so they're happy enough.'

'But I asked about you?'

'It's like I've told you before, I've missed you, Jack, but remember it was you who suggested the break and, as things stand, I don't know what the point …'

'Look, Celia,' interrupted Jack. 'I've been doing a lot of thinking while I've been away, and Damian and Sue have been a big help.'

'Damian and Sue?'

'Oh, sorry, Damian is someone who stopped my car getting flooded. Look, it's a long story but I'll cut to the chase. Damian and his wife, Sue, took me to church.'

It was now Celia's turn to interrupt. 'To church? You are joking! What church?'

'Oh, one in Manchester. Since then we've been in regular contact and we've become good friends. I'd love you to meet them. I've told them all about you. Anyway, the long and short of it is that I have decided to become a Christian.'

'Jack, slow down a minute. The act of going to church, even regularly, doesn't make you a Christian! It's not about religion, it's about a personal relationship with God.' Celia paused for a moment and reached across the table to hold his hand. 'Listen, Jack, if you are just doing this for me ...'

'No, it's not like that. It really isn't. In fact, I was worried that that was how you might take what I wanted to tell you. You once told me that just attending church no more makes you a Christian than sleeping in a garage makes you a car. I understand that. They invited me to something called an Alpha course, where you could listen to short talks over a meal and even ask questions if you wanted to. Anyway, at the end of it I asked Christ into my life. I really do feel like a new person. As you know, I just couldn't get why you saw your faith as being so important. Now I do, Celia. I honestly do!'

'Oh, Jack, that's great. I'm so thrilled for you. I can hardly believe it!'

Just then Jack's phone rang and he looked at the caller ID. 'It's from Mum,' Jack said, as he pressed the button to take the call.

'Jack, it's me, love. I'm afraid I've got some bad news for you. Your father collapsed and has been rushed to hospital. He's in the acute coronary care unit. I thought you needed to know right away.'

'Oh no, Mum! How serious is it, have they said?'

'They asked if we had family and when I told them about you they said that I should let you know right away.'

'I'll get the first plane home that I can. How are you coping, Mum?'

'To be honest I'm in a bit of a spin at the moment, love, but it'll be good to have you back here as soon as you can make it.'

As soon as Jack pressed the 'end call' button, Celia asked, 'Is it your dad?'

'Yes, he's had a heart attack, and it's pretty bad from what I can make out. I'm going to have to …'

'Excuse me, sir, are you ready to order?' asked the waitress as she approached the table.

'I'm sorry, we're not going to be able to stay.'

'Oh, that's alright, sir,' the waitress replied, with confusion in her voice that they realised she was trying to mask.

'I'm sorry that I've got to leave so soon,' Jack said to Celia apologetically. 'The moment I'm on the road I'll phone my PA to sort out the flights so that by the time I get to Manchester all I'll need to do is to check out of my hotel and return my hire car at the airport.'

'Please give my love to your mum when you speak to her.'

'Yes, of course,' said Jack. 'Oh, there's just one other thing.'

'What's that? Is there anything at all that I can do?' asked Celia.

'Yes, just one thing, if you don't mind. Will you marry me?' asked Jack, pulling her towards him.

'Of course I will.' Celia held him close, as if she would never let him go.

18th December 2002
Estonia

When Jack arrived at the coronary care ward of the hospital, he found his mother sitting alone in the visitors' waiting room and immediately concluded the worst. He moved quickly towards her and, enveloping her in a consoling hug, asked how his father was.

'He's under sedation at the moment. That's why they've asked me to wait in here. They actually suggested I go home and get some rest, but I can't leave him, Jack. I don't know what I would do if anything happened to him and I hadn't been at his side.'

'You still need to get some rest though, Mum,' said Jack. 'What are the doctors saying?'

'The next few hours will be critical. I didn't want to worry you while you were away, but he hasn't really been well for the past couple of weeks. He didn't seem to be in any pain, but he has been very tired – hardly any energy at all some days.'

'Mum, you should have told me. I would have come home straight away, you know that.'

'Believe me, Jack, I suggested it more than once, but your dad wouldn't hear of it. He said that the tiredness would pass and we would have worried you unnecessarily. He seems to have been doing a lot of thinking just lately. Sometimes when I would come into the room he would just be sitting there, staring into the distance. Whenever I asked him what was on his mind he would just wave his hand as if batting away my concerns and tell me not to worry. You know, I honestly think that he anticipated this. Later, when I sat with him in the ambulance, he told me that he'd written two letters. One for you and one for me. I wanted to break down and cry right there and then, but I knew I needed to appear strong for him. Jack, I just don't know what I would do if he's taken.'

Jack pulled his mother towards him again, and held her close. He thought of the many times the roles had been reversed when he had been just a little boy; those times he had fallen over and scraped his knee and she had cleaned the wound and reassuringly told him everything was OK. Or when he had had nightmares and his mother had sat beside his bed – staying with him until he eventually dropped off to sleep.

'I love you, Mum, you know that, don't you?'

'Of course I do, son, and you know that your dad and I love you too and are so very, very proud of you.'

Drawing away from the embrace a little, she looked up at him and said, 'By the way, did I tell you that Celia came round to say goodbye to us before she left for England? It was so nice of her. What a lovely girl she is, Jack.'

'Yes, Mum, you did tell me, and I told her how much you and Dad appreciated it.'

'You told her? Do you mean you've been in touch with her again?'

'Yes, we had lunch, or almost had lunch, together a couple of days ago. In fact, she was with me when the news came through about Dad. I've got some news for you too, Mum.'

'News? What news?' Her eyes searched her son's face and he could see the hope there.

'I've asked Celia to marry me, and she has said yes.'

'Oh, that's wonderful, Jack, it really is. I'm so happy for you and I know your dad will be too. We both felt you were so right for one another. We really did.'

Wesley Troughton's funeral took place just a few days after Christmas.

It was only when the ceremony had ended, and all the many family, friends and colleagues who had packed the church that day had made their way home, that Jack and his mother had the courage to open their respective letters.

Celia had flown over to be with Jack and, when Jack had made sure that his mother was OK, he and Celia donned their coats and took a stroll into the garden in order to give Sarah some space to be on her own.

'It's so sad,' said Celia, 'that your father never heard about our good news.'

Jack squeezed her hand.

Later, as the evening began to draw in and they were making their way back to the house, they looked across the lawn and saw that the lounge curtains were still undrawn. Through the French windows they watched Sarah as she sat in her favourite chair. To one side of her was the conspicuously vacant armchair where her husband would normally have been seated. On the other side, the lamp on its table cast its yellow light onto her lap, revealing a newly opened letter. Even from where they stood, they were able to see the tears that slid down across her cheeks. They quickened their pace, both instinctively feeling that in lingering they would be intruding into a private space.

Shortly after they arrived at the house, Celia went to her room, leaving Jack alone to read the letter his father had left for him.

Jack steeled himself as he removed two white sheets from their envelope, unfolded them, and read:

Dear Jack,

The fact that you are reading this means that I have not had the opportunity to speak to you face to face and share some of the things that have been running through my mind of late. I have written a similar letter to your mother. I remain comforted in the knowledge that should anything happen to me, she will always be totally safe and secure in your care.

You know that I have always found it less than easy to express my feelings openly. I wish I had been better at that. But I am sure you also know how much I love you and how proud your mother and I are of you. One of my greatest joys in recent years has been to have you working alongside me in the business. At first it was about me 'showing you the ropes', but in the last few years it has been you that has taken Shoreside forward. You have achieved a grasp of new technology and the latest innovations in the industry that I was never able to fully get my head around. When you jokingly called me 'old school' you were absolutely right, and I have no illusions about the fact that where the company is today is largely due to you.

Jack, this is primarily what this letter is about – the business. If anything happens to me, there are two options for you to consider. One is to fully take the helm, and I think that that is instinctively what you will feel you need to do – at least in the short term.

I am sure you know that all I have ever wanted over the years is that you and your mother are well provided for and, most of all, happy. That is why I want to mention a second option.

Son, I know that you have thrown all your energy into the business and I could not have wished for a better partner – but deep down I am not at all sure whether this is what you really want to do with the rest of your life. What I am really trying to say is that when I am gone, if you want to dispose of the business then that is alright with me. Discuss it with your mother, of course, but at the end of the day, the choice is yours.

One last thing, Jack. I don't know where you are in your relationship with Celia, but girls like her don't come across one's path as often as you may think. I hope that things work out between you, and that you will decide to be together and be as happy as your mother and I have been.

Your loving father.

Jack read the letter through again with a huge lump in his throat and sat silently for some minutes before folding it up and placing it back in the envelope. He then put it in the inside pocket of his jacket and made his way upstairs.

The following day, Jack dropped Celia back at the airport. Jack had been amazed that Damian and Sue Clarke had taken the trouble to fly over for the funeral, and it turned out that they were on the same flight as Celia for the journey back to the UK.

There had hardly been any chance to get further than the briefest of introductions during the funeral, so Celia had appreciated the opportunity to get to know them a little better during the two hours spent in the airport lounge as they waited to board. She felt that there were so many reasons for her to be grateful to them. They had been instrumental not just in Jack becoming a Christian, but in her and Jack getting together again.

By the time the plane had touched down, Damian and Sue knew that they would come to love Celia every bit as much as they loved Jack.

That evening, when Jack and his mother were alone together for the first time, it was Sarah who first broached the subject of the letter. Jack passed his letter over to his mother to read, though he felt it inappropriate to ask in any detail about the contents of her letter.

When his mother had read it through, she slowly drew her eyes away from it and said to her son, 'I don't think I'll ever feel the same way about Christmas again. At any other time of the year there would be an anniversary of us losing him – but Christmas is supposed to be about family. It's going to be so strange. I'm just going to have to try to cope and, however hard it may seem now, I suppose I will. Everybody does, don't they? In the past I've been far too quick to tell other people, "Don't worry, time is a great healer." But when something like this comes to your own door, you find yourself looking at such matters from an entirely different perspective.'

They both sat in silence for a minute or two before Jack said, 'Did you notice what Dad said about the business, Mum?'

'Yes, I did, and he touched on the same thing in my letter too.'

'What did you feel as you read it?'

'To be honest, Jack, I was surprised. He had poured so much of his life into it, as you know. I think I always assumed that he wanted you to take the business on. But how typical of your dad – all he really wanted was what was best for us. Anyway, as he wrote in the letter, in the end it's going to be your decision.'

'The strange thing is,' said Jack, 'I never once said anything to him that could have given him the slightest impression that I was finding Shoreside unfulfilling.'

'But that's how your dad was, wasn't it? There would be times when you were a boy and you would come home from school and he would ask how your day had been and you would say, "Fine, Dad, it's all good," and he would say to me later in bed, "You know, I think Jack's worrying about something," and then the next day, or perhaps the day after, it would all spill out and you would let us know how you really were. I think he knew you better than you knew yourself, sometimes.'

'You know, I think you could be right,' Jack answered. 'One thing for sure is that any relocation of the office will now most certainly be put on hold – not because I want to sell the business but because the last thing we need at the moment, Mum, is any further uncertainty.'

2006
Three years later

Jack had taken over the reins of the company immediately after his father had died and, as he'd decided, all thoughts of relocating were placed on the back burner. His mother's sister, Elizabeth, who had lost her own husband a year earlier, had been invited by Sarah to come to stay with her for a short break, and the arrangement had worked so well for both of them that they had considered making the arrangement permanent. This had been a great relief to Jack, as it meant that his mother would not be on her own on those occasions when he found it necessary to travel abroad on business.

Jack and Celia had married on 3rd May 2003, and Jack had been more than happy to cover the costs for all of Celia's close family to come to Estonia for the wedding.

His mother had said that there was plenty of room for her son and new daughter-in-law to stay with her but, knowing that his aunt had moved in and Sarah had company, they had decided instead to rent a villa in the area after their return from honeymoon.

The years slipped by, and by 2006 the business was going from strength to strength. Jack and Celia could hardly be happier together – the only cloud in the sky being their disappointment that the baby they longed for had so far not materialised.

Monday 6th February began as the most ordinary of days. Jack had left for work at around 7am. Celia, who was looking forward to having friends round for coffee mid-morning, had arranged to meet Jack for lunch at a favourite bistro in the centre of town at 12.30pm. It was a pleasant day and, as the restaurant was not too far away, Jack decided to walk so that he would be there as Celia drove into the restaurant's car park.

He watched as Celia signalled before turning towards the entrance, her face breaking into a smile as she noticed her husband.

Then, seemingly out of nowhere, a black SUV with dark tinted windows and moving at great speed careered across the path of Celia's car, smashing violently into the door on the driver's side.

In terror, Jack raced towards the scene shouting Celia's name, as if, by doing so, he could shorten the distance between them or accelerate the pace at which he could get to her side.

He wrestled frantically with the passenger door to get to where she lay slumped and bleeding across the steering wheel. But he could see immediately that the damage the SUV had inflicted would make it impossible for him to free her without help. Searching wildly for his mobile phone, he pressed the number to summon an ambulance. His pinpoint focus was so directed at the body of his wife that he was almost unaware of someone opening the driver's door from inside the SUV, dropping stealthily to the ground, racing towards the nearest alley and out of sight. But for the briefest of moments he registered the man's face – as quickly as a camera's shutter wrests an image from a chaotic environment and imprints it in its digital memory.

Having called the emergency services, and seeing he could do no more for Celia before they came, his next instinct was to find and challenge the person who had inflicted the carnage. He could see that the SUV had suffered little damage compared with the mangled metal of Celia's small car. His head darted from right to left as he ran towards the gathering spectators to question them, but then he remembered seeing the man race off. He pulled up sharply as the wail of approaching sirens accosted his ears. His first thought had to be for Celia, and so he quickly turned back towards her car.

Long before the cutting tools had freed her body from the mangled wreckage, he had known that she was dead. The paramedics produced a stretcher and, with all the sensitivity that they could muster and conscious that her husband's distraught eyes were now fixed on their every move, they carefully bore her body towards the ambulance.

The police were already taking statements from witnesses, who would later all confirm that the collision had been entirely caused by the SUV ploughing into the woman's car. Some also related that the driver, a man of Asian appearance, had fled the scene – though no one could give any further details beyond the fact that he was tall with a muscular frame and in his late thirties. None of them would have been aware that when the culprit had concluded that the driver of the other car was almost certainly dead and the heavily pregnant passenger in the back seat of his vehicle was most likely dead too, he had made an instant decision to flee.

The perpetrator, tired and breathless from the ordeal, slunk into a shadowed doorway somewhere in the nearby labyrinth of alleys in order to phone his bosses and relate what had occurred. But their immediate thoughts were not in the least for his welfare. All they wanted to ascertain was how certain he was that both parties were dead. If there was any chance that they could be identified, and this issue traced back to them, then the man who was known to most as 'The Handler' would be counting the hours to his own demise. He had told them that the girl had refused to wear a seat belt. He guessed that at the point of collision, her head had snapped back. Had she been sitting in a normal position, her neck would have been in line with her head restraint. However, owing to her condition she had been sitting at an angle, so that when the impact occurred and her head went back, its momentum was impeded not by soft leather but by the metal frame around the side window of the SUV. He said that his last glimpse before he exited the vehicle included the trace of a thin line of blood that was trickling down from her ear and across her cheek, and his bosses' minds were somewhat put at ease.

The reality was, however, that his passenger was not dead – at least not yet.

When the rear doors of the first ambulance had been securely locked and the driver was moving to the front to climb into his seat, Jack, who had been providing someone with his personal details, instinctively moved towards it. Celia was in there and he wanted to be with her, even though she was no longer alive. Immediately, the attending police officer countered his approach and, with kindness and firmness, he took hold of his arm and drew him back.

'There's nothing more you can do at the moment, sir. Just let them take her away from the area here, if you will,' said the police officer in a quiet, authoritative tone that conveyed that this was not the first time he had had to negotiate the pain of someone who had lost a person they loved in such circumstances.

It was at that point that Jack's attention was drawn to another movement at the side of the SUV, and he witnessed the body of a woman being removed from the crashed vehicle and moved cautiously onto a stretcher.

He came to the conclusion that she must still be alive as, once secured, a blanket was not placed over her face – though the rest of her body was completely covered.

As the back door of the second ambulance was opened and the bearers moved the stretcher towards it, one of the ambulance men momentarily stumbled before regaining his stance. The stretcher was quickly levelled, but not before the right arm of the unconscious woman had slid sideways from the cover of the blanket and revealed the dark mark of a serpent enclosed in a pentangle. Jack recognised it immediately as the same image it was reported had been on the bodies of the women taken from the metal container at the dockside.

The days that followed were by far the darkest that Jack had experienced in his life. When his mother had been informed, she was totally heartbroken. Sarah and Celia had enjoyed a far closer bond than simply that of mother-in-law and daughter-in-law. Sarah had treated Celia more like the daughter that she had never had.

All his friends were incredibly supportive, especially the many he had made at his church. But he struggled to see any purpose or plan in a beautiful life being so violently snatched away from him so early in their marriage.

The first emotional struggle had been a sense of incredible loss. The second was the need to find and bring to justice the person who had not only been the cause of his wife's death, but who had also fled from the scene to escape both prosecution and any sense of responsibility.

His pastor had connected with him daily in the days that followed the accident, either by phone or in person, and it was in the most recent of these visits that Jack had addressed with him some of the conflicting messages that were jostling around in his brain.

The church he was part of was mainly made up of the local community, but there were also a number of expats like himself who were either working in Estonia or who had decided to remain in the area in retirement. The minister of the church, Clive Clifford, a man in his mid-forties, was from London originally and had moved to the Tallinn area some years previously.

'Dealing with the loss of Celia is hard enough,' said Jack, as he ushered Clive into his lounge and pointed him towards a comfortable chair. 'But it's the things I hear from people who are meant to be offering me comfort that confuse me the most. I find their perspective incredibly odd, as well as hurtful – even when they couch their words in pseudo-spiritual language.'

'You mean stuff like, "There must be some sin in your life or Celia's life that God should have allowed this to happen",' suggested Clive.

'Exactly, how did you know?'

'These people always seem to come out of the woodwork at times like this!' the pastor responded. 'They usually glean their theology from flaky TV preachers or out of paperback books written by people who ride doctrinal hobby horses. And the problem with hobby-horse riders is that they usually want all the road for themselves. There is no debating with them. They always consider themselves on a higher spiritual plane than the likes of you and me and in possession of far deeper revelation. They have become devotees of their spiritual gurus and nothing as inconvenient as truth is allowed to get in their way or change their point of view. If you have read the book of Job, one of the oldest books in the Bible, it deals with suffering. I can assure you that these so-called "comforters" have been around since time immemorial, Jack.'

'And then,' said Jack, 'there are those who say that I should immediately forgive the person that wrenched Celia out of my life. I know that as a Christian I'm supposed to do that, but surely God considers justice as every bit as important as forgiveness. This person needs to be brought to account and I am going to do all in my power to make sure that he is – however unspiritual that may appear to be to others.'

Wisely, Clive chose not to spring back with an immediate response, and the two men sat opposite one another in silence for a moment or two. His pastor used the pause to reflect on how much Jack had changed in the years that he had known him.

Yes, he was struggling with the loss of his wife – but who wouldn't be? He couldn't help but think how this conversation might have gone in the early stage of Jack's Christian life. For a start, there would have been far more anger expressed than was now the case, and apart from that – he smiled to himself as the memories resurfaced – a few years ago every other sentence may well have been peppered with some choice expletives. Jack was a work in progress. But then, so was he and every other Christian that he knew. He waited until he felt it right to continue and then said, 'How about if we talk a bit about the "forgiveness thing", then, Jack? Are you OK with that?'

'I'll tell you if I'm alright with it, Clive, when I've heard what you are going to expect me to do, because I'll tell you now there is no way that I want to believe in a God that lets people off the hook, as some people appear to believe.'

'I can assure you that this is not about anyone getting away with anything. It's not like that. With all that you've got going on around losing Celia, the last thing that you want to have to handle is the feelings you have towards the driver of the car – as understandable as that may be. God lifts that weight from your shoulders by asking you to believe that He is able to deal with stuff like that. All the anger and angst that you can muster is not for a second going to affect the person whose actions robbed you of your wife. Anger, bitterness and hate are all wasted energy that has the potential of screwing nobody up but you, my friend.'

'I suppose you're right,' agreed Jack, 'but believe me, it's not easy.'

'Of course it's not easy; nothing as important as this ever is.'

Jack knew that this sense of relinquishment – leaving the matter in God's hands – was certainly not going to be easy for him. He was not a control freak by any means, but he certainly liked to be in charge of his own destiny and his own choices. As a Christian, he was learning that he was no longer at the centre of the universe, and that took some adjusting to! The will of God came first, and his role was to align himself with God's purpose as revealed in the Bible. He remembered that Damian had once likened the Bible to a highway code, in that a person could not pick and choose which bits they liked and which parts they didn't. It did not just dispense good advice or provide the luxury of selective alternatives. You could not opt to drive on the left side of the road on certain days of the month and on the right side on others. At the time, Jack had thought the analogy was a bit trite, but now he was beginning to catch the drift of what Damian had been trying to convey.

He found it easy enough to accept the parts of the Bible where it says that God accepts and forgives *us* despite our failings. It was less easy, however, to accept that this meant that we were called upon to similarly forgive others.

'Well, what about this, then, Clive?' continued Jack. 'The night I asked Christ into my life I was asked if I was willing to accept that, like everyone else in the world, I had failed at some point – "sinned", as I now know the Bible calls it.'

'Yes, I'm sure that would have been right,' agreed Clive.

'Well, next I was asked to ask God to forgive me, would that also be correct?'

'Right again.'

'OK, then,' Jack went on, 'so if anyone is to be forgiven, then forgiveness must first be appealed for and, if that is the case, if the person who took Celia's life does not *repent* – is that the word? – of what they did, then God would not be in a position to forgive them. Is that also right? Because if that *is* the case, then any position I take becomes totally irrelevant anyway.'

'I can see where you seem to be going with this, Jack, but there are two perspectives here that we have to be careful not to mix up. Let me give you an example – and I'm sorry that we seem to be using Celia's death as some kind of case study here.'

'Listen, Clive, I'm the last person who wants to do this, but I have to get this straight in my head if I'm going to have any chance of making some sense of all of this. To be honest, I thought that when I became a Christian everything would slot evenly into place, and I have to say that that does not seem to be happening right now.'

'But that's the point, Jack,' countered Clive. 'You are at least thinking, and that is good. You don't have to leave your brains at the door every time to come to church. Of course, faith and trust have a huge part to play in our lives, but that doesn't mean that we opt out of wrestling with the big and sometimes painful issues such as the ones you are dealing with right now.

'People talk about "blind faith", but there is really no such thing. If you or I exercise faith we are simply saying that God is omniscient and knows everything. This means we understand that He has a better perspective of what's going on than we have. I have to say, Jack, that there have been times when I've made judgements about people, only to find out later that I had got things catastrophically wrong once I found out all the facts. God doesn't have that problem. But listen, are you really sure that you want to continue talking like this? Perhaps we should pick this up at some other time …'

'No,' Jack retorted. 'I want us to keep going. This is important to me.'

'OK, then, let me put something else to you. At this moment it seems pretty clear that the driver of the SUV realised that his actions would have long-term consequences if he was found by the police. And so, leaving your wife and his passenger for dead, he decides to flee the scene. Now let's imagine how you would feel, even how you would react, if you ran into him by chance in a few minutes' time.'

'Do you really want me to answer that? I think it's pretty obvious. Perhaps I'm not going to lay into him, however much I might feel justified in doing so, but I would most certainly try to restrain him until the police were called.'

'Right then, let's now imagine that someone less restrained than you finds him and beats the living daylights out of him and leaves him in almost the state that he left Celia.'

'I can't see where you are going with this.'

'Hold on for just a moment, and I'll explain. Let's imagine that he's left for dead and then later the facts come out.'

'What facts?'

'Hang on, Jack. Look, I know this is purely hypothetical, and as things stand we both know what really happened, but what if it turned out that he'd had a seizure and blacked out seconds before the crash occurred and was then thrown from the vehicle after the impact and is still wandering around out there in a state of amnesia?'

'But that's ridiculous!'

'I know it's very improbable. Of course it is. All I'm trying to say is that if judgement had been taken out on him before the facts came to light, the alleged perpetrator would now be doubly a victim. In the first instance he would be the victim of a medical issue over which he had no control, and then of a retribution that was completely undeserved. What forgiveness does, even of people who are clearly at fault, is that it removes not only the corrosive anger from our spirits – that burns up no one except us – but it also takes the weight of judgement off our shoulders. That's all I'm trying to say.'

'Well, at least I understand what you're saying, but even if I park my anger against him and leave everything to God, he still has to come to justice.'

'Of course he does,' agreed Clive, 'and even if he escaped justice in this life he would have to face the judgement of God in the life to come. I know that you want to get this sorted as quickly as possible, but let me add another note of caution.'

'What's that?' asked Jack.

'Well, in the same way that I suggested you didn't try to do God's job for Him, could I also ask that you leave the police investigation to them?'

'I hear what you are saying, Clive, but all I can say just now is that I will promise to try.'

27th February 2006
Estonia

The church had been packed for the funeral and, apart from close family, there were also a few of Celia's friends from her time at university, as well as some from Gloucestershire who had travelled from the UK to attend.

Jack had heard via a friend who worked at the hospital to which the woman in the SUV had been taken that the condition of the patient was now no longer critical, although the baby she had been carrying had died as a result of the accident. Jack knew that if he was to learn anything about the driver, then the only way that he could do that was via the woman who had survived. The problem, as he saw it, was that even though he knew her condition had stabilised, he did not know if she was well enough to talk and, even if she was, the chances were that she would not be willing to talk to him.

He thought back to the advice that Clive had given him when he had discouraged him from getting involved. 'Just leave it to the police,' he had said. And in one way Jack could see the sense in this – especially with the likelihood that legal proceedings would be taking place. However, despite all the facts that he was marshalling that told him to back off, something at a deeper level was telling him that he needed to somehow make contact with the girl.

Jack's friend at the hospital had been reluctant to convey any more details than she had already provided, but eventually he learned that the patient was on the ward immediately outside the intensive care unit on the ground floor and that her first name was Elena.

He was aware that the chances of him being given admittance to see her were so slim that they bordered on the impossible. He also knew that there were so many unanswered questions around what had taken place that day that there may even be security outside her room – perhaps even a police presence. Nevertheless, he concluded that he must at least try.

Arriving at the hospital, he followed the signs to reception and glanced around to see who might be the best person to approach. There were already a few people around the desk. One woman had an elbow resting on the counter like someone waiting at a bar to be served. She was probably resigned, he thought, to being there for some time. Perhaps she was waiting for a friend or family member to be discharged. A couple of nurses in pale blue uniforms on the other side of the desk busied themselves among a forest of folders and files.

There was one woman who appeared to stand out from them all and Jack concluded that she must be the one in charge. She was slim, tall and wearing an immaculate white uniform, and Jack thought she was perhaps in her early fifties, but he also knew that he was notoriously poor at guessing people's ages – especially those of women.

As Jack appraised her, she turned her head inquisitively towards him, her grey eyes peering through rimless glasses and scrutinising him as he moved forward.

As her gaze fastened onto him, like a ground-to-air missile locking on to an aircraft that had intruded into its airspace, he instinctively knew that any charm offensive was unlikely to work here.

As he neared the desk she raised her arms to adjust her grey hair more tightly behind her head and into a bun. His mind immediately shifted similes, as he now concluded she resembled a vulture about to swoop.

'Excuse me, madam,' Jack began, emitting a wide smile that was not reciprocated, 'there is someone I am concerned about that has recently been discharged from intensive care and who now, I understand, is in a room of her own and might be able to receive visitors. Her name ...'

Before Jack could continue he was interrupted by the woman, who had now removed her hands from the back of her head and placed them on the reception desk in front of her. As she did so, she placed her weight on them in such a way that her body leaned closer towards him. Was the vulture now about to pounce? he wondered.

'Two things, sir, if I may? The full name of the patient and your relationship to her?'

Jack knew that if he said that he only had her first name, then any answer to the second question would be superfluous.

He was just about to offer a reply that he trusted might have at least a modicum of credibility when they were both interrupted by a flurry of white coats with appended stethoscopes sailing in from an adjacent corridor towards the reception area.

'Ms Rodriquez,' one of the furious-faced doctors began. 'How many times have I asked you to be more careful when you direct important people to my rooms?'

'I'm sorry doctor, what …?'

'Please allow me to finish, Ms Rodriquez, I have been waiting for the past twenty minutes to receive Monseigneur Conti, of St Mary the Virgin, at my cardiology clinic. When he had not appeared, I found I had to go looking for him, and where do you think that I found him?'

'I don't know, doctor. I just asked him to sit on the row of seats down that corridor and told him that he would be called in when you were ready.'

'But my office is not in that corridor, is it, Ms Rodriquez? It's in the next one along, and I ask you again, where do you think I might have found him?'

'I don't know, I'm sure, doctor,' came the stuttering reply.

'Well, I'll tell you, Ms Rodriquez! I found this senior cleric sitting adorned in the full regalia of his office in a row of seats and attracting the bemused attention of every passer-by. He was understandably curious as to why he was also attracting sniggers and why people were furtively whispering to one another behind their hands as they passed. The mystery, however, was soon solved, Ms Rodriquez, when he stood up and read the signs on the wall behind him. You had directed this reverend gentleman to sit in a row of chairs outside the clinics for prenatal counselling and sexually transmitted diseases. Now, Ms Rodriquez ...'

Jack thought that this was the perfect moment to leave and, sliding past the ongoing altercation, followed the signs for the intensive care unit in the knowledge that Elena's room was adjacent.

To his surprise there was no one either outside or inside the cubicle apart from the patient herself. He looked through the oval glass window and saw a dark-haired young woman lying in her bed and apparently asleep.

A drip led from a bag suspended from a metal stand to her left arm, just above her wrist. Jack realised that if he woke her and she cried out or called for help, not only would his journey have been fruitless, but he could also find himself in all kinds of trouble. But he had come this far so, pushing the adverse consequences to the back of his mind, he slipped through the door and slowly approached the bed. Before he spoke, he took in the appearance of the woman who lay there. The left side of her face was bruised but he knew that in time that would heal. What concerned him more was the pallor of her skin.

'Elena?' Jack whispered.

There was no initial response, but when he spoke her name again and just slightly louder, she began to stir. Opening her eyes, she seemed to be trying to remember where she was and why she was there. She looked first in front of her and then her head moved slowly to the right and towards Jack.

'Who ... who are you?'

At first it was just a question wanting an answer and with no emotion attached. But as she saw there was a man in her room who she clearly did not recognise, she became increasingly and visibly anxious. Jack realised that because he was not wearing a white coat, she would obviously conclude that he was not a doctor. She appeared to be trying to marshal her thoughts but, through the jumbled memories, struggled to take in the situation. She showed signs of increased anxiety brought on, no doubt, thought Jack, by a sense of feeling both vulnerable and defenceless.

'Help! Someone, help!'

The sounds came as a croak and hardly reached Jack's ears, let alone those of anyone who might already be in earshot of the room. Her eyes darted around; Jack wondered if she was searching for an alarm button but could not locate one. She tried to lift herself in the bed but, overwhelmed by weakness, fell back.

'You're not a doctor! I know the doctor. Who are you?'

'Elena, it's alright!' said Jack, in an attempt to reassure her. 'There is nothing to be afraid of. My name is Jack. I have just come to see how you are, that's all, and to find out if there's anything that you want – anything at all.'

'I lost my baby! I lost my baby! They told me it was a girl. I never even got to hold her.'

'Um ... yes ... I heard that,' said Jack, at a total loss as to how to respond. 'How are you, Elena? What are the doctors saying?'

'Who did you say you were? Why are you here? Have you come from them?'

Jack realised that, for better or worse, he had to explain who he was.

'My wife was in the other vehicle,' he offered. 'I'm afraid she didn't survive, so both of us ...'

'It wasn't my fault. Please don't blame me. I was just a passenger.'

'Hey, hey ... it's OK, Elena. Of course it wasn't your fault! Everybody knows that it wasn't your fault.'

At this, the terrified young woman in front of him appeared to relax, at least for a moment.

Jack glanced at his watch. He must have been in here for at least five minutes. How long had he got? How much could he ask without distressing her even more? Perhaps he should leave now.

'I'm sorry for your loss.'

'Excuse me?' said Jack, unsure of what he had just heard.

'I said I am sorry for your loss. I'm sorry that your wife died. I really am.'

Lost for words for a moment and fighting back rising emotion, Jack tried hard to compose himself. He had experienced genuine warmth from family and friends, but to hear this from someone he had only just met, someone, he guessed, who had been sold as a commodity between criminal gangs and endured things he could not even begin to imagine … It was almost too much.

'Do you know what Elena – you and me – we are in the same boat, aren't we?'

'How's that, Mr Jack?'

'Well, we've both lost someone who meant the world to us. For me it's my wife, and for you it's your baby. I know she didn't live long enough for you to get to know her. But she was still your baby. Isn't that right?'

The young woman said nothing. She just lay there and the tears that had welled up were now running down her cheeks unrestrained.

'Listen, I've got to go now, Elena. Is it alright if I call you Elena?'

'Yes, of course,' came the broken reply.

It was the simplest of questions, and Jack did not know it, but those last eight words meant more than she would ever be able to express. It was the first time for as long as she could remember that anyone had genuinely asked permission before they said or, especially, did anything to her.

Jack had assumed that this might be the case, and that was why he had posed the question in the first place.

'Listen, Elena, I have to go now, but I will come back. Would that be OK with you?'

'Yes, Mr Jack, please, please, come back.'

'It's not Mr Jack. My name is Jack Troughton, and Elena, listen to me carefully, you will need to remember my name because you might be asked if you are willing to see me. Do you understand?'

'Yes, Jack Troughton. I will remember – and Mr Troughton, just one more thing.'

'What is it, Elena? I need to go very soon. I think I hear voices outside coming this way.'

'Just one important thing: please – don't trust XCO bar.'

Jack had no idea what this meant, but had no time to stay for clarification. He simply reached over, squeezed her hand gently, slid out of the room and along the corridor and, not risking the use of the main entrance, exited the hospital via a service door.

Making his way around the building to the place where he had left his car, he opened the door, engaged the engine and drove off.

28th February 2006
Estonia

'You did what? You are joking, tell me you're joking. I can't believe what I'm hearing, Jack.'

Clive Clifford moved the handset from his ear and looked at it, as if by doing so he could get more sense out of the phone than he was getting from his friend. Returning it to his ear, he continued. 'You mean you went to the hospital and, without permission from the staff or permission from the patient, you actually went into her room uninvited? The room of the person who is linked to the crash? Tell me I'm not hearing this, Jack! I told you … '

'Listen, Clive, I know what you told me, and in many ways it makes no sense …'

'Makes no sense? This is crazy!'

'I know, I know, but I just had to do it. The girl's in a mess. She lost her baby. Her life may be under threat.'

'What are you talking about, Jack – her life may be under threat? What does that mean, for heaven's sake?'

'Well, just think about it. The driver of the SUV who ran off probably thought that both of the women had died in the crash, leaving no witnesses and no trail back to him. We already know that the vehicle was running on stolen plates. If he, and the gang he works for, find out that Elena survived – in fact, I would be amazed if they don't know already – then they will want to ensure that she doesn't live to give testimony in court.'

'Jack, if the police believed that there was any threat to her safety, there would have been a guard on duty outside her room and there wasn't – you seem to have walked right in unchallenged, from what you've just said.'

'Well, I'm going to visit my mother later this morning and then, in the afternoon, I'll go across to the hospital and see if I can learn any more from her.'

'For pity's sake, you can't be serious.'

'Got to go now, Clive – catch you later. Oh, and just one other thing, have you ever heard of a bar called the XCO? It might be a nightclub or something like that.'

'No, there's nothing like that in this area. Perhaps out of town but not around here, I'm sure. Why do you ask?'

'It's nothing – just something strange that Elena said. Anyway, must go.'

The call ended and the dial tone resumed.

Clive removed the handset from his ear, looked at the receiver again, shook his head, and placed the handset back in its cradle.

'Hi, Jack,' said Sarah Troughton, smiling broadly and extending her arms to welcome her son as he stepped towards her at the front door of her home.

'How have you been, Mum? Are you OK?'

'I'm fine, son, but what about you?'

'I've just been trying to keep myself occupied. There's been a lot to do at the office and, apart from that, there's the whole thing surrounding the accident.'

'Are the police any nearer to finding the man who caused it?'

'Not as far as I'm aware. It looks like he just vanished into thin air. Anyway, no one is telling me anything, that's for sure.'

'You're looking very tired, Jack. I know it's understandable, but what concerns me is that when I've looked at you recently, it reminds me of how your dad was. I just don't want you to …'

'Mum, there's a big difference. I am a lot younger than Dad was, and I don't have the health challenges that he faced either. I'm OK, don't worry. I really am.'

'Well, I'm not so sure. I know it's over three years since your father passed, but don't forget the letter he left you. You know he wanted you to be happy, not just busy. What he wrote to you …'

'I know what he wrote, Mum, and I know he released me from feeling I needed to be tied to the business for life, but the company is doing well and, even though we never relocated, I think there's still plenty of scope for expansion. Anyway, why are you bringing this up at this point?'

'We are human *beings*, Jack, not human *doings*. Deep down, your dad knew that Shoreside was not something you wanted to be involved in for life and I have always thought the same.'

'So why are you bringing this up now?' asked Jack. 'You've been thinking this through, haven't you? So I find myself asking why.'

'Well, I suppose I have; but something else has happened just recently …'

'What do you mean, "happened", Mum?' Jack extended an arm to her shoulder and drew her closer, examining her face for any clue to what 'happened' might mean. 'You're not ill, are you? Nothing's wrong?'

'No, son, of course I'm not ill. A few aches and pains that come with my age, but – it's just that I had a letter from your uncle Ronald in the States asking how I was, and … well, he asked about the business and so forth.'

'But you haven't heard from him for ages. I remember you saying only recently that you wondered why he hadn't been in touch. I mean, how many times has he contacted you since Dad died? Twice … three times at the most?'

'He's a very busy man. He has lots of responsibilities. He's become very successful over the years. Well, Jack, I'll come right to the point. He wants you to get in touch with him.'

'Me? He's hardly had anything to do with me all my life. Why would he want …?' Jack paused for a moment to collect his thoughts. He visited his mother regularly and had thought it strange that she had invited him round specially today. Then she was alluding to his stress, and now mentioning Ronald.

'I get it, Mum. He wants to take over the business. That's it, isn't it?'

'Not take over, Jack. He can't do that. The company belongs to you, you know that. But I think he may wish to make you an offer and, knowing him, I think it would be a generous one.'

'Mum, I don't want to be unkind, but I've just lost Celia. This is hardly the best time for me to be making long-term decisions.'

'I know that, son, and I told him that …'

'Told him, Mum! You mean you have discussed this with him?'

'No, not discussed it exactly. Look, I know it's a bad time, but he has the chance of taking over a big firm based in New York. It's a major player in the transport industry and one that wants to expand into Europe. Shoreside is small compared to his other acquisitions, but he thinks it would be an advantage if he could add Shoreside to his portfolio now.'

'Oh, that's great, Mum. He wants to "add it to his portfolio", does he – as if he's just moving a pawn on his conglomerate chessboard? It's my livelihood – it's *our* livelihood, Mother!'

Sarah knew that Jack only addressed her as 'Mother' when he was upset. She could understand his feelings. Of course now was not the ideal time. She may have been 'just his father's wife' in some people's eyes, but she still had a strong eye for business and always had. She was acutely aware that, from a management point of view, there was a very narrow window of opportunity. It was not a decision that could be put off for long and she knew her brother-in-law would place a strong offer. The way the world economy was going, who knew what could happen in the future?

But there was more than that at stake here. She was not primarily thinking about the business. She was seeing it through a mother's eyes. Jack had been looking under pressure long before the accident, though she had never wanted to point it out to him in case he was hurt. There was no question of him being in competition with his father's memory, but he was becoming almost as driven as Wesley had been. It had never affected his relationship with Celia – they were too much in love for that – but he had certainly been burning the candle at both ends as the workload had increased. Yes, it was debatable whether she should have brought the matter up at this point, but she had considered it a risk worth taking.

'All I'm asking you to do, Jack, is to think about it. It wasn't that I wanted to spring anything on you. But there is a time element involved in this. If you do decide to contact your uncle, he will be better placed than me to tell you exactly what he has in mind.'

'I'm sorry, Mum, of course I'll think about it, but it's all come as a bit of a shock. And I'm sorry if I was abrupt with you. I've just had what you might call a *robust* phone conversation with a friend and, well … what with all this …'

'It's alright, son. I honestly didn't know the best way to bring it up. Look, all I'm asking is that you give it some thought, that's all. Let's leave it there, but it would be nice if you could at least let your uncle know one way or the other.'

Sarah made them both a coffee and brought out a plate of flapjacks. He always complained that they were bad for his waistline, but had never been known to refuse.

That afternoon, Jack made his way back to the hospital and climbed the steps towards the front entrance with not a little trepidation.

'Hello, Ms Rodriquez, and how are you?' Jack said, as he approached the reception desk with the same smile that had failed to bear any fruit twenty-four hours earlier and which he was not counting on now to secure him any particular advantage.

'My goodness, you've got some cheek coming back here. You've got some nerve and no mistake – and how do you know my name?'

'Well, that name tag on your uniform is a bit of a clue,' said Jack, still retaining the smile, 'and anyway, I overheard the doctor talking to you.'

'Right, well, I think we will draw a veil over that, shall we?' replied the receptionist, her authority noticeably diminishing as the embarrassing memory resurfaced. 'It's not right what you did, though. You know that, don't you?'

'Yes, I know, and I'm sorry, but I really did need to see her.'

'It's just as well that when we checked on her it was clear that she was glad that you'd made the visit. In fact, I noticed that she was much more at ease and brighter than she has been since she came in. We had not had a smile out of her, or any sign of warmth as far as I can remember, until yesterday. She also mentioned that if ever you were to call again we should be sure to let you …'

'Oh, that's wonderful,' cut in Jack, as he angled his body in the direction of the corridor that led to her room. He was standing poised to move, as if waiting only to be released by a word from Ms Rodriquez in order that he might continue on in the trajectory he had already commenced.

'Hold on, Mr Troughton – it *is* Mr Troughton, isn't it? – if you would, hold on. I would be happy for you to see her again – if she was here, but she's not. She's been moved.'

'Moved? Moved where?' asked Jack, anxiously.

'I'm not at liberty to say.'

'Why on earth not?'

'Those were my orders.'

'Orders? Orders from whom?'

'I have just told you, I'm not at liberty to say. Please do not question me any further. That's all there is to it and I think you should leave now. I'll bid you good day, Mr Troughton.'

With that, she turned on her heel and headed away from him, through a door marked clearly in red, 'Private'.

Jack was nonplussed as he made his way back out of the hospital. Out of the corner of his eye he noticed a police car parked at the kerb in front of him, but gave it only a cursory glance. He was just making a turn to the right when he heard the electric buzz of a car window being lowered, followed by a voice that called across to him, 'Mr Troughton, a minute of your time, if you please?'

Jack heard it as part-question and part-command, so turned back towards the police vehicle. There were two policemen in the car, the one who had spoken and his driver. The driver kept his gaze forward as Jack peered in, and the officer who had spoken continued.

'Mr Troughton, would you be able to spare a few moments for a brief chat?'

'And you are …?' enquired Jack.

'I am an officer dealing with the tragic crash in which your wife was killed. I wonder if you could accompany us to the police station if at all possible. We won't keep you long, and of course my driver will deliver you back to your car, which I assume is somewhere in the vicinity.'

Jack thought that he was probably going to be given an update on the case and, welcoming any news that might be forthcoming, inclined his head in assent. When the officer saw that he was moving towards the rear seat he made the slightest of backward nods to the driver, indicating that the door should be released. The driver clearly understood for, as Jack bent forward he heard the click that indicated he was free to enter.

The police station was a spartan building and the interview area was sparsely furnished. The room had a metal table, which Jack noticed was fixed to the floor, and three dark blue plastic chairs with metal frames. There were two at one side of the table and one at the other, and a recording machine at one end of the desk. Jack was asked if he would like tea or coffee, and when he indicated that he needed neither, was invited to sit on the single chair.

The officer who had initially approached him sat, to Jack's surprise, not immediately in front of him but slightly to the side and a fraction back from the table. A second man then entered the room. It was neither the driver nor anyone that Jack had previously seen. The second man took the chair directly opposite Jack, so he assumed that it was he that was going to conduct the interview. Jack noted that neither of the two men had introduced themselves. He had watched enough TV to know that the first thing anyone did in a scenario like this was to give their names to the interviewee – together with their rank. Neither of these officers had done so.

Jack's first inclination was to invite them to say who they were, but decided against it as he concluded that that might appear somewhat aggressive and he wanted to maintain a good rapport with them in order to elicit as much information as possible.

'Mr Troughton, first of all let us apologise for two things,' began his interviewer. 'The first is to do with the room we are in. There is nowhere else where we could chat. This is a small station with few amenities. The second apology is for the abrupt nature of our approach to you. My staff had attempted to telephone you first thing this morning but the line was engaged, and then, when we tried later, there was no reply.'

'I'm sorry about that,' responded Jack. 'I was on the phone to a friend before leaving to visit my mother.'

'That's alright. We understand,' said the man, reassuringly.

Jack considered it very strange indeed that they had known precisely where he would be when they had approached him. If they had contacted his mother she could not have told them, as he had not mentioned to her during their conversation where he was going after he had been with her.

The officer who had initially invited him to the station said nothing. He sat with an expressionless stare, watching Jack's reaction to each of the questions as they were put.

'Could you please tell me why I am here?' enquired Jack. 'I assumed when I agreed to come that it had to do with the accident in which my wife died. I'm expecting that you will be able to update me with any progress that has been made. For example, have you managed to find the driver of the SUV?'

Jack had felt from the moment that he had entered the room that he was on the back foot and was finding the present exercise more than a little intimidating. The police station may have been small, but he was sure that these men would have had a private office of some sort that was a little more welcoming than this.

'One thing at a time, Mr Troughton. First of all, can we point out to you that this is not a formal interview. Let's just call it a chat, shall we? You will notice that nothing is being recorded. However, my colleague may take a few notes along the way, if you don't object.' Jack was not given an opportunity to object, as his interviewer continued without a pause: 'Now, Mr Troughton, can you tell me why you were at the hospital this afternoon?'

'I was visiting someone,' responded Jack.

'Well, you didn't visit for very long, did you? You were only in the hospital for a very short time – only a couple of minutes, in fact.' Before Jack could reply, he continued: 'And would this person you were visiting be the same person that you visited yesterday?'

'Yes, it was,' responded Jack.

'And could you please tell us the patient's name?'

'If you knew I was there yesterday,' retorted Jack, a little more forcefully than he had intended, 'you probably know precisely who it was that I was there to see.'

'We do, actually, but we must confess that we were not a little surprised about your interest in this person. Please tell us why you wanted to see the woman in question?'

'I thought that would be fairly obvious,' said Jack, thinking that this was now morphing into more of an interrogation than an interview. Surprisingly, though, he was conscious of feeling far less intimidated than he might have been. Perhaps it was the adrenaline or the fact that he was now becoming more annoyed than nervous.

He had done nothing wrong, yet here he was being treated as if he were the criminal who had fled the scene rather than the person who had watched his wife die.

'And why should you think that we would find this obvious?' the officer continued, without acknowledging or even recognising Jack's change of tone. 'Some people might go so far as to suggest that you are guilty of interfering in a police investigation. I need to point out to you that, if you are, you could be in serious trouble. It could even be construed that you are seeking to pervert the course of justice. If that is not your objective, and for your sake we sincerely hope that it is not, you could be meddling in something far bigger than you could possibly imagine. Do I make myself clear, Mr Troughton?'

This was not a 'good cop/bad cop' scene from the detective films he had watched over the years. This was 'bad cop/bad cop'. Officer two had yet to speak, but his gaze remained fixed laser-like on Jack's every response – words and body language included. Jack's mind immediately flashed back to the damaged metal container on the dockside nearly four years ago. Like frames of a film, his thoughts momentarily jerked towards the bodies of the women being carried out of the containers and then jumped to Elena as she lay helplessly in a hospital ward.

The voice came again, but louder this time.

'Do I make myself absolutely clear, Mr Troughton?'

'Look, my wife has been killed in a road accident – in my view, murdered.'

'Yes, we are very sorry about your loss, Mr Troughton, we really are,' offered the interviewer, in a tone that was as emotionally sterile as the tiles on a morgue wall.

'Yes,' continued Jack. 'I heard what you said, but my wife has been killed and the man responsible has fled the scene. It appears to me that the highest priority now should be that this person is found. Unless I have missed something, no one seems the slightest bit nearer discovering where or who he is. It seems plain, at least to me, that he clearly thought that both my wife and the other woman had been left for dead and that there were no witnesses. However, there were two.'

Out of the corner of his eye, Jack saw the officer who had been meticulously scrutinising him almost imperceptibly shift his position on his chair as he heard this.

'Two, you say,' asked the first officer, 'and exactly who would they be?'

'Well, obviously the woman who has survived,' answered Jack.

'You mean the woman that you visited yesterday.'

'Yes, Elena.'

'Oh, it's Elena, now, is it? On first name terms now, are we? And what information did *Elena*,' he gave her name particular emphasis, 'convey to you?'

Jack was now aware not just of the second officer moving his position more noticeably, but also that he was leaning slightly forward as if wanting to take in every nuance of what Jack was saying.

'She actually told me very little, as it happens. I only had a couple minutes with her before I needed to leave.'

'You mean before you fled, Mr Troughton. Would that not be a better way of putting it? *Before you fled.*' The last three words were delivered with emphasis. 'In fact, you had no right be there in the first place, did you, Mr Troughton? You were there without permission, if I am not mistaken, from either the hospital staff or the patient herself. But anyway, you said there was a second witness. So who might that be?'

Jack paused for a moment before replying.

'Well, me, of course. I was there, remember. I saw everything. I not only witnessed my wife's death, but I also saw the face of the man who ran from the SUV.'

At this, the second officer broke his silence and, in a voice that betrayed the very slightest tinge of nervousness, said, 'And do you think that you could recognise the man who fled if you saw him again?'

Jack had been focused on the help being given to his wife. Others had reported a thickset, muscular man of Asian appearance. Jack had probably taken in far less than others had, given the state he was in, but he had noticed that this second suggestion had most definitely rattled the second officer from his silence. Jack was not prepared to lie but, at the same time he wanted to hold on to what appeared to be an advantage, and simply added, 'Well, I was there at the time, wasn't I?'

He had been there and for the briefest of moments had captured the man in his vision. Jack's answer hung in the air, with neither officer apparently knowing what to do with it. They already possessed the statement that he had given at the time of the incident, which had provided no more detail than other witnesses had given when they were questioned. But this was the first time anyone had thought to ask if he would be able to recognise the driver if presented with the opportunity to do so.

Jack had clearly not indicated anything to the contrary. In fact, how could he respond more accurately unless he was presented with a line-up? No one could be sure unless their memory was tested – and some got it right and others didn't.

It was Jack who then took up the conversation again. 'So, have you moved any further on in your investigations, or are you no further forward at all? I assumed when you approached me earlier that you wanted to speak to me about how things were progressing, but now it appears that everything remains at a standstill.'

'All we are prepared to say at this stage is that we are continuing with our investigations,' said the first officer defensively.

Jack knew that this was a meaningless catch-all phrase which could have been made by any police force anywhere in the world. It conveyed either that they knew nothing at all, or that they knew a great deal that they did not want anybody else to know. He had had enough of this and knew that they had no basis on which to question him further. Moving to a standing position, he said, 'Then if there is nothing more you want from me, I will be on my way, if you don't mind.'

Both officers seemed taken aback, almost affronted, that he had taken the initiative to leave, but they seemed to know he was right. There was no way they could keep him here, even if they wanted to.

'I think you said that someone would be kind enough to take me back to my vehicle at the hospital car park?'

'Very well,' said the interviewing officer. 'You may go, but be assured that we may need to talk to you again at some point.'

'Well, I trust that, if that is the case, then on that occasion there will be a record of our conversation – especially if you intend to charge me with anything. Obviously, in that event, I will also want to have the benefit of my lawyer with me. Oh, and just before I leave,' Jack continued, 'could you please provide me with the address where Elena has been taken? I assume it is another hospital?'

'I'm sorry, Mr Troughton, we cannot do that,' said the first officer. 'That is not for you to know. So if you would please make your way towards the foyer, one of our drivers will join you shortly.'

Jack had only to wait for a moment or two before another officer appeared, and he was then conveyed towards one of the cars parked in the forecourt of the station. The young man opened a rear door for him and, once inside, moved around the car to access the driver's seat. Jack noticed it was the same man that had earlier driven him to the station.

'You obviously know where you're taking me,' Jack said to him.

'Yes, sir, back to the hospital, I believe. Is that right?'

'Yes, thank you,' replied Jack. 'You can drop me on the main road where you picked me up. My car is in the parking area at the rear. I can easily walk from there.'

The officer did not speak again during the short journey, until they had arrived at their destination. At this point the driver, while applying the handbrake, said, 'OK, sir, I'll leave you here. You can get out now. I have released the door.'

Jack thanked him, closed the door and was just about to walk away when the officer called out, 'I hope that wasn't too much of an ordeal for you today. He can come over quite strong sometimes, our Inspector Escobar.'

'What did you just say?' asked Jack.

'I just said people find Inspector Escobar a bit intimidating sometimes. He rarely conducts the interviews himself – he just sits there and watches.' And with that, the young officer pulled away.

Jack stood motionless for a minute – almost in a daze.

'Escobar! Elena didn't say "Please don't trust XCO bar", she said, "Police – don't trust Escobar!" Could he be in on it all?' Jack thought anxiously to himself. 'Could Escobar be in the pocket of the sex traffickers?'

Jack fished out his keys, found his car, joined the rush-hour commute and made his way home. When he opened the door, he absent-mindedly picked up three letters that had been delivered in the morning's post. Most of his mail came to the office, and the post that had come to the house was usually from Celia's friends. They seemed to send one another cards all the time; mostly friends from church writing notes of encouragement or extending invites to coffee mornings. Of course, these were now things of the past, Jack mused. He dropped the mail on the hall table and headed for the kitchen.

He was too tired to start cooking and certainly didn't want to venture out for a meal. With Celia gone, it was very hard for him to eat out alone. If he did, he knew all he would see was the empty chair across the table from him.

Going into the kitchen, he opened the fridge door and selected a ready meal. After a day like today, comfort food was an easy choice, and within just a couple of minutes the ping from the microwave indicated that the cottage pie was ready.

When everything was cleared away, he turned on the TV and switched to the BBC channel to find out what was going on in the UK. London mayor, Ken Livingstone, had been found guilty of bringing his office into disrepute and, despite tomorrow heralding the first day of March, Britain was in the grip of the severest weather of the winter so far. He moved to the programme list but found nothing of interest. The thing he could not get out of his mind was the involvement of Inspector Escobar. It raised so many worrying questions. If he was working for this criminal gang, how safe was Elena now? And what could Escobar be doing in terms of suppressing evidence, or even alerting the gang to any evidence that was currently available? The problem now was that he knew no one in the police force who had any influence, or that he could even begin to trust with his suspicions. But there was at least one thing of which he was certain – Elena's life was definitely in danger. And it was then that he had an idea.

1st March 2006
Estonia

The moment Jack returned to the office he searched in his files for any details relating to when he and his father had been contacted by Customs to attend the opening of one of their containers. He knew it was about four years ago and during the summer. He needed the precise date but, more importantly, the name of the person who had overseen the investigation.

It did not take him long to find what he was looking for. The date was 6th August 2002. 'Here it is,' he said to himself. 'Her name was Pamela Abbott!'

He lifted the phone and dialled the number that he had retained for her department. After a couple of rings, a man's voice enquired as to whom was calling and the nature of his business.

'I'd like to be put through to Ms Pamela Abbott, please. It is in regard to some enquiries that she was involved in with my company a few years ago. I would like to speak to her with a view to setting up an appointment to see her. It's an urgent matter and so …'

'I'm sorry, sir,' the voice on the other end interrupted. 'I am afraid that that will not be possible. Ms Abbott does not work in the department any more. She accepted a promotion around eighteen months ago.'

Jack was disappointed, but perhaps the man to whom he was speaking could still be of some help.

'Do you have any contact details for her that would help me get in touch?' Jack continued.

'I cannot see why that would be of any use to you if your enquiry relates to a matter that involved this department. Could I put you through to her successor? I have the extension number right here.'

'No, that's OK, I really wanted to speak to her personally if at all possible.'

'Well, I'm afraid that I cannot release any personal details to you. This would, as you might understand, breach our policy regarding data confidentiality.'

'Yes, I fully understand that, but could you at least tell me the department she is with?'

'Certainly, sir, I am happy to do that. Her office is not situated at this address, but I can give you the number for reception at the place she now works, if that would help.'

'That would be great. I would appreciate that,' Jack replied, pleased that what he thought had been a dead end now seemed to be opening up, if only a fraction.

Jack made the call. It took a great deal of effort, and not a little patience, but eventually he was put through.

'Hello, Mr Troughton, how nice to hear from you. This is a surprise. I trust you are well and your father ...'

'My father passed away, I'm afraid – heart attack.'

'Oh, I'm so sorry to hear that. I was so appreciative of your understanding when we took up so much of your time unnecessarily on that dreadful day. You were both very considerate. Anyway, how can I help you today? By contacting me here, you have learned already that I am no longer involved with the work I was engaged in when we first met, so I'm not really sure how ...'

'No, it's not anything about that. Look, it's a sensitive matter that I can't really talk about over the phone. Is there any chance that you could spare me a couple of minutes sometime soon to chat, face-to-face?'

There was a few seconds' pause at the other end, and Jack assumed she was weighing up what it might be that he wanted to talk about, and even considering if it might compromise her, or her department, should she agree to speak to him. So, before she could reply, Jack added reassuringly, 'It's nothing either about you or the work that you do. I'm basically looking for some advice, I suppose, and I felt you might be the best person to help.'

'Well, I must admit I am intrigued. Though, if it's not official business, I'm not sure that it would be right to meet at my office. If you are in my vicinity at around lunchtime we could meet then. It's not something that I would really consider normally, but frankly, given the wild goose chase we put you through a few years ago, perhaps it's the least I can do.'

'Lunch would be wonderful,' responded Jack.

She suggested both the venue and the time that would suit her best, and a couple of hours later they were sitting across the table from one another. The café that had been chosen was typical of the many that were situated around the perimeter of Tallinn's medieval cobbled squares. Red and white striped awnings sheltered the diners from the sun and, when both had ordered a light lunch and it had arrived, it was Pamela Abbott who was the first to move from the small talk to ask why it was so important that Jack meet her and with such apparent urgency.

'I was wondering as I was walking from my office what this could possibly be about. You're not in any trouble are you, Mr Troughton?'

'Oh, not at all. Well, not in the way that I think you mean. And please call me Jack.'

'Well, I'm glad to hear that at least ... Jack ... and you might as well drop the Ms Abbott – especially if we are not discussing anything on a professional basis.'

Jack knew that the next few minutes of conversation had a huge element of risk attached to them. He had only ever had two conversations with this woman and even those had a space of almost four years between them. Could he really bring her into his confidence? However, he quickly concluded that he had little option.

Ever since he had become a Christian, he had committed every day to God in prayer and this morning had been no exception. There were just so many things going on around his life just now; his mind was all over the place, and the last thing that he had wanted was his mother raising the added complication of the future of the business. Yet since she had mentioned it, he had been unable to push it completely to the back of his mind, much as he had wanted to. Perhaps accepting his uncle's offer might not be a bad idea. Commercially, Shoreside was doing well. But was that what everything was really about – making money? Was that really the bottom line? He had once thought so, but over the past few years, and particularly since that chance meeting with Damian that had gone on to open up a whole new spiritual dimension to his life, he wasn't so sure. And now, with what had just happened … he needed a different focus.

He had always wanted to 'make a difference'; that was just how he was wired up. But make a different to what? His bank balance? His material security? He knew that there was nothing wrong with either of those things per se, but what had he remembered Clive saying when he was preaching? 'Possessions only become wrong when they begin to possess us.' Had that happened to him? He wasn't sure. Perhaps it had. And now that Celia was gone, what really mattered, after all?

'Mr Troughton … Jack … are you still there?'

The voice had seemed to come out of the distance, but it had the desired effect of bringing Jack back to the moment.

'Oh, I'm sorry. Yes … my mind seemed to have wandered for a second or two,' he said, apologetically.

Jack then went on to relate the account of Celia's death – the man running from the scene – the woman who had survived – the crude tattoo on her body that was the same as had been found on the women who had been discovered in the rusted container at the dockside. He told her everything except the final episode of the story – the part that involved the risk. He paused, not because he did not want to go on, but because he wanted to somehow gauge the reaction of his listener to what he had recounted thus far.

'This is horrendous, Jack, truly frightful. Losing your father and then your wife being killed in such desperate circumstances! I really don't know what to say.'

It was clear to Jack that Pamela Abbott was genuinely sincere as she expressed her sympathy. From the moment she had entered the restaurant he had noticed that her body language had expressed a certain degree of tension. She had sat with her back straight, almost perched, on the edge of her chair as if she might be called upon to leave at any moment. Even as the waitress was taking the order he had noticed her glancing at her watch. In fact, her posture had been so pronounced she might as well have said the words right out: 'How long is this going to take? What is it you want? How soon will I be able to leave and get on with the rest of my life?'

Jack thought he was good at reading people. He sometimes got it wrong, but usually he thought himself not very often far off the mark. Right or wrong this time, it did not matter. Her body language had now clearly changed. She was sitting right back in her chair. She seemed noticeably more relaxed and, when she did lean forward, it was evident she was giving Jack her total attention.

'As I said, Jack, I am staggered at your story. You poor thing! How awful. But what I can't see is how you think I might be able to help.'

Jack went on to relate the rest of the story. He covered Elena's warning to him about the corrupt police officer, though stopped short of mentioning his name.

'But, Jack, I still can't see … I don't know …'

'Listen, Pamela, let me lay it on the line. You had an influential role in your department when I first met you. You've now been promoted to a role with even greater status. The thing is …' Jack continued hesitantly, 'I just don't know who I can trust. I can't share this at the local police station. I have no idea if the officer concerned is working alone or whether there are others, even more senior to him, that are on the payroll of the organisation. I need someone to introduce me to a figure who is way beyond the rank of anyone that I would normally have the chance to access. I don't know who that person would be and, even if I did, it's unlikely they would ever listen to me.

'What it boils down to is that I'm guessing that you might have the ear of the kind of person that could be crucial in this whole thing. I honestly believe that this is a matter of life and death. I know I can't bring Celia back, but I can at least try to do something to prevent other people being harmed. For all I know, the gang may have got hold of Elena or, God forbid, she may even already be dead.'

Pamela Abbott slid back in her chair and cupped her chin in her hands, signalling to Jack that she needed a few moments to think.

After a while, she folded her arms in front of her and looked directly across at him.

'You know, Jack, there is one person that comes to mind. He is certainly a very high-ranking officer. I've met him on a couple of occasions at formal dinners connected with my profession. Our paths have crossed enough times, however, to place us in the category of firm acquaintances, if not friends. I could speak to him, I suppose, but of course I can't guarantee that he will agree to see you or, even if he does, whether he would be willing to take the matter forward.'

'But are you prepared to try?' asked Jack hopefully.

'Yes, I'll certainly try but, as I have said, I'm not sure whether any outcome, even if there is one, will meet your expectations. You see, you need to understand how the police force in Estonia works.

'The highest-ranking police officer holds the title of National Police Commissioner. The central agency is the Estonian Police Board, which manages, directs and coordinates the activities of all police units under its administration. Then there are the police units of which there are three: the Central Criminal Police, the Central Law Enforcement and the Forensic Service Centre. There are four territorial police units, called Police Prefectures. The local police chiefs are called prefects. As I am sure you will realise, in any organisation that has strong leaders within clearly defined departments, there can be those who are jealous of their own space – defending their territory, if you like. It can get complicated and sometimes justice can be the loser. Do you hear what I am trying to say, Jack?'

'Well, I can only guess. I have seen enough American crime dramas where the local police don't want to give way to the FBI or CIA, and I'm sure that back home in the UK there must be similar tensions.'

'What I am saying I suppose, Jack, is that we have a lot of incredibly busy people who are all trying to do their job with huge caseloads and insufficient budgets ... so don't hold your hopes up too much. They are professionals under pressure.' With a quick glance at her watch, and realising she needed to get back to the office, she rose from her seat, extending her hand. 'I need to go, Jack. I promise I will do what I can. If you hear from anybody, it will be unlikely to be me. If nothing materialises, then at least you can be sure that I will have done my best. If something does come up, then I suppose you will be contacted by the relevant authorities. I need to go now.' She was moving towards the door, but before leaving, she turned and asked, 'Can I cover the bill?'

'No, not at all. My invitation … my pleasure. Oh, and thanks.'

Jack headed back to his own office. His position in the firm gave him all the flexibility he needed time-wise, but it was only when his PA alerted him to the list of people who had tried to reach him and were still waiting for answers that he realised how much all this was eating into his schedule. There would be no doubt that he would be coming in a lot earlier and getting home later over the next few days.

When he eventually pulled into his drive that night, he arrived with the sense that as least as far as today was concerned, the schedule was a little more back on track.

On unlocking the door, he picked up just one letter and was about to drop it on the hall table when he noticed the three that were there from yesterday that he had not opened. The two manila envelopes he decided to open last as they would probably be business related or bills. He turned his attention first to the one that remained. It was white and A5 in size. The outside was blank and so obviously delivered by hand. He opened it and slid out a photo of his mother taken outside her house. There was no accompanying note.

'Who on earth would send me a picture of my mother?' he said to himself and then turned the photo over.

He caught his breath and dropped both envelope and photograph on the table, in a gesture that implied that by putting even the slightest physical distance between him and those two objects he was, by that act, separating himself from the consequences of the seven words he read that had been written in large letters: 'Back off if you value your family.'

For a moment or two he just stood there transfixed, and then, gathering himself together, he paused a second or two longer.

He had been about to snatch them up from where they lay when it occurred to him that he was looking at something that constituted evidence. He realised that he should not handle the picture further as there could be fingerprints that could lead to the sender. Fortunately, he had drawn the photo from the envelope by the edge and, between finger and thumb, had rotated it around as he read what was on the back. But then a second thought came to him. 'But what good is evidence that can't be presented to the police?'

Earlier that day, as he had spoken to Pamela Abbott, the thought had occurred to him that by following through the whole issue with the danger that Elena was in, he may well be placing *himself* in a position of exposure and vulnerability. However, he had dismissed the thought immediately. This was not only about Elena. This was primarily about Celia and what had happened to her. It was also about people whom he had never met – the women lying dead at the dockside and those who, right now, were under the control of a gang that had its tentacles around so many broken lives. It had actually also occurred to him that perhaps 'making a difference' in this kind of context could be what the future held for him. There was no doubt in his mind at all that the photo in front of him was a game changer. He had lost two of the most important people in his life. His father had died and his wife had been killed. There was not the slightest chance that he was now going to allow his mother's safety to be put at risk.

It was a long time before Jack got to sleep that night. There were now more variables in the equation than he could comfortably process.

6th March 2006
Estonia

Jack reached his office shortly after ten. As he entered the reception area, he was surprised to see Mia waiting for him. His new PA had been with the company for just a couple of weeks and, in her apparent desire to please and make a good impression, sometimes created an aura of nervous fussiness about her. Jack was hoping this would wane with time. He wondered why she was in the reception area rather than her office, and he was hardly in the door before she hurried towards him.

'I know you asked that I keep today totally clear of appointments for you, Mr Troughton, but there is a man upstairs waiting for you. He says that it's urgent. I made it clear to him that he would need to make an appointment and that you had no space in your schedule today, but he insisted and …'

'It's alright, Mia, don't worry, it can't be helped. I know you did your best. I'll deal with it. Did he say who he was and what he wanted?'

'No, he said he would only speak with you. I'm sorry, Mr Troughton, I tried, but he was so insistent.'

As Jack reached his floor and made his way towards his office, he watched as a well-built man in his late forties stood to his feet and walked towards him. Jack assumed he must be at least six foot two. He was immaculately dressed in a dark grey suit, white shirt and maroon silk tie.

'Mr Troughton, your PA has explained to me that you have a very full schedule today, but I think, when I explain why I am here, you will probably create some space for us to have a talk.'

'I hardly think that is likely, Mr …?'

'I'll introduce myself once we are in your office, but if I say that Pamela Abbott was the person who suggested we might meet, then I think you will understand.'

Jack opened the door, ushered his visitor in and extended his arm towards a group of heavily buttoned green leather Chesterfield armchairs at the far end of the room, alongside a coffee table, indicating that his visitor should make himself comfortable.

'Would you like tea or coffee?' offered Jack, knowing that, if this was who he thought it was, he was not going to start the paperwork that he had planned to work on any time soon.

'Coffee would be good, thank you.'

At this, Jack pressed a button on the intercom on his desk and, when there was a response at the other end, said, 'Mia, please bring us in some coffee.'

When both men were seated opposite one another, the visitor introduced himself.

'My name is Markus Poska. A couple of days ago I received a call from Ms Abbott, who suggested that we should perhaps meet one another. She mentioned to me something of the circumstances in which your wife died, and first of all, please accept my condolences. It must have been a terrible ordeal for you.'

Jack appreciatively raised his hand to acknowledge the courtesy, but did not interrupt.

'I am not at liberty to share my rank, or even the department to which I belong, but you can be confident that my seniority is such that you can talk to me without any fear that our conversation will be in any way compromised. I will also need your assurance that anything that I may convey to you will be held in complete and absolute confidence.'

Jack gave him the necessary assurance and Poska continued.

'Firstly, some questions of clarification. I understand that you were a witness to the accident in which your wife was killed, and that you saw the face of the driver of the vehicle.'

'Yes, that is correct,' said Jack.

'And can I therefore assume that you would recognise this man if you saw him again?'

'Yes, I believe so,' affirmed Jack.

'You *believe* so? How certain are you that would be able to identify him?'

'I am certain that I could.'

'That's good.' Poska glanced over at Jack's desk. 'I see you have a computer terminal.'

'Yes, of course.'

'That's good. For reasons that I think you may understand, it would not be appropriate for me to ask you to visit a police station to look at photographs of possible suspects, but we could use a computer here to access a number of encrypted files for you to look at.'

Jack was just about to respond when there was a knock on the office door, followed by Mia carrying in a tray. She placed it on the coffee table and, when she had made sure that each of the men had taken a cup and saucer and were aware of the croissants that she had brought in, she left the room.

'So I assume from what you have just said,' continued Jack, 'that you are aware of my concerns about possible corruption within the police department.'

'Sadly,' responded Poska, 'there is nothing "possible" about it. We are fully aware of it and, in regard to the people trafficking problem, we are also aware of Escobar's involvement.'

Jack was taken aback. He had been careful not to mention to Pamela Abbott the name of the officer concerned.

'We have been aware for some time that he was in the pay of the gang that was running the girls,' continued Poska. 'We could have moved in on him before now, but we wanted to hold back a little in the hope that he would lead us to people higher in the organisation. To have arrested him prematurely would be like sending flares into a night sky. We would get a result of sorts, and purge a few corrupt policemen out of the system, but the long-term effectiveness of the operation would be negated. It would simply only serve to scare off the main players.'

'But if they have abducted Elena from the hospital …' interjected Jack.

'Elena has not been abducted,' Poska assured him. 'We realised the danger she was in as a potential witness. It was one thing holding Escobar on a long leash, but we could not do that if the woman's safety was going to be in any way jeopardised. It was, in fact, my department that decided to remove her for her own good. She is in a safe house and has all the medical attention that she needs. Naturally, the local police force is not aware of the location.'

'So what happens now?'

'Well, to be totally honest, the fact that you may be able to identify the man who drove the vehicle that caused the accident means that you may be in danger as well. These people are ruthless, as I'm sure you already realise.'

'I can assure you that a safe house is not going to work for me,' responded Jack. 'I've got a business to run. I can't be cooped up on the off-chance that someone might want me silenced – and anyway, how long would that kind of protection need to go on for?'

'I think we should take one step at a time. At this point we don't know if you are a witness, in the sense that, although you were at the scene of the accident, you could positively identify anyone. Look, let's go over to your computer. I assume that there is a password that we will need to get in? And could you ensure that we are not disturbed by any of your staff for the next few minutes?'

Jack moved round to the front of the desk on which his computer stood and tapped in a few keys before stepping back to allow Poska access. Knowing that he would need privacy to put in passwords of his own, he left Poska to do whatever he needed to do while he slipped out of the office to make sure that the two of them would not be disturbed. By the time he returned to his desk, there was already an array of faces displayed before him on the monitor.

'What I want you to do is look carefully at these images,' said Poska. 'Take all the time that you need. We know who the suspects are, but have included in the file a number of images of people who look very similar, but who have no connection at all to the case. It may appear that we are making this unnecessarily difficult for you, but we need to know that your evidence is incontrovertibly conclusive.'

'I fully understand,' said Jack. 'Can we make a start?'

Now it was Poska who moved out of the way, in order for Jack to have a full view of the screen. Poska had been right: there seemed to be an awful lot of people who looked very much alike. However, it was not long before Jack sat back in his chair and, pointing to the image displayed, said with total confidence, 'That's the man! No doubt about it. I am 100 per cent sure!'

Poska looked across to the screen and, with a sigh that betrayed the relief that he felt in getting a positive result, said, 'Thank you, Mr Troughton. This is exactly the same image that Elena picked out.'

'You mean she has been through this process already?'

'Well, of course. She did it at the safe house. Naturally, it was easy for her as she saw the man on a day-to-day basis. You only saw him for a few moments, so it was important that you were able to confirm the identification. We don't know his exact name. Elena said that within the gang he was always referred to as "The Handler". This may be because he was usually the one who primarily controlled the girls, but I suspect it has also to do with his ruthlessness in dealing with whatever problems turned up for the gang. Elena has made it clear to us that, given the things she has witnessed herself, this man was not only more than willing to be involved in gratuitous violence but, as is so often the case with these people, was also a sadist.'

As Jack heard these last two words his mind jumped immediately to the envelope that had been delivered to his home together with the photo of his mother. The man who now stood in his office may be the only person in law enforcement that he could trust at this precise moment. Jack signalled back to the armchairs and, as Poska moved in the indicated direction, Jack removed the envelope from his briefcase. As Poska eased himself into the chair, Jack proffered the thin package in his direction.

'This was delivered by hand to my home,' he explained. 'You will see that I have put it in a plastic cover in order to protect any fingerprint evidence that there may be on it. That's how you people work, isn't it?'

Poska did not reply. He took the plastic folder and, without opening it, said, 'You just need to tell me what's inside. I won't be opening it myself just now. I'll get some of my forensic people to look over it when I get back.'

Jack related when it had been delivered and what the envelope contained. When he had finished, Poska said, 'You did well by doing your best not to contaminate any evidence that there may be. However, I have to say that these people are very clever. This would hardly be the first time that they would have attempted to intimidate people in this fashion, so they've probably covered their tracks anyway by using plastic gloves. We won't be able to say for sure until our experts have had the chance to have a look. Could I ask if you have security cameras at your house?'

'No, I'm afraid not,' replied Jack. 'Nor at my mother's.'

'OK, well, we'll see what, if anything, we can elicit from this, then – but I wouldn't hold out too much hope at this stage.'

Poska started to get up, indicating his need to leave and, as he did so, Jack rose, took his hand, and shook it warmly.

'Thank you for being so frank with me, Mr Poska, and I would be especially appreciative if you could offer some level of protection for my mother.'

'Yes. We will keep an eye on her. It was good to meet you, Mr Troughton. I would appreciate it if you could let my office know if your travel plans are likely to take you very far from this vicinity in the next few weeks.'

Poska handed him what appeared to be a business card.

'There is just a single number for you to keep hold of. It's staffed twenty-four hours a day. It will obviously not connect you directly to me but, depending on the urgency of your communication, it will most certainly be forwarded to me if necessary. You can depend on it.'

Jack spent the rest of the day clearing his desk of as much of the backlog of company business that he could. With all that was going on around him, it was almost helpful to be focusing on something other than this current dilemma – even if it was only for a few hours.

A little after 5pm, Mia came in to say that she was leaving for home and to update him on some calls that she had taken during the day and which he might need to know about. There was nothing of any real urgency and, once she had left, he picked up the phone and dialled Damian's number. He knew that it would be around 3pm in the UK.

'Hello, Damian Clarke here,' came the response as the call was answered.

'Hi, Damian, it's Jack.'

'Jack! How are you? Where are you phoning from?'

'From my office. I haven't disturbed you, have I?'

'No, not at all, good to hear from you.'

'Listen, Damian, I can't go into too much detail on the phone right now, but I was wondering if there was any chance that my mother could come and stay with you for a few days – a couple of weeks, maybe – at some point soon? I want her to take a break, and ...'

'Of course she can, Jack,' Damian interrupted. 'Sue and I would love to have her with us. It would be a pleasure. Is she alright?'

'Oh, absolutely fine. Fit as a fiddle. To be honest, I haven't even spoken to her about this yet. It's just that there's a whole lot of stuff going on at the moment surrounding Celia's death. It's complicated. Damian, I know I'm not being very coherent – and I will explain it to you when I can, I promise – but I just want her to get away for a while, that's all.'

'It's OK, Jack, no need to go into detail. Look, you have a chat with her and then let us know what dates you are thinking about, and we'll take it from there.'

'Thanks, Damian, I really appreciate this. I'll be in touch. Say hi to Sue for me, won't you?'

'Of course I will. Get back to me when you can.'

When the call had ended, Jack realised that he needed to talk to his mother soon. But how was he going to do it without making her anxious? It was alright Poska saying they would keep an eye on her, but even with all their resources, he knew that there was a limit to what even they could do. Jack resolved to drop by his mother's house later that evening. He was just about to close the door on his office when the phone rang. He was surprised to hear Damian on the line.

'Hi, Jack, I'm glad I caught you. Listen, I just mentioned our conversation to Sue, and she reminded me that we are going on holiday in a couple of weeks' time and will be away for about a fortnight. I don't know how I could have forgotten that.'

'Don't worry about it, Damian. To be honest, I felt a little embarrassed about contacting you right out of the blue in the first place. It's not a problem. I appreciate you letting me know right away, though.'

'No, you don't understand, Jack. This might be the best possible thing.'

'How do you mean? In what way?'

'We're going on a cruise to New York, out of Southampton. Why don't you ask your mother if she would like to join us? We'd love her to come along. Honestly we would.'

'New York?' said Jack incredulously. 'I'm not following you. How long are you going to be in the States? I was just thinking of her getting a break in the UK. I'm not sure she would be up to the pace of a place like that. I was really thinking on her having a rest for a couple of weeks.'

'Well, that's why Sue and I think it's ideal. We love cruises but we're not into all the stops and the trips! We are doing a round trip. It will take fifteen days and that will include just one sightseeing trip in Nova Scotia and one in New York. Sarah would not need to even get off the ship if she didn't want to. Think about it, Jack. We booked a few months ago, but we happen to know, through adverts in the Sunday supplements, that there are some pretty good discounts for the places that haven't been taken up. As long as her passport is up to date, and she can get the travel insurance in time, she may be able to grab a bargain.'

Jack thought for a moment. This could be the perfect solution. There was no way that those thugs could reach her if she were crossing the Atlantic.

'Damian, are you really sure you and Sue don't mind?'

'Don't mind? We would love her to come. Anyway, your mum could order her day as she wished. She could be with us as little or as much as she liked. We could even just meet up at mealtimes, if she wanted. Have a chat with her and see what she says. However, if she would like to come, she would need to start getting things in motion pretty soon.'

'Wow, thanks, Damian. I was going to drop by to see her tonight. Please thank Sue for me.'

Jack drove to his mother's house straight from the office. He had thought of ringing ahead but concluded that if he did, she would insist on making him a meal.

When she answered the door, she was delighted to see her son on the doorstep. Nevertheless, Sarah Troughton, apart from being an intelligent woman, knew her son better than anyone else in the world and it seemed she sensed that this was not just a casual call. When they had settled down in the lounge, she broached the subject directly. Jack was almost relieved when she did so.

'There's no pulling the wool over your eyes, is there, Mum? Yes, you're right. I have come around to see you for a particular reason.' He was just about to launch into a prepared speech when the door opened.

'Jack, how lovely to see you,' a voice said. 'Sarah never mentioned to me that you were coming!'

'Aunt Elizabeth!' said Jack, putting his coffee aside and rising to kiss her on both cheeks. 'How are you? No, it's an impromptu visit in a way.'

'He says it is, Beth, but I think I know better,' Sarah laughed.

'Well, if it's a private matter, Jack, I'll come back to see you before you go.'

'No, it's not private really,' said Jack, realising that he was now having to play his strategy by ear and concluding that it was probably best if he came right out with what he had to say.

'You remember Damian and Sue Clarke, don't you, Mum?'

'Yes, of course I do. Lovely people. They are alright, are they? Not unwell, I hope?'

'No, they are fine, Mum. What it is, is that they are going on a return cruise to the States in a couple of weeks and they wondered if you would like to accompany them. You always said that you would have liked to go on a cruise one day, but then, Dad was never in favour, was he? Always worried it would be too crowded. Now you could go and you wouldn't be on your own. How about that?'

'To the States? With Damian and Sue? Where in the States? How did all this come about and why now?' asked Sarah, incredulously.

'Well, it is to the States, to New York in fact, but you would only be there for a day. As I said, it's a round trip – fifteen days, to be precise. We were on the phone to one another earlier today and, to be honest, it was me who suggested that you needed a break. Then they came up with this idea. I know it's all a bit sudden, but it could be just the thing, don't you think?'

'It's very sudden, and anyway, even if I wanted to, I couldn't leave Beth here on her own.'

'Of course you could,' interjected Beth. 'It sounds lots of fun. What a wonderful opportunity!'

'But how would you manage?'

'How do you think I would manage?' laughed Beth. 'I love your mother to bits, Jack, but even we get under one another's feet sometimes. You know, it might even be a break for me,' she said throwing Jack a mischievous wink.

'Well, I don't know, I really don't,' said Sarah, pensively.

However, by the time Jack had left the house that evening, everything had been agreed. Aunt Elizabeth was fully in agreement, and his mother, though adopting a semi-reluctant posture of being mildly bullied, was inwardly excited about the whole idea. Over the next few days the arrangements were put in place and the passage was booked.

During the weeks running up to the date of the cruise, Poska's department pulled together the remaining strands of the investigation. The trafficking gang were arrested in a dawn raid and there were also simultaneous arrests of a total of eleven corrupt police officers, of which Escobar was one. Of course, no one thought for a minute that this was the end of sex trafficking. On the contrary, this contemporary expression of slavery was growing exponentially all across the globe – as was the people trafficking that took advantage of those who wanted to migrate for socio-economic reasons. No one believed that this was going to end any time soon.

In this respect, Poska's intervention may have only been a drop in the ocean but, as far as this network was concerned, their operation had been almost completely closed down. The forensic thoroughness of surveillance and evidence gathering over many months had borne fruit. It had appeared that the net had brought virtually every fish into the boat, large and small, and, in consequence, bail had been denied to everyone involved. The gang's lawyers had been overruled at every step. Members of the judiciary had made their decision after considering the very real possibility of flight, the level of violence and the virtual certainty that anyone not kept in custody might well embark on a process of witness intimidation.

Poska was quick to assure Jack that there was no immediate threat to either him or his mother. However, he was also equally honest in pointing out that in the months that would follow, especially around the time when the cases would come to trial and Jack emerged as a key witness, things may not be quite as clear-cut.

Elena, on the other hand, could face the future in the knowledge that she would remain under witness protection in the short term and, when sentencing had occurred, provision would be made for her to move to another country, with new papers and an entirely new identity.

25th March 2006
The Atlantic

Sarah Troughton had flown over to stay with Damian and Sue for a couple of days before making the trip to Southampton to board ship. Damian and Sue had ensured that Sarah was in the stateroom next to theirs, and at 7.30pm they went down together for the first meal of the voyage. The options that were offered when booking were a table for two, four, six or eight. They had chosen 'six'. The meal at which everyone met for the first time was often marked by a slight nervousness. The question in most people's minds was whether they would get on well with the passengers that had been allocated to their table for the entire voyage.

Once through the double doors into the restaurant, the head waiter had one of his staff show each guest to their table.

When Damian, Sue and Sarah were shown to their seats, they found that their three dinner companions were already seated. A couple that Damian guessed might be in their late sixties introduced themselves as Chuck and Daisy Winters from Stone Mountain, Georgia. The next person to greet them was obviously, from his accent, a fellow Englishman. He introduced himself as Simon Bellenger – a tall, athletically built man in his thirties. By the time the first course had been ordered and served, it seemed evident to all that everyone was going to get on very well indeed.

The third night into the voyage was the first of the formal nights, and it was only when Damian had taken a white dress shirt from the hanger and was rooting around in a drawer to no avail that he realised that he had forgotten to pack a bow tie.

'I can't believe it,' he said to Sue. 'You know how meticulous I am with my lists. I know this was on there, so how could I not have packed it?'

'Damian, hold on, it's not the end of the world,' Sue said, calmly. 'With 2,300 passengers on board, I'm sure you're not the only person to have forgotten something. Look, I can drop by the men's store on deck three and pick one up for you. I need something myself from the cosmetics department so I'll get your tie while I'm there.'

When Sue reached the men's department she immediately realised how right she had been. By the time she had selected the black tie she found that there was already a queue at the till. Slowly the queue edged forwards. No one appeared stressed except the young salesman, who looked as tense as a coiled spring.

When it was Sue's turn to be served, and given that she was the last in the line, she thought it might be a good idea to assure him she was not in a rush by engaging in a little small talk. On glancing at his name tag, she saw 'Anthony' adjacent to the shipping line's logo.

'It's been a busy afternoon, has it, Anthony?' Sue began, in the most sympathetic voice she could muster. 'Or do you prefer Tony?'

'Oh, Anthony please, dear, if you don't mind. I can't stand Tony. It's awful, don't you think, when people shorten names?'

'Well, I don't mind personally,' said Sue, 'but if you do – then Anthony it is.'

'I've been run off my feet, dear, I really have, and it's all the fault of Megan Mellor in "high-end watches".' As he said this, he extended an accusing arm full length and pointed in the general direction of the adjacent department. 'I've taken about as much from that Megan Mellor as I can stand, let me tell you!'

'Oh, I'm sorry,' offered Sue, as she realised that, like it or not, she was being drawn into the intimate details of a debacle that was going she knew not where. But by now Anthony had swivelled back to face Sue and, with one arm by his side and the other on his hip, continued. 'Every time she wants to change shifts I comply, even when it's not convenient, yet the only time I want her to stand in for me, like today, she refuses. "It's much more important that I cover high-end watches than sell the bits and pieces that you sell," she told me earlier – cheeky madam. High-end watches? She doesn't know a Rolex from a Timex. Anyway, dear, I mustn't burden you with my trials, must I? How can I help you?'

Sue handed him the black bow tie and, with a flurry of wrist and arms, Anthony processed her cruise card, placed the tie in a bag and handed it to her.

'Thank you for listening, dear. You've got a peaceful aura about you. Has anybody ever told you that? I can see it, anyway. People tell me it's a gift.' And with that he busied himself with tidying some memorabilia on a nearby shelf.

That evening at dinner, much of the conversation centred on what it was like to live in Georgia. Chuck and Daisy were interesting conversationalists and they were thrilled when Sarah relayed the experiences that she and Wesley had had when they had been in the States on business. Sarah especially mentioned the warm hospitality that had been extended to them while they were out there.

'And then, of course, there was the food – corn on the cob, grits and Brunswick stew,' enthused Sarah. 'Oh, we loved it so much there, and hearing your accent, Daisy, seems to bring it all back.'

'I hope you mean the memories of Georgia, and not the stew,' said Chuck with a grin. 'Our accent can be a bit strong to some folk. I believe it might even be called a drawl.'

'And how has your day been, Damian?' Simon asked.

'Pretty uneventful – but that's good. We're all here to relax, after all. Well, I say relax, that was apart from the fact that when I was getting ready for tonight, I realised that I hadn't packed my tie. But it was hardly a crisis. Sue was able to buy one from the store without a problem. She assured me that with more than 2,000 passengers on board, I wouldn't have been the only one to have left something behind.'

'There was quite a queue when I got there,' said Sue. 'They appeared to be understaffed and the man that was serving seemed to be getting himself in something of a frazzle by the time it was my turn to be served.'

'That'll have been Anthony, then,' said Simon.

'Yes, it was,' said Sue, surprised. 'Have you met him as well?'

111

'I've known Anthony for years. We were partners for some time.'

'In the same firm?' interjected Chuck. 'Fancy that, you on the cruise and your colleague on the staff. That must feel a bit odd. Did you know he worked for this shipping line when you booked?'

'I think Simon means something else,' offered Sue. 'I picked up fairly quickly in my conversation with Anthony that he might be gay …'

At this, Daisy Winters appeared to be moving her fork around her plate at an accelerated speed, and Chuck was looking at his Beef Wellington with focused attention, as if somehow questioning the right of the pastry to be enveloping the meat.

'Don't you have gay people in Georgia, Mr Winters?' asked Simon, with just the hint of a smile, though without the slightest acidity in his tone.

'Well, I'm sure that there are homosexuals there like everywhere else. It's just that … well, it's just that my wife and I don't run into them very much, that's all.'

The speed at which Daisy was moving her salad around her plate showed no sign of abating. Simon thought it best to move the conversation on as expeditiously as possible.

'It's a long story and possibly not one for the dinner table,' he continued. 'Suffice to say that we are not together now and haven't been for over a year. I decided to come on the cruise to get some space to think. I had no idea that Anthony worked here and actually, had I known, I would probably have booked with another line.'

The awkwardness was momentarily rescued by the waiter asking if everyone was happy with their meal, his enquiry probably rising out of a learned sensitivity to changes in atmosphere around tables, thought Simon. Waiters knew that not all tables 'clicked', but maybe the waiter had believed that this one had done so from the outset. His interjection was met with smiling appreciation from everyone, and he drifted away with his mind appearing a little more at ease.

The following courses were eaten to the accompaniment of Damian, Sue and Sarah, each in their own way, trying to bring the conversation and the relationship back on line. But there were moments when it was very much like a ship's captain trying to negotiate the vessel around an iceberg.

At dinner the following night, everyone appeared to approach the dining table with a measure of apprehension. Sarah, Sue and Damian hoped that normality would surface and that there would be no atmospheres to cloud the rest of the voyage. Simon settled himself into his chair and, even before the waiter laid the napkin across his lap, was smiling profusely and addressing himself to the Winters with an enthusiasm that was designed to communicate that no offence had been taken on the previous night and 'Let's all be friends again'. It was evident that the Winters had talked the matter through in their stateroom before they came to the table, for they too were signalling by tone and body language that they wanted nothing more than to bring everything back on to an even keel.

31st March 2006
New York

There were only two stops on the transatlantic crossing. The first was in Nova Scotia and the second, New York. The vast majority of passengers disembarked at New York as their final destination or as an interim stop on their onward journey. Those who booked for the round trip most often took one of the pre-booked excursions that lasted for the day that the ship was docked.

Damian, Sue and Sarah were in the latter category and had met for an early buffet breakfast at the restaurant before disembarking. They had chosen the option that gave them the most free time. They were to leave the dockside by coach to Macy's department store, and from there they planned to visit the Empire State Building, the Chrysler Building, the Rockefeller Center and the site where, nearly five years earlier, two planes piloted by terrorists had tragically brought the twin towers crashing down in flames.

Having had their cruise cards scanned on exit, they made their way to the coach area and selected the one that matched the number on their excursion receipts. Sarah and Sue had been looking forward to Macy's but were surprised at how locked in time the store seemed to be in comparison with those in the major cities in the UK. They thought the escalators looked like something from the 1950s, with their wooden slatted steps, rather than the brushed grey metal that was usual back home.

However, it was the shoulder-to-shoulder crowds that surprised the three of them the most − not so much in the store, but along Fifth Avenue and around Times Square. By the time they reached the Rockefeller Center, everyone was ready for a coffee. Having found a pavement café, two cappuccinos were ordered for Damian and Sue, and a vanilla latte for Sarah, together with three pecan croissants.

'So, how are you all enjoying New York?' came a voice from the next table.

'Simon, we didn't see you on the coach!' exclaimed Sarah, the first to recognise him as the three heads turned.

'I wasn't on your bus. The Macy's tour was oversubscribed and they put on a couple of extra vehicles. I think mine may have set out about an hour or so earlier than yours.'

'Well, why don't you pull up a chair and join us, rather than sitting there on your own?' suggested Damian.

'I think I might, if that's alright with you. Whether it's on ship or shore, we appear destined to eat and drink together,' said Simon with a smile, edging his chair nearer.

'Our table on board seems to have moved on from that awkward moment a few days ago,' offered Damian. 'I think you handled it very well, if you don't mind my saying so.'

'Oh, thank you,' answered Simon.

'Given that you and Anthony used to be together, it must have been so strange when you came across him on the ship,' suggested Sue.

'It certainly was, but I have to say that it wasn't an acrimonious split. It was odd, in a way. The direction of my life was changing and Anthony found that difficult to deal with – that's probably the long and short of it. I've tried to look at things from his point of view and I can probably guess how it must have felt from his perspective. Strange how it all happened, really – and all because of an old Bible, would you believe?'

'An old Bible?' asked Damian, interested.

'Yes, Anthony and I had gone into Cheltenham, shopping, and he said that he needed to pop into a store for something. He said he would only be a few minutes and that actually was about as long as he took. However, during those few minutes something was about to happen that would change the course of my life forever.

'While waiting for him, I'd taken a seat on one of the benches that were located around the pedestrianised area outside the shops. Immediately I sat down, I saw that someone had left an old book on the bench. Initially, all I wanted to do was to move it out of the way so I could sit down, but as I picked it up it was clear that it was a Bible. It had clearly been well-used over the years, almost to the point of falling apart.

'It looked as if it had been there for quite some time. There must have been a light shower earlier because the cover was a bit wet. What was particularly strange was that if anyone had wanted to discard it, it would have been very easy to do so, given there was a bin right next to the bench. Anyone wanting to throw away the Bible could not have failed to see it.

'Anyway, I picked it up and placed it in a carrier bag I had with me. Then Anthony came out of the shop and we headed off towards the Montpellier area where we'd parked our car. I didn't say anything to him at the time. In fact, I never mentioned that I had found the Bible at all. Neither of us was in the least bit religious, and I probably thought he would find it rather odd that I had taken any interest in picking up something like that in the first place.'

'This is an unbelievable coincidence!' exclaimed Damian. 'I can hardly believe it!'

'You mean that we have bumped into one another on this excursion, or that Anthony and I find ourselves on the same cruise?' asked Simon.

'Neither, actually,' said Damian. 'You won't believe this, Simon, but a person we knew had the very same experience – and I think that was in Cheltenham, too! Perhaps happened on the same day.'

'You're kidding me!' said Simon, incredulously.

'I'm not. In fact, she was married to a man who, if can you believe it, is Sarah's son.'

'Your son, Sarah?' exclaimed Simon. 'That's amazing!'

'Yes, my son, Jack, was married to Celia. She once told me she picked up a Bible in Cheltenham – in very similar circumstances to yourself.'

'But it can't be the same Bible, because I've still got mine,' said Simon.

'And my daughter-in-law kept hers,' added Sarah. 'So someone must have placed the Bibles deliberately – though I can't for one moment imagine why.'

'So you're a Christian, are you, Sarah?' enquired Simon.

'Well, I'm not sure that I would describe myself in that way, at least not to the degree that Jack and Celia …' Sarah glanced across the table. 'Or even like Damian and Sue here. But tell us, what on earth has this got to do with you and Anthony not being together?'

'I can certainly do that, but we'd all better keep our eye on the time,' Simon said, glancing at his watch. 'We need to head back towards Macy's in plenty of time to connect with the tour bus.'

It was not until they were back on the ship, had had their evening meal and were seated with drinks in the lounge later that evening that the four of them took the story up again.

'Well, where were we?' asked Simon.

'We were asking you how finding the Bible affected your relationship with Anthony,' said Sarah.

'Right, OK. I think it was about three or four weeks later when things came to a head. At first I found myself just dipping in and out of the old Bible – almost opening it at random if I remember. I then thought it would be a good idea to start at the beginning and work my way through. However, I very soon gave up on that idea. The first couple of books were alright, but I soon found it a bit heavy going – a lot of stuff about Jewish rituals and things like that. After a while I jumped forward to the New Testament, from the birth of Christ onwards. I was intrigued by what I read but then, once I'd got through the first five books it started getting a bit more difficult to get to grips with again. The thing is, I found I just couldn't stop once I'd started. I became almost mesmerised by the life of Jesus.'

'Well, I have never read the Bible through,' said Sarah. 'But I did read, when I was much younger, the bits about the life of Jesus and frankly I cannot recall any reference at all to the gay or lesbian lifestyle. So if Jesus, the founder of Christianity, didn't think it was worth mentioning, I can't see why what you read, Simon, should have proved so apparently disruptive for you. If two people are in love, straight or gay, I don't see that it's anyone else's business.'

'I fully understand where you're coming from, Sarah,' continued Simon. 'As you might imagine, I of all people get that. I'm sure you realise that I spent several years of my life holding that same viewpoint very strongly – that was of course before I became a

Christian. So I appreciate the point that Sarah is trying to make. In the Old Testament, prior to the birth of Christ, adultery is declared to be wrong. More than that, it became a sin punishable by death. However, when Jesus saw a group of men about to stone to death a woman who had committed adultery, He intervened and stopped them.'

'I should think so too,' said Sarah, a bit more vociferously than she had intended.

'Yes,' continued Simon, 'but after He had intervened, and she had profusely thanked Him, He then told her to go home in safety but also to stop her sinful lifestyle.'

'So this is why you broke off with Anthony, is it?' asked Sarah.

'It's a bit more complicated than that,' Simon replied. 'Anthony quickly picked up that things were different between us. Yet I felt that I could hardly tell him what was going on in my mind and especially the root of my new thinking.'

'Why on earth not?' enquired Sarah.

'Well,' replied Simon, 'it's because we'd had numerous discussions on this subject in the past, but from the same side of the argument. We almost hated Christians, especially those that came from what we saw as the religious right in the States – anti-gay, anti-abortion, anti-everything. We openly despised everything about them. To be frank, if Christians had said about me the kind of things I said about them, they would have been prosecuted for being homophobic. And that realisation was one of the things that disturbed me the most during those very difficult days.'

'Disturbed you in what way?' asked Damian.

'I was defending our lifestyle as legitimate under the banner of tolerance. I was chanting in Gay Pride events "Love not hate" – yet hate was at the very core of everything I felt towards anyone that disagreed with us. I was quick to slate Christians for hypocrisy – and sometimes with good reason! – but I was beginning to see that I wasn't exactly immune. As I read the teachings of Jesus in contexts such as the one I mentioned earlier about the woman caught in adultery, I could see that He was able to love the woman without loving her lifestyle. When I was shouting tolerance, I was only really asking, actually demanding, that the world be tolerant with us. However, when it came to being tolerant with those who had opposing views to my own – that was a different thing altogether. I simply raged against them. I hated them. Sometimes I wondered if I would have willingly acted violently against Christians if the opportunity had arisen and if I could have got away with it. As I said, I began to see my position as totally hypocritical. I wanted tolerance only for us. Also, I was astounded when I read in that old, battered Bible that the biggest critics of Jesus were not the ordinary people but the ultra-right-wing religious establishment – the Pharisees. They called him, of all things, the friend of sinners. I knew then beyond a doubt that I wanted to commit my life to someone like that, and I still do. Anthony, as you might imagine, just couldn't see it – and so that's how it ended.'

'Are you really telling us, Simon,' asked Sarah, 'that you swapped a loving relationship with Anthony for something you read in an old book, the most recent parts of which were written 2,000 years ago. I can't believe you did that!'

'Wow, Sarah, I think that's a bit unfair,' interjected Damian. 'Simon doesn't see the Bible as the irrelevant text of an ancient culture – and neither do Sue or myself.'

'Well I didn't mean to offend, I'm sure,' said Sarah. 'It's just that …'

'No need at all to apologise,' interrupted Simon. 'As I just said, I held the views that you are expounding for a long time and expressed them far less graciously than you have done just now. The long and short of it I suppose is that I felt in the first instance that I had become aware of the facts about God through what I read in the Bible. Then later I became acutely aware that God was, as a person, "knowable" through Jesus Christ. I feel that God speaks to me through the Bible and through prayer. I also have this consciousness that He is with me all the time. So much so that it's almost impossible for me to remember what it was like not to experience His presence in my life. Jesus is as real to me as any of you sitting in front of me are.'

'But you are gay, Simon … you're gay!' said Sarah in exasperation. 'How can you admit to that disposition and then feel the need to repress your identity? It seems so unfair – frankly unjust.'

'I don't see it as any different,' said Simon in response, 'to the fact that when a married straight man is attracted to another woman, he is able to decide not to progress his feelings to a relationship. I don't want to be insensitive, Sarah, but if your husband made a decision to be faithful to you rather than have an affair with someone else – would you rush to the conclusion that he was unjustifiably repressed? I really don't think so.'

'Well, if you put it like that ...' said Sarah a little uncomfortably, and clearly somewhat taken aback.

'You know,' said Simon, 'it's getting a little late so I think I'll head back to my room. Listen, I trust we're all good – no one's offended, I hope?'

'Of course, we're all good – at least I am,' said Sarah. 'I feel like I'm learning stuff, or if not "learning" then at least looking at things from a different perspective. And believe me, that's something that's not easy to do when you get to my age,' she added, smiling.

2nd April 2006
The Atlantic

'April Fools' Day was yesterday,' Simon said to Sue, as she drew her coffee to her lips and looked over the top of the cup towards him with a smile that was on a spectrum somewhere between teasing and mischievous.

'No, honestly, he was there, he really was,' insisted Sue. 'I saw him with my own eyes.'

'He couldn't have been. I was there myself and I would have seen him. There is no way that Anthony would have been at the church service.'

'I can assure you that he was,' insisted Sue. 'He was sitting on his own in one of the boxes.'

Simon was aware that the place where the service was held consisted of tiered seating and that, in addition, there were private boxes that could be hired for a fee when the evening entertainment was taking place. However, they were rarely used, if at all, when a church service was being conducted as most people liked to be part of the congregation that, at any other time, would have been an audience.

'That's amazing. It really is. I thought he would be the last person …'

Sue and Simon were sitting in one of the coffee lounges dotted around the ship when Simon noticed that the subject of their conversation was at that very moment striding purposefully in their general direction – something more noticeable on a cruise ship, where almost everyone, guests and staff alike, either strolled or sauntered. However, it was evident that Anthony had not seen them, and he was about to march right past them when Simon called across, 'Anthony!'

At the sound of his name, Anthony stopped, swivelled around and looked across the lounge for the source of sound. His eyes locked first on to Simon – who he greeted with an 'Oh, it's you! I thought I recognised that voice' – and then swung over to Sue, adding, 'but I don't think I know you, do I?'

'This is Sue. She and her husband are on the same table as me in the restaurant.'

Sue thought she saw his face relax ever so slightly as he heard the word 'husband'.

'Why don't you join us for a minute?' invited Sue, as she indicated a spare chair alongside them.

Anthony's eyes hovered over the chair thoughtfully, as if questioning whether it was what it purported to be and then, as if concluding it was safe to alight, sat down, crossed his legs in one swift action and, addressing Sue more than Simon, said, 'Well, I suppose I can take a minute or two. Anyway, I think I've seen you on the ship haven't I, dear? I have got quite a good memory for faces. Are you enjoying your cruise?'

Anthony had crossed his arms and pivoted his body noticeably towards Sue and at the same time away from Simon.

'You told me I had a good aura,' said Sue smiling, 'and yes, I am enjoying the cruise, thank you.'

'Oh, did I? I can sense that in people, you see. Some people have got it and some people haven't. And then some people have it and lose it.'

With that, he pointedly swivelled his head towards Simon and then swiftly back to Sue. She felt that it was a far less accusing action than a casual observer might have thought – the body language reflecting more an affectionate connection with Simon than anything else.

'You won't remember me, I'm sure,' said Sue. 'You must see hundreds of people every day. If I remember, you were having a hard time with one of your colleagues who worked on the watch department ...'

'Oh yes, that was the witch Megan Mellor, dear – or can I call you Sue?'

'Of course you can call me Sue.'

'I shouldn't be horrible about her. I felt quite guilty, talking about her like I did. From what I've heard she's got problems of her own. People who are hurt tend to hurt others, don't they?'

'I think you're right,' said Sue. 'I often think that myself.'

'Guilty enough to drive you to church, then?' enquired Simon playfully.

'Me in church? Don't be ridiculous …' and then, immediately realising that he must have been seen, he admitted, 'Well, I did go, but just to see what it was like. I didn't think you would see me from where I was sitting, Simon, even if you were there yourself.'

'It wasn't me who saw you; it was Sue,' explained Simon.

'That doesn't make sense. How would Sue make a connection between you and me?'

'Because I told her about us.'

'You *told* her! You mean you've been talking about me behind my back, Simon?'

'It wasn't like that, Anthony,' said Sue. 'Simon was telling me about his life, and it was clear that you were an important part of it.'

'*Were* being the operative word,' rejoined Anthony pointedly.

'You still are,' said Simon. 'I hope we can always be friends – even close friends – it's just that the relationship has changed. You know that.'

'Oh, I know that,' rejoined Anthony. 'Anyway, let's not go there.'

'Alright,' said Simon, 'but why were you at the service? Explain yourself.'

'I just wanted to see what it was that was so important in church that made you make the choices that you did.'

'So, having been there, what did you conclude?' enquired Simon.

'To be honest, I found it all a bit weird. I don't want to be rude, but why the seventeenth-century language for a start? It's the twenty-first century! And why, when the people were singing, were most of them just mouthing the words – just like we used to do in assembly at school? Anyway, some were not singing at all. The worst, though, was all the "repeating bits" as far as I'm concerned.'

'You mean the responses,' offered Sue.

'Well, whatever they're called. It was all "we are wretched undeserving sinners" and that kind of thing – nothing positive – quite dreary really. Is that really how your God wants us to relate to him, Simon?'

'You have got a good point there,' Simon admitted. 'We don't have that kind of format in our church, and the language and music are far more contemporary.'

'We're not knocking the way they worship, though,' interrupted Sue. 'In their tradition they see it as expressing humility before God. Though I do agree with Simon that it does come over a bit one-sided. God is not an accusing taskmaster but a loving father – and I agree that that didn't really come over as it might have done in the service.'

'Was it all bad, then?' asked Simon.

'None of it was "bad", I suppose,' said Anthony. 'It was just that, frankly, I couldn't see the point. To begin with, I concluded that everyone was breaking into their holiday routine out of some Christian duty. However, I have to admit that, as I looked round there were those, even you, Simon, who looked as if the event had real meaning for them. And when you were singing, or worshipping I think you call it, it was as if you really were communicating with someone you knew. To be honest, I was happy to think you had found something that gave some substance to your life. It's just a pity that by embracing that, it unfortunately excludes me. The whole history of LGBT has been about exclusion, hasn't it, Simon? It seems that Christianity is just another expression of it – or should I say "oppression" of it?'

'It's nothing to do with being gay, Anthony, honestly,' said Sue. 'Two of my friends – Simon has never met them – are not gay, but had to wrestle with relationship issues after they met as well. Becoming a Christian is about choices and often lifestyle choices too. There's no question about that. Sometimes those choices can be hard to make. At the core, it's about adjusting our life to God's will, which, I can assure you, is always best in the long run. God is not going to adjust His will to ours. He's not a politician who, like a weather vane, changes direction according to the way every wind blows. His primary aim is not to get elected. He is God, after all.'

'Well, I'm not sure that's true,' countered Anthony.

'How do you mean?' asked Sue.

'Well, Simon here obviously "voted for God" and presumably so did you.'

'But it's not the same,' said Sue. 'People vote for politicians and so give them status. God chose us and, by doing so, gives us status by bringing us into His family – making us His children. In fact, the Bible goes even further. It says that before we consider choosing to follow God, God chooses to draw us to Himself.'

'What are you saying, Sue?' said Anthony with emphasis. 'Are you trying to make me feel wretched on purpose or what? First I find out from Simon that he has chosen God over me. Now you are telling me that even God chose Simon over me.'

Sue could see where Anthony was coming from and instinctively reached across to him and put her arm around his shoulder. For a second it seemed that Anthony would recoil, and almost did, and then noticeably relaxed as Sue continued. 'Let me ask you a question. Why did you *really* go to the church service this morning? Was it really just to spy on Simon, or was there something else?'

Anthony thought for a moment. It would be so easy to be dismissive and avoid the honest answer. After all, he hardly knew her. In fact, he did not know her at all. Didn't she, after all, represent all those who had oppressed and rejected gay and lesbian people, passed laws against them in the past and even had them imprisoned until only a few decades ago? Then he thought back to the bullying he had had at school after he 'came out'. None of those bullies had been Christians – far from it. And the rejection he had experienced in the street, especially walking along with a gay partner: had these people all been Christians? Of course they hadn't. That was nonsense.

It was almost as if Sue knew what he was thinking when she said, 'Before you answer that, Anthony, let me apologise for the unfeeling and ungracious ways some people calling themselves Christians *have* acted towards the LGBT community in the past.'

As she said this she brought to mind the horrendous image of an elderly, wizened-faced man in a baseball cap that bore the legend 'Thank God for AIDS' that the American media had blazoned across some of its front pages a few years back. She had felt ashamed at the time and she felt ashamed now. The position he had taken had nothing to do with her, but that was hardly the point. The point was that that image represented a small minority of ignorant people whose spirit in no way reflected the teachings of Christ, but it had managed to convince a lot of gay people that God was against them.

'I'll tell you why I really went,' said Anthony. 'It's true I wanted to get a sense of what it was about, but there was more. I suppose it was to do with my unhappiness about lots of stuff that's been going on inside. It's not so much about my gay identity as much as about the way I always seem to get so angry … so vindictive …'

As Anthony had seated himself between the two of them, now it was Simon's turn to reach out and put a hand on his shoulder.

'Hey, come on, stop it, the two of you, you'll have me in tears,' said Anthony. 'I'll end up breaking down in front of all these people in a minute if I'm not careful. What's going on?'

Simon quickly glanced around the coffee area before adding, 'I wouldn't worry about it, Anthony, everyone seems to have their noses in their cappuccinos, lattes and mochas – none of them appear to be worrying too much about us.'

Breathing deeply, and moving from the edge of a sob to the edge of a laugh, Anthony felt himself settle.

'All this is good news, not bad,' said Sue.

'Oh really, and how do you work that out?' enquired Anthony.

'Well, one of the sure signs that God is "choosing" us is that we feel drawn to Him. Sometimes that takes the form of asking questions we never used to ask, feeling challenged about things that never used to challenge us and …' here she paused before saying, 'going to places like church services that we never imagined ourselves going to before.'

'Do you really think so?' said Anthony, moving back nearer to tears again.

'We most certainly do,' said Simon and Sue in unison.

10th April 2006
Estonia

'So tell me, how did the cruise go, Mum?' asked Jack in their first phone conversation since she had returned.

Sarah had been back in Tallinn for a couple of days before Jack had made contact. Normally he would have been on the phone to his mother within a few hours, but there were some things that he had to get in place before he talked to her for the first time. He had already fully explained everything to Damian, and Damian had left Sarah with the impression that her son had been tied up with some business abroad for a little while. In fact, Jack had done everything that he had needed to do without actually leaving the country.

'It was wonderful,' said Sarah. 'Damian and Sue were kindness itself. I told them at the outset that they must be free to do their own thing for the fortnight without worrying about me, but we were like one big family the entire time. And we met some lovely people as well. It could not have gone better. But how are you, Jack? You've been OK, have you? There's been nothing to worry about at your end – you know, with everything that's been going on? I know you and Damian have been in touch so I'm sure he would have told me if there was a problem.'

'Everything's fine, Mum,' answered Jack. 'There is nothing to worry about at all. Listen, the reason I'm phoning so early is to see if you're free for dinner tonight.'

'I'd be delighted to cook something for you!' said Sarah. 'It will be lovely to see you ...'

'No, I booked a table at that place I remembered that you and Dad liked so much, and they're holding the table by the window.

I've said that if for any reason you couldn't make it I would let them know within the hour. How are you fixed?'

'That's lovely of you, Jack. It would be great. What time will you pick me up?'

'Would 7.30pm be OK?'

'Of course it would.'

'Wonderful! I'll see you then.'

Everyone wanted to book the table overlooking the harbour and it was usually necessary to book days in advance to secure it. But Jack knew the owner.

'You're looking well, Mum,' said Jack, as the waiter drew a chair back for Sarah. 'Cruising obviously suits you.'

'I could get used to it very easily. The problem is that they say that the average person puts on seven pounds for every week aboard.'

'Ah, but you're not average are you, Mum? If you haven't walked it off, I certainly bet you've talked it off.'

'Oh, you cheeky thing,' replied Sarah, her eyes dancing in a smile. 'Anyway, why the big occasion? It's been a long time since you took me out for a meal.'

'I'm just glad to see you safely home,' replied Jack.

'Why, did you think I wouldn't make it back?'

'No, don't be silly. You know I didn't mean that.'

'Excuse me, sir, would you both like wine this evening?' asked the sommelier, as he hovered over them with a large format list encased in maroon leather.

'The house red will do for me,' Sarah said as, with a polite gesture of her hand, she gently brushed the menu aside. 'This is an expensive place as it is without you going to …'

'No,' remonstrated Jack, as he accepted the list and ran his finger down the page. Turning the list towards the sommelier he said, 'We will have this particular pinot noir, please.' Then, turning to his mother, he added, 'I think this was a favourite of both Dad and yourself, wasn't it?'

'Yes, it was,' confirmed Sarah, 'on special occasions, but …'

'There is no "but" about it. The pinot noir it will be.'

'Will that be all for now, sir?' asked the sommelier, backing slowly away.

'Yes, and a bottle of sparkling water.'

'Certainly, sir, your waiter will be with you shortly.'

'So what is the special occasion?' asked Sarah, quizzically.

'We'll leave that until we've ordered,' said Jack. 'We'll come to that soon.'

They were halfway through the entrée before Sarah said, 'Come on, Jack, you'd better tell me what all this is about. I think I'll develop heartburn if you keep me in any more suspense.'

'I thought you might have guessed already,' answered Jack. 'It's about the business. I've had a change of heart and come to the place where I agree with you that we should, just as you suggested, let Uncle Ronald have the company if he really wants it.'

'I never expected that for a moment. What a surprise,' said Sarah. 'I thought that last time we spoke you were intent on holding on to the firm because you imagined that that was what your dad would have wanted. In fact, if I remember rightly, you went so far as to imply that your uncle's motive was to wrestle the firm from your control.'

'I know, Mum. I think I was being overly defensive at the time but, anyway, I have spoken to him.'

'You have what?' said Sarah. 'You've spoken to him? You've been out to the States while I was on the cruise? So that's why you sent me off …'

'Hold on, Mum, who's being defensive now? Of course I didn't "send you off". You told me that he had made a generous offer and I have spoken to him at length on the phone and I agree that his offer is every bit as generous as you suggested. To tell you the truth, I have already given my assent. I knew you were on board with the idea anyway, as you had been the one to put it to me in the first place.'

'But what about your Aunt Elizabeth? What does Beth think about it all?'

'She's fine about the whole thing,' answered Jack.

'You mean you've talked to her about it already as well?'

'Well, yes, if I'm honest, Mum, I have. I wanted to cover as many of the bases as I could before you came back.'

'Well, you certainly seem to have done that, haven't you? Good grief, I suppose next you will be telling me you have had the lawyers draw up the agreement and have secured a suggested date for completion.'

Jack paused for a second, then reached across the table and laid his left hand on his mother's arm. 'The fact is, Mum, that I have. I thought you would be happy. As I've just said, this was your idea to start with, not mine.'

'Well it was,' agreed Sarah. 'I mean it still is, I suppose. It's just the suddenness of the thing. I listened to Ronald because I could see how much you were taking on yourself and I didn't want you ending up like your dad. I don't want to lose both of you – or see you work yourself into an early grave, even if you survive me. So what did Beth say about this when you spoke to her? Does she want to stay out here or return to the UK?'

'It's all really down to you, Mum,' said Jack. 'You make the final choice and I'm sure she'll be happy to go with whatever you decide. If you want my advice, I suggest that you sell the house as well as the business. Then Aunt Elizabeth will return to the UK with you. I know you both get on so well. I've even found a place you can rent in the short term while the house is being sold. There will certainly be a lot of finance at your disposal when everything has gone through, and there's no reason at all why you couldn't have a small property over here as well, so you could visit as often as you liked. If you think about it, you could have the best of both worlds. I guess Aunt Elizabeth would be as happy to move between the two just as much as you would. Think about it – all the freedom to do what you want and be where you want, while you both enjoy good health. Who wouldn't want to take advantage of a choice like that?'

'But why all the haste?' asked Sarah. 'I think it's good you have come to the decision you have, and even thoughtful of you that you have progressed matters while I've been away, if I'm honest. It's just that I can't understand what all the rush is about. The house market is not so volatile that we have to make a decision to sell right away, and the business will be going to a trusted member of the family. Why can't we just bide our time and go with the flow, as you often put it?'

They had reached the coffee stage by this time, and Jack used the few seconds it took for the waiter to position the cups in front of them to marshal his thoughts before continuing. How much should he tell his mother? If he said nothing, he could not adequately explain the speed he was proceeding at. If he told her everything, she might become anxious.

'Do you know what?' said Sarah. 'I think that this has got something to do with those girls who were found in the container and even Celia's death. I'm not as stupid as you think, Jack. Are you telling me that you are in some kind of danger? Because, if you are, you know I would want to do anything I could to take the pressure off you. You realise that, don't you, love?'

'It's not about me, Mum, and I don't for a minute think that you are stupid. I should have guessed that the only person in the world who has known me all my life would be able to read me – at least a little bit. No, I don't think there is any imminent danger, but we are talking about some dangerous – even evil – people. I just thought that if you had decided that you wanted to sell up, then why hang around, when we have the resources at our disposal to make the move whenever we want?'

Jack knew that, although he had every reason to believe his mother and aunt would have nothing to be concerned about once the transition had taken place, the same could not be said for himself. Cartels of that type had tentacles all over the place. Of course he believed in divine protection, but he also lived by the advice that he understood was attributed to Oliver Cromwell: 'Trust in God and keep your powder dry.'

By the time he had dropped his mother to her front door later that evening, the matter had been settled. Everything would be put in motion for the sale of the house at the same time that the transfer of the business would be made to his uncle.

Before retiring, he switched on the sports news to learn that the 70th Masters Golf Tournament had been won by Phil Mickelson, shooting at 281.

It would be almost a year before the trial would take place and, by the time that it had, Sarah and her sister had secured and settled in their new home in Murieston, Scotland – seventeen miles from Edinburgh.

They had also taken Jack's advice and purchased a small property in Tallinn, a few miles from Sarah's old home. They planned to rent it out on short-term contracts to holidaymakers through the year, though they would block off certain periods exclusively for their own use. Whether they used the dates or not was immaterial. They just wanted to be sure that they had a bolthole in Estonia should they have a mind to travel there.

Jack's uncle had taken over ownership of Shoreside engineering and was already further expanding its operations internationally – something that both Jack and his father had always hoped would happen.

Elena had been given a new identity and, it was believed, had moved to somewhere in the UK. But no one really knew for sure, except the security branch of which Poska was a significant part.

As for Jack, he was spending much of his time as a business consultant, working mainly within Europe but sometimes further afield, as his reputation grew alongside his experience. He had most recently secured a major contract with a business based in Geneva.

But the threat to his life was far from over.

30th June 2007
England

The car park barrier lifted and a grey Lexus accelerated away from Glasgow Airport. Jack Troughton glanced at the clock on his console and registered that it was 3pm precisely. Eleven minutes later, as he accessed the A74 heading south, he was unaware that two explosions had taken place in the area that he had just left. One would be reported worldwide and the other would not. Neither of the incidents had been connected.

The first was a terrorist attack. It would later emerge that a dark green Jeep Cherokee loaded with propane canisters had been driven at speed into the glass doors of the airport terminal. There would be no fatalities other than one of the perpetrators. The second explosion would be in the multi-storey car park. It had written off a red Toyota Corolla as well as severely damaging other cars in the vicinity. There had been no fatalities at the second incident and no one had been injured. The target of the second attack was the car that had, minutes earlier, been parked in bay 1131 – a Lexus.

As Jack pulled intro Killington Lake Services his phone rang. The caller ID revealed who was ringing as he pressed the 'receive' button.

'How are you doing, Damian?'

'I'm more concerned about you, Jack, are you safe?'

'What do you mean – safe?'

'Haven't you heard the news?'

'Just got off the plane from Geneva about three hours ago. What news?'

'There's been an incident at Glasgow Airport. Just seen it come up on the TV. I knew you were flying in there today and I just wanted to check you were OK. Thought you might have had the radio on as you were driving.'

'I'm absolutely fine. Were many people hurt?'

'The area is sealed off, of course, but nothing has been said about casualties as yet.'

'Wow! It must have happened while I've been on the road, then.'

'Well, as long as you're safe. Incidentally, Sue was asking what time you would be arriving at our place, so we can have the meal ready.'

'Listen, how about the three of us going out for a meal tonight, on me? I haven't seen you guys for a while and it will save Sue worrying about cooking. We've got a lot to catch up on.'

'No need to worry about Sue – it would be me that would be cooking tonight anyway.'

'In that case, we are definitely going out for a meal,' laughed Jack.

'Well, if you insist on missing out on one of my specials, then we'll see you later. Do you think you could make it by seven thirty?'

'Yes, I'm sure that won't be a problem.'

'OK, that's great. See you around seven-thirty, then. Bye … bye … bye.'

Jack pressed the 'end call' button and wondered why people always seemed to end a phone conversation like that. After all, they never opened it with 'Hello, hello, hello'. Then he realised he had caught himself doing the very same thing on more than one occasion. He supposed it was a kind of subliminal communication that said 'I wish we could talk longer – sorry the call has to end' – or perhaps he was overthinking an issue that didn't really exist.

Damian and Sue had been very supportive since Celia had died. Some people within his circle had seemed to cut him off socially – not because they didn't care, he knew that, but because they simply didn't know what to say – especially in the light of how she had been killed. He assumed it was mostly the 'intruding into private grief' thing. Damian and Sue had been different – always seeming to gauge how he was feeling and managing to respond to his mood appropriately.

After exiting and locking the car, he made his way to the restaurant area. Then, a flat white ordered, he edged his way within sight of the nearest TV monitor, where small groups of people were either sitting or standing as they sipped their own coffees. Occasionally, as more details emerged, someone would turn to a total stranger, with whom ordinarily they would probably never have interacted, and expressed their horror. It wasn't too long before the rolling headlines began to repeat themselves and Jack became aware that everything that had so far been released about the airport attack had already been conveyed. There were still a couple of hours before he would reach his friends' home in Manchester and so he headed back onto the motorway.

Jack checked his rear-view mirror before signalling in preparation to move into the middle lane, but held back because he saw that a silver BMW was already signalling. When he eventually eased his car to the centre, the BMW moved into the overtaking lane and then the driver, maintaining the same speed as him for long enough to stare and make eye contact, sped off into the distance.

Jack wondered if he had been driving badly, but was sure that he hadn't. Anyway, the man in the other car – a white guy in his thirties – didn't appear to be angry or upset. It was as if he was checking to see who was driving. Had that really happened, or was he being paranoid? He had dismissed the anonymous threats he had received over the past few weeks, but even so, from time to time they still managed to edge their way back into the centre of his consciousness. Nevertheless, he made a mental note of the BMW. Given everything he had experienced of late, one could never be too careful. Had he known what had happened in the airport parking space he had recently vacated, he would have reached an entirely different conclusion.

Jack switched on the car radio and listened as 'Makes Me Wonder' by Maroon 5 emerged from the speakers.

'It was certainly him. There's no doubt about it.'

The BMW driver had pulled over at the first opportunity in order to use his phone.

'You are absolutely sure that you weren't mistaken?' questioned the voice at the other end.

'Not a chance. The number plate tallies and I'm positive it was him. I pulled alongside him as I drove by. It was Troughton and no mistake.'

'Why didn't you fix the device to the car rather than put it under it?' the voice said.

'If I had secured it to the car, then anyone moving the vehicles on either side could have set it off. You know how little room there is to negotiate in those multi-storeys. How was I to know that the remote would jam?'

'People here are not happy – not just with the outcome but with you too. You had better sort this out, and fast. They've got the girl away and I assume she's living somewhere with a new identity, and we need something better than just going for his relatives. He has no wife or kids, anyway. Our operation has all but closed down and we will never get territory back or regain respect if we lose face in front of our competitors. We're seeing signs already that they are starting to move in on us.'

'Well, there is always his mother ...' suggested the driver.

'Don't be ridiculous, you idiot! Are you serious? We get hit at this level and the only retaliation we can muster is to terminate an old woman! We'd be a laughing stock. Listen, I am telling you now – you better sort this mess out. This is not just about you any more. I was the one who assured them that you could handle this. You weren't the first choice and you convinced me you had everything covered. It's my neck on the line as well as yours. If you can't handle things, then I ...'

'Of course I can handle things. I'll just need a few days.'

'Why a few days?'

'Because he didn't travel home from the airport. He's heading south. I tailed him for 140 miles before I pulled alongside him.'

'Heading south? What do you mean – south? Why aren't you following him now, then?'

'Look, I've got a plan.'

'Got a plan! You had a plan and now we are teetering on the edge of chaos. I'm sick of the sound of your voice. I don't want to hear it again until you can promise me that Troughton is dead.'

Two hundred and fifty miles away in Tewkesbury, Gloucestershire, Elena sat on a bench in the grounds of its Abbey, a site on which a place of worship had been present for almost 1,400 years. She read through the application form for the second time.

So much had happened in the past year. A new identity – she was Sasha, now – a new home, a new language, some acquaintances ... but few friends. If she was totally honest, *no* friends – at least no one in whom she felt free to confide. It was not that people were unapproachable or that there had been no overtures of friendship towards her. It was simply that she remained continually concerned that if she let people close, something could slip out; some unguarded statement or whatever. It was just too big a risk. Loneliness was one thing, but the threat of discovery, once she had weighed it all up, was worse – far worse.

To begin with, the language had been the principal barrier. She had learned English at school back home as a child, but in those days it was just another lesson on the timetable to her and something to be endured rather than enjoyed. More than once in the past year she had wished she had paid more attention to it. But she had studied hard over these months and fortunately had had the time to do it. She could hardly believe that her new identity had also been accompanied by a bank account – something that she had never had, or even dreamed of having, when growing up in her village.

Of course, the money would not last forever and that is why she was applying for a position in a care home. She realised that it would involve menial, perhaps even unsavoury, tasks, but she did not mind. It would be a job and, anyway, she would be helping people. She had watched her grandparents grow old and remembered the helplessness in her mother's eyes as she failed to find the money for the medical bills that could have softened the severity of their condition – or at least lessened the struggle with their pain.

Her father had gone off with another woman when she was still a child and her mother had been left to cope on her own with her and her two sisters. But at least her mother no longer had to suffer the violent alcohol-driven rages that had become almost a daily occurrence. There was a sense of relief when he had gone, though that was soon followed by a sense of emptiness. He had proved to be neither protector, nor provider, nor parent – but nevertheless, he was still her father.

A wind rustled the leaves in the huge beech tree across from where she sat, and for a moment she thought the breeze would blow the paperwork out of her hands. She tightened her grip on it, as if by consolidating her hold it would help her gather together the threads both of her thoughts and her resolve.

When she had sat in what passed as a marketplace in her village and had been approached by the handsome man who complimented her and told her she should be a model, she could never have conceived for a moment what those words would lead to. He had spoken of contacts abroad and a passport, not just to another country but to another life.

Looking back, she could not believe how naïve she had been. For as long as she could remember she had spent her days like someone craving for water in a desert, stumbling towards the oasis that always dissolved into a mirage moments before she believed it was within her grasp.

Fairy-tale dreams had turned into a nightmare worse than she could ever have imagined. The hope of a secure home had long ago evaporated into a 'castle in the air'. There were no handsome princes – at least, none that she had ever met. Even before the encounter in the marketplace, she had narrowly escaped abuse by a leering uncle who had only been fended off by the screams that had brought her mother to her rescue.

It was not that she was stupid. She thought people always seemed to parallel material poverty with intellectual deprivation, but that was not so. At school she had excelled in those subjects that she found interesting and applied her mind to. Outside the classroom, writing had been her creative escape; even poetry sometimes. But she had stopped that when the prose became too dark. The sentiments were accurate enough; it's just that rereading them had only served to underscore the narrow corridor that was her experience. Someone had once told her that the root of the word 'anxiety' was best interpreted in that expression and she thought that must surely be right: no way to move forward with safety, no way to move back and no room for manoeuvre.

When the handsome stranger had offered the way out, it was as if she had suspended every semblance of rationality. He had called himself Bohdan, but she had no idea if that was his real name. Anyway, it didn't matter now. She should have known that there was always 'free cheese in a mousetrap'. But 'knowing' had to do with 'thinking', and the cotton-wool dreams of her heart proved stronger than any fabric of logic that she had been able to muster on that fateful day.

The stranger had taken her to the city. She had been treated like a princess to begin with, and then he had introduced her to his friends.

They had beaten her, humiliated her and drugged her. It had begun with a slap across her face. Stunned, she caught sight of Bohdan. His look did not convey horror, pity or even a semblance of remorse. There was not a scrap of shame in his cold demeanour. His stare was blank. His eyes were empty. He had been bait, and she had been hooked in every sense of the word. She knew that his name meant 'God's gift', but in reality he had played the part of the devil's snare.

She had been too traumatised to notice that by the time the next slap had landed he had turned away and left the room – his job having been done.

She could not know how many had raped her, though she could certainly recall the blissful detachment in the seconds after the needle had later entered her arm. However, when the drug had worn off, the horror rushed back into her consciousness like a tsunami that swept everything before it. How to hold it back? How to escape its constant progress every waking moment? As time went by, the needles became her only solace. Beaten and drugged into dependency – now a commodity and little more than meat – she, and others like her, were totally under their masters' control.

She had heard that in some places they moved girls in metal containers. It made no sense. There were lots of other ways to traffic people from one place to another. Perhaps the border controls had become more stringent or the guards harder to bribe.

But the fact was, she was alive and, at least for now, her identity hidden. How long it would stay that way she had no way of knowing.

'So let me get this clear. Your name is Sasha Sellick and you have been in this country how long?'

The woman behind the desk, who had previously introduced herself as Maureen Stibbes, organised the file in front of her and Elena watched as the woman's eyes darted from the papers on the desk to engage her own and then back to the papers on the desk again. The interview had commenced.

Elena guessed her interviewer must be in her early fifties. She was stockily built, but Elena would not have described her as obese. Her fair hair, probably its original colour rather than dyed, was swept tightly back from her face and gathered behind her head in something between a bun and a very short pony tail. As she asked this first question she used the index finger of her right hand to ease the bridge of her glasses further up her nose towards her forehead as if, by doing so, it would bring greater focus to the process she had just initiated.

Elena explained the length of time she had been in the UK and knew instinctively what the next question would be.

'And you have had no employment at all during your stay. Am I correct in that or have I missed something?'

'No, you are absolutely correct, Ms Stibbes.'

'Well, I'm sure that you understand that this immediately creates two problems for me. The first, and by far the most important, is that I have no references from any employment you have been engaged in in the UK from which to draw upon. Your CV is, for all intents and purposes, empty.'

She continued the process of glancing down at the file and sharply back up, repeating the process with such rapidity that she reminded Elena of the hens that fed in her yard back home – one eye on their grain and another on their surroundings.

'I see, however,' the head went back down again, 'that your references from where you come from are exemplary. My problem, as you might expect, is my difficulty in verifying them.'

'I understand that, Ms Stibbes,' said Elena, in as contrite a voice as she could muster.

'The second question that leaps out at me from these pages relates to how you have managed to exist financially up to this point. Now , I know that asylum seekers and refugees get benefits from the hard-working taxpayers in this country but that …'

'Excuse me, Ms Stibbes,' interrupted Elena, 'but I am neither an asylum seeker nor a refugee …'

She wanted to add that, if she had been, that would not create an issue of shame for her. She knew better than most the trauma of poverty, and the powerlessness to escape it, but did not think it was wise to make a point of this at this juncture. Responding to this woman's ignorance in order to score a point was not going to secure her a position. There were times and places to express her feelings and put people straight, but this was probably not one of them.

'Well, what I meant to say – I am sorry if you were offended by my comments – was that you seem to have secured a permanent address and it would appear you are managing to meet the demands of rent. How have you managed to do this without gainful employment, if you prefer me to put it that way?'

'When I came here I brought some savings with me that, though modest, have meant that I've been able to cover my living expenses without recourse to other income – social security or otherwise.'

'Well, I suppose there is something to be said for that,' said Maureen Stibbes, with an air of pompous self-righteousness.

Elena could not help but wonder how this woman would have fared if born into the straitened circumstances she and her family had had to endure. However, taking a short controlling breath before each answer, she proceeded to what she hoped would soon be the end of the interview.

When that point had been reached, and the vertical movements of Maureen Stibbes' head from face to file had finally finished, Elena looked across to her interviewer, whose eyes were now locked on the file in an attitude of focused contemplation.

After what seemed to Elena an eternity, but could not have been much more than a minute or two, the head moved up and the eyes locked back on to her.

'Sasha, I am going to be absolutely honest with you on two counts. I can call you Sasha, can't I?'

'Of course, Ms Stibbes,' said Elena, a little warily.

'The first is that we at Cotswold Mews have the highest standards. We have a duty of care primarily to our residents, but

141

also to our staff. This means we cannot employ any Tom, Dick or Harriet that waltzes in off the street and asks to be part of the CM family.'

'I hope you do not see me as just waltzing in off the street, Ms Stibbes,' responded Elena. 'I have complied meticulously with all aspects of the application process and both read and signed your company's vision and values statement.'

'I know, dear, I know you have,' replied Maureen, with a marked change in her attitude and demeanour, 'and that brings me to my second point. I am going to be open with you, Sasha. This business has a large turnover of staff, especially at the level that you have applied to be working at. Retaining people is a very real problem for us. It sometimes feels like we are hatching eggs on an escalator. As soon we think people have settled with us, they up sticks and move away, for better pay and better conditions, usually.'

'Up sticks?' asked Elena. 'I don't quite understand.'

'Oh, it's just a turn of phrase, don't worry about it,' responded Maureen. 'The residents, we like to call them guests,' she went on, 'do not need continual medical help. There are other places that cater for those with problems of that nature. Don't get me wrong, we have a GP who visits regularly and is as attentive as his schedule allows, but the work that you would be engaged in, if you accept this appointment, will demand a great deal of patience. You won't find people here with severe dementia, but there are those that suffer with quite monumental mood swings which demand more from our staff than just simple tact, believe me. I'm sure that you will have also read the duties and expectancies that the role you have applied for entails within the application folder we sent you, especially the issues that surround caring for the personal hygiene aspects of our guests.'

'Yes, Ms Stibbes, I have,' said Elena.

'And what are your thoughts on that? Do you think you will be able to cope?'

'I'm sure I will, Ms Stibbes. It won't be a problem at all, really it won't,' Elena responded, hoping she was making the point clear.

'There will, of course, be a trial period of a few weeks in which you can evaluate whether this is the place where you want to be and, for our part, we can see if this is the best position you are suited for. So what I am really saying is this – if you really want the job, the job is yours.'

'Thank you very much indeed, Ms Stibbes.'

'Well, if you're sure, all I can say to you, Sasha, is – welcome to Cotswold Mews.'

2nd July 2007
Murieston, Scotland

It was Beth who first heard the doorbell. Neither she nor Sarah were expecting anybody, so they could not imagine who it might be on a Monday morning. Perhaps it was a parcel.

As she went down the hall towards the door, Beth glanced through the window, even though she knew that whoever was on the front step would probably already be outside her line of sight. She glanced up and down the street to see if there was a post office van or delivery vehicle, but could see nothing ... nothing except a silver car parked on the other side of the road and some way off.

'Good morning, madam, I am very sorry to trouble you,' said the short, stocky man who was standing on the doorstep. 'Would you be Mrs Sarah Troughton, I wonder?'

'No, I'm not. I'm her sister. How may I help you?'

'I am Gabriel Porteus ... I was wondering if Mrs Troughton is at home.'

'I'm sorry, who did you say you were? I don't think we know anyone of that name,' responded Beth, cautiously.

By this time, Sarah had made her way down the hall. She spoke over her sister's shoulder to the person standing there.

'I am Sarah Troughton. How can we help you?'

'My name is Gabriel Porteus. I'm a friend of your son. I've been trying to reach him but without success on a matter of some urgency, and wondered ...'

'Excuse me, but how did you get hold of this address? We've only recently moved into the area. How is it you don't know where my son is but have managed to find me?'

For an instant the man felt wrong-footed. What she was saying made sense. He needed to think fast. He couldn't risk breaking the momentum. She must not become suspicious – that would ruin everything. He had no idea why he had concocted the name 'Gabriel Porteus' as he had entered the estate of smart looking executive homes, but it had seemed as good as any at the time.

It had taken them ages to get this address and it was more by luck than judgement that they had discovered where Sarah Troughton lived. One of their contacts who worked for the estate agent in Tallinn had overhead a conversation that Sarah had had with the lawyer completing the sale. He had asked where she was moving to, and the town of Livingston had been mentioned; she was moving there with her sister. The next part had been harder. Livingston, Scotland, was a large and expanding town. However, judging by the money they had got for the old place, it was pretty certain that Sarah Troughton and her sister would be living in the better part of the area. That had narrowed the search down to Murieston. From there it was just a matter of going to the local newsagent in the hope that these women took a daily newspaper. When he had asked the assistant if she had any idea where two 'relatives' had moved to – two ladies in their early sixties – it had been simplicity itself.

He had been told that the Scots were friendly people, and that had been the Achilles' heel. All he wanted was an address, and he had got it from a talkative shop assistant.

'Well, he used to talk a lot about you,' the visitor continued. 'Is there any chance that I could come in? I promise not to keep you long.'

Sarah and Beth hesitated for a moment.

'If he is a friend of Jack's, then it surely must be alright,' said Beth.

Once they were seated in the lounge, Sarah asked, 'So, how did you say you got our address?'

'Well, as I was saying, Jack mentioned you in conversation a great deal, and when he said that you had moved to Scotland, I told him that I had been over here on business quite a bit and so I asked him, in passing, where you had moved to. He said Murieston. I happened to be in the area so … Has he changed his mobile number, do you know? I simply can't reach him …'

He thought he had better keep some consistency to his story, just in case that mouthy woman in the shop happened to mention something the next time they were in there.

'No, but he's probably not answering the phone. I can understand you not being able to pin Jack down. He's all over the place at the moment. He is a very busy man,' said Sarah.

'He's a business consultant, you know,' added Beth, with more than a hint of pride in her voice. 'Sometimes he stays here with us. When he travels any distance around the country he's in hotels, and only recently he has returned from Geneva.'

Sarah's worried glance made him think that she was just a little anxious that her sister was conveying so much information.

'So you are expecting him here soon, then, are you? Him having just returned from Geneva, that is?' enquired the visitor.

'Why exactly did you say that you needed to contact Jack? The matter was urgent, I think you said?' interjected Sarah.

'It's most urgent. He has been doing some work for the company I am employed by and we decided to act upon his recommendations. I had met him at a restaurant to complete the contract with him,' the man went on, 'and he was kind enough to drop me back later to the hotel I was staying at. This was about three weeks ago. I had a briefcase with me, which I had put in the back of his Lexus. It had some very sensitive information inside. So sensitive, in fact, that we had not committed it to our computers. It was just hard copy. When Jack dropped me off at the hotel entrance, I got out and it wasn't until he had sped off into the distance that I realised I had left my briefcase in his car.'

'But I'm sure that Jack would have contacted your hotel or your company as soon as he found it?'

'Well, it was on the floor,' said the man. 'He wouldn't see it unless he'd been carrying passengers. I never leave anything of value on the back seat in full view. I usually ask that it be put in the boot of the car but, as the journey to the hotel was so short and we wouldn't be stopping anywhere en route …'

'But I can't understand why you or your company didn't try to reach Jack after you discovered you had left the briefcase behind,' said Sarah. 'After all, you must have had all his contact details when you engaged him to work for you.'

The man shifted about on his chair, hoping his nervousness would not be noted. It was like being interrogated by Interpol. He had to see their point, though. He could feel his story slowly crumbling under their scrutiny. It even crossed his mind to abandon the charade and force what he wanted out of them. He was more used to extracting what he wanted by violence; not this ridiculous verbal swordplay. This was not his style at all. He wanted to play to his strengths, but he could not risk any more mistakes. Whatever he did here, he would have to tidy up afterwards. He may be in an upmarket housing estate, but it was a housing estate nevertheless. It was all too risky. He would have to stay on the same tack.

'He doesn't seem to be answering his phone or replying to his emails. Then, as you have said, he has been abroad so we haven't been able to make contact. I need those documents back very soon. My bosses are not a little upset that I have let all this happen. I could even lose my job because of it. So, as you might imagine, any help you can give me, however small, would be very much appreciated.'

He could see in the face of Sarah Troughton's sister that she was the type to be moved by sob stories.

Beth was always moved by sob stories. She was the kind of person who would be reduced to tears by any film whose plot was even marginally emotional. She knew that Jack would not want this gentleman's career to be in jeopardy because, however inadvertently, he had driven off with his case.

Without even glancing across at her sister for any sign of assent, she said, 'Well, all we know is that he planned to travel down to see some close friends in Manchester. As we haven't seen him for a while, we arranged that he would come round here for a meal tomorrow evening. Would you like to leave your contact details with us so we can pass them on to him when he comes? We'll make absolutely sure he knows how urgent it is, and I'm sure that he'll be in touch as soon as he possibly can.'

'That would be absolutely amazing,' the man said, taking out a small notepad from his inside pocket and jotting some numbers down. 'If he phones either of these two numbers he will get through to me. One is my office and the other is my mobile. This really is very good of you. Thank you for giving me so much of your time, you really have been most kind.'

'Would you like a cup of tea before you go? We're sorry we never thought to offer you anything,' asked Beth.

'No, that's perfectly alright,' the visitor said, relieved that he had gleaned all the information he needed. 'I have to be going. Anyway, thank you for being so helpful.'

The three of them stood simultaneously, but it was Beth who led him to the door. When she had waved him goodbye, she returned to the lounge to find Sarah sitting back in her chair with her arms opened wide in questioning exasperation.

'Why on earth did you tell him all that, Beth? We haven't got the slightest clue who he is! I was trying to signal to you to stop, but you just went on and on – even offered him tea, for goodness' sake. What on earth were you thinking?'

'I'm sure there is nothing to worry about. He seemed perfectly OK to me – and so polite too.'

'Beth, take a moment to think. Why do you imagine we are we here in Scotland?'

'Well, because your business has been sold and you always wanted to come back to the UK.'

'But why else?' asked Sarah.

'Well, there was that trouble when the trial took place – but that was ages ago. If anyone had wanted to get to Jack, I'm sure that they would have done so by now.'

'Well, I hope you are right, Beth, I really do,' responded Sarah. 'Whatever you say, I'm worried. There was something he said that is niggling at the back of my mind, but I can't seem to put my finger on it.'

The man headed back to the car with the assured step of a confidence trickster who had laid bait and had had the pleasure of seeing it taken. He slumped into the driving seat and smiled before switching on the engine. The two phone numbers he had given them were as bogus as his cover story. Troughton would never get to use them because Troughton would be dead long before he ever reached the house.

3rd July 2007
Murieston, Scotland

It was as the two women were discussing what they would make for Jack's homecoming meal that Sarah looked across to her sister in panic and alarm.

They had been chatting over which of his favourites they might make. They were at a stage in their lives when recipe books seldom entered into the equation, especially when it came to Jack's culinary preferences. Both of them were well able to prepare his 'specials' with their eyes closed. He had simple tastes; some might even have described them as 'comfort food'. On the occasions when they had presented him with more elaborate dishes that took more time to plan and prepare, though he was always appreciative and effusive in his praise, deep down they knew what it was that he really preferred.

Sarah had been crossing the kitchen carrying a Pyrex dish when it smashed onto the white tiled floor as her hands came up to her face in terror.

'Jack's in grave danger, Beth! We've got to warn him! That man was an imposter. Even now it may be too late.'

'Sarah, whatever is the matter? What do you mean, imposter?'

'It's the car, Beth! It's the car! Porteus, or whatever his real name is, said that he left the briefcase in the Lexus, but he couldn't have!'

'Why couldn't he?'

'Because Jack only bought the Lexus a few days before he left for Geneva. When the man said that he had had a meal with him three weeks earlier, he was driving a Mercedes. Only if he had seen him drive to the airport, or drive from it, would he have known that Jack drove a Lexus. We have to get hold of him right away!'

Sarah did not have to swipe her finger far through the contact list on her phone before she came to 'Clarke'. She would use the landline, though, instead of the mobile. She did not want to suffer any poor connections, particularly now of all times. The phone was answered on the fourth ring.

'Thank God!' Sarah exclaimed, under her breath.

'Hello, Sue Clarke speaking.'

'Hi, Sue, it's Sarah here. Can you put me on to Jack right away?'

'Are you OK? Is anyone ill? Are you alright, love?'

'Listen, Sue, I know I must sound rude, but I must speak to Jack right away. I'll explain later, but I need to talk to him now. Can you put him on, please?'

'I'm afraid I can't, Sarah, he's just left – about twenty minutes ago, I reckon.'

'Oh no!'

'Sarah, what on earth is the matter? Shall I put Damian on?'

'No, I need to contact Jack but there's some problem with his phone, I understand. What shall I do?'

'There's nothing wrong with his phone as far as we know,' replied Sue.

'Well, he's not switching it on or answering it or something. I don't know which!'

'Jack always keeps his phone on,' continued Sue. 'He has to because of his work. The only time he switches it off is when he's in a meeting or something like that. And I know it's working because he's just spoken to Damian about something he left in his room. I think it was a phone charger or something.'

'Thanks, Sue. Listen, I know you believe in prayer, so please pray. I can't go into it now, but I will get back to you. Please, please pray!'

Sarah hit the 'end call' button and immediately punched in the number for Jack's mobile.

'This is all my fault!' Beth cried in the background.

'Get a grip, Beth! It's not anybody's fault. It is what it is. Blaming ourselves isn't going to help. Let's hope Jack picks this up.'

'Hello, Jack Troughton. Who am I speaking to?'

'Oh, Jack! Thank God – are you alright?'

'Of course I am, Mum. What's wrong?'

'Jack! I don't know how far you are from the next service station, but I need you to pull in there. Jack, please do as I ask and, when you park, try to find a space away from the main body of cars. And when you get parked, watch out for a silver car!'

As soon as Jack had pulled into the next service station and had parked, he called his mother back. Sarah related to her son everything that had happened. The first thing on Jack's mind now was how to prioritise what he should do next. His mother had said that she would phone Sue to apologise for the abruptness of her call, but Jack had said that she didn't need to do that as he would need to phone Damian anyway and try to work out a way forward. It had become obvious that the driver of the 'silver car' – the BMW he'd seen before, he realised – would try to target him at some point between where he was now and his mother's home.

However, he concluded that his mother had been overcautious about the imminence of the attack. There was no way that the man would use a service station to make an attempt on his life, as he would know that the parking cameras would record every vehicle entering and exiting. Nor was it likely anything would take place on the motorway itself. Again, it would be the presence of cameras that would be the deterrent. Jack lifted the phone handset and hit the speed dial for Damian, who answered on the first ring.

'Is that you, Jack? Is everything alright? We had this call from Sarah …'

'I know. It seems that some guy got into her home.'

'You mean broke in – forced his way in?' asked Damian, anxiously.

'No, she and Aunt Elizabeth are OK. He invented some story to worm his way into the house, with the intention of getting to know my movements.'

'You mean your mother told him where you were?'

'No, she didn't tell him your address. You and Sue have got nothing at all to worry about.'

'I'm not worried about us, Jack. I'm just surprised, given everything that has gone on, that your mother would …'

'It wasn't my mother. It was my Aunt Elizabeth. You know how trusting she is. I'm not really blaming her. I'm not blaming anyone.

The problem is that he now knows that I'm due at their place this evening. My guess is that he'll choose a spot fairly close to my mother's house. If anything is going to kick off it is probably going to be somewhere within a mile or two of Livingston.'

'Have you contacted the police yet?'

'No, I wanted to phone you first, but that is certainly the next thing on my list.'

'I've just had an idea,' said Damian.

'What's that?'

'I am going to drive out now and meet you in Scotland.'

'No, I am not going to allow anything to happen that might put you or Sue at risk.'

'Listen, Jack, you know Sue would want me to help if I can. But I'll talk to her first if it would make you happier.'

'But I can't see the point of you coming all that way!'

'I'll tell you the point. This bloke is going to be looking for a Lexus, not a white Hyundai. What I suggest is that I come and meet you somewhere within ten miles of Livingston, where you can park your car and then we can go the rest of the way in my car. When we've parked, we can contact the police.'

It was four and a half hours before Jack and Damian were able to meet up. There was no point swapping cars any earlier on the route as both vehicles needed to be accessible. The place that they had chosen meant that the Lexus could be parked safely until they needed it again. They approached the police station together.

'Just hang on a wee minute, let's get this straight,' said the desk sergeant in his distinctive West Lothian accent. 'You are telling me that a man came to your mother's house yesterday morning to get your address, left without in any way threatening her, and you are therefore suggesting on the basis of this somewhat flawed logic that I should believe that your life is under threat as he is waiting somewhere in our beautiful Scottish landscape to assassinate one of you two gentleman from down south?'

'That's exactly what my friend is saying,' said Damian. 'You only need to check with the Estonian Special Branch.'

'The Estonian Special Branch!' said the sergeant in a voice laced with a combination of incredulity and sarcasm. 'I can't smell anything on the breath of either of you, but perhaps you're taking some kind of special medication, because that's the only way I can account for such a pile of nonsense as this. I suppose you know that wasting police time is a criminal offence. It's something we can charge you with and, if that happens, it will leave you with a criminal record should either of you two numpties not already have one. And you say – Mr Troughton, was it – that a silver BMW passed your Lexus after you left Glasgow Airport and its driver glanced over at you while overtaking. Is that more or less the gist of it?'

'Yes, that's right,' said Jack, hoping that at last they were beginning to be taken seriously.

'Well, I can tell you,' said the sergeant, drily, 'if we arrested every driver on our roads that looked askance at another motorist, there would be more people in jails in Scotland than out of them. Oh, incidentally, you are talking about a Lexus? Because when I watched you enter our car park on my monitors here …' at this he jabbed a thumb behind him without taking his eyes from them, 'I saw you with my own wee eyes come into our compound in a white Hyundai.'

'That's because we switched cars a few miles back,' said Damian, irritated.

'Oh, I get it now,' said the policeman with a wry smile. 'You concluded that it would be more cost-effective to have a sniper's bullet penetrate a Hyundai than a Lexus … and you boys call us Scots thrifty! Listen, gentlemen, I will take all of your details, including your mother's home address.'

'So you are taking us seriously, then?' asked Damian.

'If you ask me, I think that this is about the most ridiculous story I have heard in all my time in the Force. I only want your details, especially yours, Mr Troughton, to save me asking for them again if ever we need them for a charge sheet.'

'So what do you think we should do now?' Damian asked Jack as they exited the police station and walked towards the car.

'Well, one thing is certain,' said Jack. 'We can't go round to my mother's house tonight. We have no idea how close Porteus – or whatever it is he calls himself – is to them. Were we to turn up in Murieston, we'd stand every chance of putting them in very real danger. I'll give my mother a ring to say that we won't be there. I assume you'll want to phone Sue to assure her that you're OK?'

Sarah and Beth had already reached the conclusion that Jack would not be coming that evening. However, it had been good to hear his voice on the phone and to know he was safe. They knew he would come to see them as soon as it was safe to do so and would be sure to phone them in advance when he was coming.

The BMW driver was parked, hidden from the road, at a place that the man had worked out Jack would have to pass, whatever route he took to his mother's house. But it was now 9pm; the night was drawing in. Where was Jack? Those women must have tipped him off. He was surprised. It was evident that they had believed every word he had said – even offering him a cup of tea in the end.

One thing he was absolutely sure of was that he must not fail this time. What he had to do, he had to do tonight. He would terminate Troughton one way or another.

He had tried the personable diplomacy route and that clearly hadn't worked. It was now time to operate in the way that had become second nature to him. The way that he knew best.

Pressing the boot-release button, he opened the car door, swung himself out of his seat and made his way to the rear of the vehicle to retrieve a small duffel bag.

He waited until he was back in the car with the door closed before unzipping the top to examine the contents. Everything was present: the gun – a Glock 19 – the Stanley knife, the jemmy and the role of duct tape.

He re-parked the BMW two streets away from his destination and went the rest of the way on foot. When he got within a few metres of the house he pulled his woollen hat further down over his ears. There was no need to wear a mask as they had already seen his face. He had concluded that by the time this was all over, he would be well away anyhow. The hat was just a precaution in the unlikely event that a neighbour happened to be staring out of their window.

He felt for the latch on the side gate. As he expected, it was bolted, but that would not be a problem. He knew only too well that these things were not made to be serious security deterrents; just to keep the opportunist burglar at bay. He would be on the other side of it in seconds – and he was.

'I think I'll just give Sue a ring before I turn in for the night,' Sarah said to Beth's back as she saw her ascending the stairs.

'OK, love,' replied Beth, without either stopping or turning. 'Try to sleep well. See you in the morning.'

Sarah thought for a moment that she had heard a noise coming from the kitchen, but dismissed it as just a figment of her imagination. She picked up the receiver and poised her finger to dial, but then stopped. There was no dialling tone. Her first thought was to contact BT. There was no time for her second thought.

A gloved hand came from behind and slid across her mouth at the same moment as she became aware of something hard being pushed into the small of her back.

'If you make the slightest sound it will be the last that you will ever make,' a voice whispered.

Sarah froze in terror.

'Now walk slowly and carefully to the table over there. I say "carefully" because if you kick anything on the way it'll be the last thing you ever do.'

As the two of them edged their way forward like partners in some macabre dance routine, the man glanced around the room. The curtains remained completely closed and, although there was a warning sensor positioned in the corner of the ceiling, the system clearly had not yet been armed for the night. Their movements would remain undetected. He pointed towards a carver chair at the end of the dining room table. There were six chairs, and the ones at each end were carvers.

Sarah sat.

With the gun still pointing at her, he pulled the roll of duct tape from his bag with his left hand, passed it to her and in the faintest of whispers said, 'Now I want you pull out a section of the tape.'

Trembling, Sarah pulled out a silver strip, and when it had reached about nine inches, the man reached down once more into his bag and in a single swift movement clicked out the blade of the Stanley knife, drew it across the roll, and severed the strip.

Sarah knew what was coming next, but was helpless to do anything about it.

The man seemed confident that she was completely clear about the consequences for her and her sister if she made the slightest sound, as he laid the gun to one side, snatched the strip of tape from her hands and transferred it to her mouth, ensuring that the nasal passages were kept clear. It appeared he did not want her to die of suffocation – at least not yet.

The next few minutes were spent in taping her hands to the armrests of the carver and her lower legs to its legs. Then his eyes scanned the room for the second time, and the slightest of smiles creased his lips as his gaze rested on what had apparently been the object of his search – a mobile phone.

He reached for it, then instinctively held his breath as he heard the sound of a toilet flushing. He was aware of a door being opened – probably the bathroom – and another one being opened and closed – definitely a bedroom.

The phone was not password-protected. He opened the contacts app and easily found Jack's number. He walked soundlessly to the kitchen, being careful to avoid the scattered shards of glass that had come from the door through which he had gained entry. He pressed the icon for the number he wanted.

'Hi, Mum, is everything OK?'

The man spoke softly into the receiver.

'I'm afraid your dear mother cannot come to the phone, Mr Troughton. The sad truth is that she is tied up at the moment and won't be going anywhere.'

'Who is this?' said Jack, a mixture of anger and anxiety in his voice. 'Put my mother on the line right now. If you've hurt her, I'm telling you …'

'Be silent for a moment, Troughton, and listen to what I am about to say to you. If you deviate from the instructions I am about to give you in the slightest detail, your mother and her sister will not survive the night. You see, I can't get to you so I need you to get to me. I know your first instinct will be to contact the police, but that would be a huge mistake, I promise you.

'I am going to give you a series of instructions via this mobile. This will create a number of waypoints on your route. Each one of them will be a location at which I will require you to pause for a few minutes in order for me to ensure that no one is following you. After I have entirely satisfied myself that you are not being followed, I will direct you to the next place and so forth. Do you understand?'

'Yes, I do,' said Jack, 'and I promise you that if you hurt a hair of my mother's head, I …'

'Please, Troughton, you are in no position to threaten me. There is no escape for you. You are going to die. The only thing you need to concern yourself about is whether you will also be responsible not just for the deaths of two others who are dear to you, but how long each of them will endure before they draw their final, merciful, breath.'

'Why are you doing this?'

'What a silly question, Troughton. You know full well why I am doing this. Friends of mine are serving very long sentences because of your testimony and the testimony of that slut of a girl. Some of them will die in prison and they, and many others, have also lost millions in anticipated revenue. If this wasn't bad enough, you have virtually closed down our organisation and so it will be my pleasure, on my friends' behalf, to close *you* down. So the first thing I want to know is where you are currently.'

'We are …'

'*We* …? What do we mean by *we*?'

'I have a friend with me. We are in a local hotel on the outskirts of Livingston.'

'Well, you better make absolutely sure that your friend remains under the same constraints as yourself. If either of you deviate from my instructions one iota, the women will die. Are you entirely clear about that?'

'Yes, I am,' answered Jack. 'You can do whatever you want to me, but please don't hurt my mother or my aunt.'

'You will get a call from me on this phone in a few minutes. What car are you driving now? I assume you have switched?'

'A white Hyundai,' said Jack.

When Jack ended the call he turned to Damian, who had been agitatedly standing nearby and trying to piece together the gist of the situation as he listened frustratingly to just one end of the conversation.

As Jack related the full account of what had transpired, Damian gasped.

'You have got to tell the police, Jack, you don't have an option.'

'How can I? This man is clever. He's going to direct me through a number of vantage points from which he can see whether or not I've been followed. If the police use helicopters, he'll pick them out in an instant. We can't send the police to the house – for all we know, he has Mum and Aunt Elizabeth at a different location by now – or even in his car with him. And we don't know who he's working with – he can't be doing this alone. It's all too risky but, apart from that, Damian, the police have already dismissed our story out of hand. I am going to cooperate with the plan and you are going to have to stay here and pray. Perhaps you could ask Sue to pray too, without spelling out the details. That would be the best help you could give me right now.'

Damian handed over the keys of his car to Jack, just as the phone rang.

There were four waypoints received over the next couple of hours. Jack realised his wait in each place was not just for the driver to assess whether he was being followed. It also gave the man the time, once he was confident his strategy was working, to drive ahead to the next location, unobserved.

'How long is this going to go on for?' asked Jack, when the phone rang yet again.

'It will all be over soon, Troughton, as will you. I want you to drive towards the house now – or at least within half a mile of it. Have you heard of the Murieston Trail?'

'Yes, I know where that is,' Jack replied.

As he had been driving about, during what were now the early hours of the morning, he had wondered why the man had not picked him off at any one of the locations that had been selected. He could think of only two reasons. The first was that he would have needed a rifle to accomplish that and Jack had concluded that he did not have one. The other reason was that a 'clear line of sight', which was an advantage as far as surveillance was concerned, was also a major disadvantage when it came to murder. If the driver could see him, then so could any potential witness who might be driving by.

This last location was perfect from the killer's perspective. The trail, a local beauty spot, had been created by the developers when the luxury housing estate had been built.

The trail consisted basically of a series of paths covered with tree bark that meandered alongside a shallow stream. Jack had walked it on more than one occasion when trying to collect his thoughts or just chill. But that had always been during the day. Right now, the area would be pitch black with no artificial lighting. The other thing was that there was no vehicular access. The trail could be accessed from only one direction and that by foot.

He was about two miles away from the location when the phone rang. Thinking it would be the driver, he pressed the 'receive' button and asked, 'What now?'

'It's me, Jack, it's Damian. I phoned Sue – and don't worry, I didn't give too much away. She assured me she would be praying but said that Psalm 91 came to her. I want to read part of it out to you:

> Whoever dwells in the shelter of the Most High
> will rest in the shadow of the Almighty.
> I will say of the LORD, 'He is my refuge and my fortress,
> my God, in whom I trust.'
> Surely he will save you
> from the fowler's snare
> and from the deadly pestilence.
> He will cover you with his feathers,
> and under his wings you will find refuge;
> his faithfulness will be your shield and rampart.
> You will not fear the terror of night,
> nor the arrow that flies by day,
> nor the pestilence that stalks in the darkness,
> nor the plague that destroys at midday.
> A thousand may fall at your side,
> ten thousand at your right hand,
> but it will not come near you.
> You will only observe with your eyes

and see the punishment of the wicked.
If you make the Most High your dwelling –
even the LORD, who is my refuge –
then no harm will befall you …'

Jack felt a lump come to his throat. In all the Bible there could not have been a more suitable word of assurance for him right at this moment. Jack thanked Damian and asked him to thank Sue. However, he had no sooner hit the 'call end' button when the phone rang again.

'What the hell are you playing at, Troughton? I'm getting more than a little concerned that you are trying to mess with me. Do you really have so little regard for the lives of your family? I've just tried to get through to you but you were engaged. Who, I wonder, would you be phoning at 2.45am in the morning, I'm asking myself? Do you take me for a complete idiot? You can never say I didn't warn you.'

'Hang on,' said Jack. 'Just calm down. I didn't phone anyone. The friend I told you about phoned me to see how I was.'

'To see if you are still alive,' the voice replied with mockery and menace.

'He's kept his side of the bargain to the letter, as have I, so what is it you want me to do now?'

'I want you to park up about fifty metres from the entrance to the trail. You are then to walk along the path to your left until you get to the edge of the stream. You will eventually come to a bench. You are not to sit on the bench but to stand in front of it.'

Jack knew exactly where the bench was. He had sat on it many times before. He also knew why the man had insisted that he should stand. It was clear now that he did not have a rifle, and a standing person was likely to present a bigger target. If the first shot did not hit an artery or a vital organ, then there would be other chances to go in for the kill once he had been immobilised.

It was also clear why he had chosen the stream, which Jack had no doubt the assassin would already be on the other side of. The watery barrier ensured that Jack could not rush him. It was true that the expanse was shallow, but Jack would have had to wade rather than run. This would slow him down considerably and he would not stand a chance. He had to admit the man had thought everything through.

Jack stood exactly at the spot that he had been told to stand, and was surprised how calm he felt. Was this because he had resigned himself to the inevitable, or was it something else? He was convinced it was. He had read in his Bible, in Philippians 4, about a peace that 'transcends all understanding'. This must be it, then – because rationally it made no sense at all.

He was glad that he had not been reduced to having to plead for mercy. No one could ever precisely predict how they would react when faced with a situation like this, so he was glad that if it was God's will his natural life should end here – at least it would end with dignity. What was more, he knew with absolute certainly that there was no 'the end', because he was a Christian. He would see Celia again. They would be reunited, that was certain – whether within the hour or in years to come. It humbled him, as well as comforted him, that after all the biblical knowledge he had gleaned, and faith statements he had expressed, when he was standing in total darkness being able to see no more than a few metres in front of him, this stuff really worked.

The anticipated voice came out of the blackness on the other side of the stream.

'Goodbye, Troughton!'

Jack had read more thrillers than he could count and watched more movies than he could remember, and they all seemed to run through the same scenario when they got to this juncture. There would be a speech from the perpetrator explaining what he was doing and why he was doing it. Well, at least it seemed he was going to be spared that.

In the stillness he listened to the metallic click of a gun being cocked and a second later he heard the shot ring out.

What he had expected least was what he heard next. It was a Scottish accent that rang out in his direction.

'Get yerself doon on yer face, Troughton! Reet doon where yer are – this is the police!'

The shot had come from the rifle of a police marksman, who had picked out the man through a night-vision scope.

Within what seemed like only seconds, police officers were at Jack's side helping him to his feet.

'Are you alright sir?' the nearest to him asked.

'Absolutely fine,' replied Jack. 'A little shaken, but absolutely fine. But my mother …?'

'Don't you worry about her, sir. She's fine too, and the lady who lives with her – your aunt, isn't it, sir?'

'Yes, that's right,' said Jack breathing heavily, more out of relief than exertion, 'but how did you … ?'

'We'll go through all that at the station later, but for now we need to get you to a hospital.'

'Oh, there's no need for that,' said Jack.

'I am afraid there is, sir. It's procedure, you see. They are likely to give you a routine check on admission and then keep you in overnight for observation. But don't worry, we will also have an officer posted on your door.'

'What for? I assume the man is dead, so what further threat can I be under?'

Jack became aware of movement on the other side of the stream as a cloud had moved and let a shaft of moonlight through the dense trees. He could just make out the silhouette of people carrying something that appeared to be a stretcher.

'He's not dead – just wounded. Our firearms officer shot him in the shoulder to ensure that he would be disarmed but not killed. You are under no current threat – as far as we know, that is,' continued the officer. 'However, we cannot be entirely sure that he is working alone. When you and your friend visited the station you were not dealt with within the standards that we would expect of our officers. Off the record, the desk sergeant who you spoke to is currently under suspension pending an enquiry – but we can leave all that until tomorrow. The Chief Inspector who now has jurisdiction over the case has stipulated that from now on everything should be done by the book and, as irritating or unnecessary as that may appear to you, that's the way it's going to be. This whole can of worms could have turned out very differently had not some apparently unconnected coincidences come together in the way that they did. You know, I think someone must be watching over you.'

'And my mother and aunt?'

'Mrs Troughton is already being checked out at the hospital. Your aunt has been given a sedative and a neighbour is staying with her for the night – or what's left of it. I understand she slept through the whole thing, until we broke down the front door, that is,' he added, ruefully.

'Broke down the front door!' said Jack in astonishment.

'We'll explain all that tomorrow, sir. On the assumption that you are as fit as you say you are, some officers will come round early in the afternoon and take an initial statement from you.'

Both Jack and his mother were discharged at 10am the following day and Damian was on hand to drive them home. The front door had been professionally boarded up. The back door, through which they were able to enter, also had signs of temporary repair, given the glass had been broken by Sarah's attacker the previous evening.

It was through this door that, late in the afternoon, Sarah gave admittance to two plain-clothes male officers and a woman in uniform.

When everyone was seated, Jack asked, 'So, tell us, how on earth were you alerted to the fact there was a problem in the first place?'

'Well, let's start at the beginning,' said one of the plain-clothes policemen who, by the body language and sense of deference of the other two, everyone deemed to be the most senior and therefore the person in charge. There had been formal introductions when they had first entered the house, but those in attendance had taken little notice, being more preoccupied with the questions that they were anxious should be answered. 'First of all, Mr Troughton,' he continued, 'we need to apologise for the offhand way in which you, and Mr Clarke here, were treated by the officer you met on your arrival at the police station. We have CCTV footage, of course, but the entire conversation was overhead by a civilian member of staff who was in an adjacent office. The door was open and she was later able to recount everything. But it was not this person who set the alarm bells ringing. That happened later, in the canteen, when the desk sergeant had been waxing eloquent about how he had "seen off two nutters" who had been wasting his time. As those listening had obviously never met you, they had no way of knowing how justified his comments were.

'However, by an absolute coincidence, an officer who had been visiting the station from down south and had only dropped in for a cup of tea before setting off home heard the words "Estonia" and "Lexus" and pricked up his ears. He quickly left the restaurant area and asked for access to a computer terminal. He then made a call to the police HQ in Fettes Avenue in Edinburgh. In turn, they contacted the most senior police officer at our station. They were clearly very concerned and indicated that they would now be taking over control of the operation, but they still needed to get hold of the person you had spoken to, with absolute urgency. The problem was that the desk sergeant had ended his shift and gone home.

'When we eventually reached him, we discovered that he had not asked for the address of where you were staying and only had the record of your mother's address. By this time it was late into the evening. We secured the telephone number of the house here and became increasingly concerned on discovering a dead line. The reason all this had taken so long was that there were other strands of the investigation that we had to pull together within a very tight time constraint.'

'Hang on a minute,' interrupted Jack. 'This doesn't make any sense. Why would the words "Estonia" and "Lexus" alert you to anything? I don't follow.'

It was then that the second detective joined the conversation.

'I trust you are aware, sir, that this was not the first attempt that this man had made on your life?'

'Of course it was. I have never met this man before today.'

'You may never have met him, but you had certainly seen him.'

Jack thought for a moment and then said, 'Well, I knew him as the driver of the BMW that passed me after I left the airport and had gone down as far as Killington Lake, but how would you make any link?'

'Because,' the detective continued, 'he had made an attempt on your life a couple of hours previously.'

'I'm sorry, I still don't see where you are going with this.'

'The explosion at the airport,' the woman officer interjected.

'Yes,' said Jack trying to work the logic through. 'There was a terrorist attack on the airport earlier that day. Damian phoned and told me about it, but that didn't have any connection to me.'

'That didn't, but the other one did,' added the senior officer.

'What other one?' asked Jack, confused.

'The one that exploded in the bay where your Lexus had been. It had been armed so that it would detonate as you entered your car. It inexplicably failed, but it did detonate a few minutes later. The person who handled, or mishandled, that operation is the person you refer to as "the driver" and the man who presented himself at this house as Gabriel Porteus. His real identity has yet to be established. However, we expect that information very shortly. The public were never made aware of the second explosion. People in London, probably politicians with a security clearance far higher than mine, made that decision and of course the police had to go along with it. When anyone pre-books at a multi-storey, the time of their entry and exit is logged but, as you know, no bay number is allocated. Those using the facility park wherever they can find a space and usually have to negotiate a couple of levels before they do so. The BMW driver had not parked on your level. Why would he, when he knew that there was going to be an explosion? But he had clearly parked at a place where he had opportunity to follow you in the event of anything going wrong – which was, of course, exactly what had happened.'

'But how did you make a connection with Estonia?' enquired Damian.

'Because when the forensic people sifted through the wreckage, they were able to identify the device as one that was identical to others they had come across that had been used by criminal gangs, and which they identified with that part of the world. It's not my department, and certainly not my speciality, but these things apparently have "signatures" that can identify them. This is also true in other areas of ballistic analysis, as you may be aware.'

'I understand that, but what I can't work out is why, if you had my registration number and the make of my car, you didn't contact me as part of your investigations?'

'There were many contributing factors,' answered the officer. 'The priority of the security forces was one, as you might imagine, with the internationally visible terrorist attack that had taken place. We were working with a finite level of resources – even taking into consideration the police presence and the operations of the Special Branch. Another issue was the fact that there were several cars that had entered and exited the multi-storey within the time frame we needed to be looking at. When you factor in things like human error – the list becomes endless.'

'So how was the link made in the end?'

'An officer had reported a silver BMW acting suspiciously earlier in the day. Not long after, as the driver had raced to catch up with you, he had committed a traffic violation in the process.'

'You mean a speed camera had flashed?'

'Precisely,' continued the officer. 'And when CCTV footage was examined, it also revealed that his plates were false. Also I'm given to understand, though I can't be entirely sure about it, one of the shots revealed your car, which had a number plate we were already processing, in the frame.

'Anyway, the long and short of it was that when we put together Estonia, Lexus and BMW – not to say a life-threatening situation – and when the line was dead at this location we had no option but to send a team here as a matter of urgency.'

'But what about the BMW? How did you find his location?' enquired Damian.

'It wasn't easy, I assure you,' said the senior officer. 'It was only when we found your mother and she was subsequently in a position to be able to talk.'

The officer who had been speaking glanced over at Sarah with affirmation and appreciation in his eyes.

'Mrs Troughton was able to give us a description of the man and, of course, we already had the details of the stolen plates that he was still using. Our cameras only caught up with him part way through his cat-and-mouse strategy with you. We already had an armed officer on standby and were fortunate to get to the final location as soon as we did.'

'Seems to me like there was a whole lot of luck and fortunate coincidence in the past twenty-four hours,' interjected Beth who, until this point, had not said a word.

'Or divine intervention and God's protection,' offered Jack.

'All I can say about this,' said the senior officer, 'is that in all my many years of experience I have never known an operation that commenced with so much chaos and mismanagement to end with such clarity and precision. It certainly is a miracle, however you want to define that – at least, from where I'm sitting.'

'I noticed you used the word "end",' commented Sarah. 'How can we be sure that this will ever end and we can rest safely in our beds?'

'I think you can be very sure, Mrs Troughton,' the officer continued reassuringly. 'We have already received intelligence from abroad about the operation that Jack knows about only too well. What happened in the courts effectively shut down the operation, and we believe that the attempt on Jack's life was a last-ditch attempt to retain a semblance of presence by these people in the criminal underworld out there. We would all be naïve in the extreme were we to imagine that this is the end of people trafficking or sex trafficking. I can assure you that it is not. What I can tell you, however, is that our friend in custody is singing like a canary, as the cliché goes. He's terrified of the retribution that he'll receive from his compatriots, given he has given further loss of face to them. He will be going away for a very long time but, in my experience, the security of a prison regime too often proves insufficient to guarantee his ongoing safety, if people really have a mind to get to him. He is clever enough to realise that it's in his very best interests to finger everyone he can think of and point us in their direction. It won't alter his sentence – he has gone too far for that – but it may mean that he will at least see his term out in one piece.

'Ironically, Mr Troughton, everyone he takes out of the system to protect himself will increase the measure of security that you will enjoy. In my view, you have not the least thing to worry about.'

October 2007
Cotswolds

'To be honest with you, ladies, I have no idea what started it off. She just began to weep hysterically. There was just no consoling her.'

Maureen Stibbes was holding one of what she liked to refer to as her weekly 'case conferences'. It was an opportunity to bring members of the core staff of Cotswold Mews together to review the past seven days, to discuss any present difficulties and to share any upcoming changes that she felt her team needed to be aware of.

Maureen was seated at a circular table in the staffroom with three of her assistants. To her left was Mawusi Addo, who had been with her on staff the longest. On her right was Gemma Belham, who had been employed for a year, and opposite her was Sasha, who still thought of herself as Elena, and who had only been working there for three months – but who in that time had earned Maureen's trust and the respect of the other two. At first Elena had been worried that the other women might have resented her being in the group. Not only had she been there for by far the shortest time, but she was also the youngest. But she worked as a team player rather than just as an individual, and she knew Maureen liked that.

'The thing that surprises me most of all,' added Gemma, 'is that up to this point I would have described Maudie Roberts as one of the most even-tempered of all the guests we have here.'

'Well, she certainly won't talk to anybody about it, that's for sure,' said Mawusi. 'I've tried, and I know we all have. How long has she been with us, Maureen? It's got to be a few years now, I would imagine?'

'That would be about right,' agreed Maureen. 'I know that she had turned eighty-eight when she was admitted and, as you know, we've just had a special celebration for her ninety-fifth birthday.'

'What was her background?' enquired Gemma.

'Well, she is Welsh and proud of it,' answered Maureen. 'I was looking at her file only recently and it appears she lived most of her life in a town called Tonyrefail. I think it's in South Wales. Yes, it must be, because she once told me that about six years after she was married, her husband was killed in a mining disaster in the Rhondda Valley – and I know that's in South Wales.'

'Did she ever remarry?' asked Gemma.

'No, she remained a widow all her life,' answered Maureen. 'Goodness, when you think of it, she must have been on her own for the best part of seventy years!'

'But what about children?' asked Elena.

'None that I know of,' replied Maureen. 'There are none on her file and no one has ever visited her who claimed to be a relative.'

'So how is her stay here funded?' asked Elena.

'Well, I can answer that,' interjected Gemma. 'As you know, I deal with the financial aspects of admissions, and it appears that when her home was sold she gave power of attorney to a long-time neighbour, who set up a trust fund for the purpose.'

'So we are all she's got as far as family is concerned, then,' said Mawusi, more in a 'statement of fact' voice than a questioning one.

'That's right,' continued Maureen, 'and that makes what's going on now all the more important. Whatever started this up, we don't know – I mean, it's been going on for days now – and we're the only ones who are around and likely to get to the bottom of it. It's distressing to see her like this, it really is. I'm not prepared to sanction any medication at this stage. We don't want to use a chemical cosh.'

Two weeks later, Elena and Mawusi were spending their day off at Cribbs Causeway, a large shopping centre on the outskirts of Bristol. It was less than an hour away by car. They had become firm friends since Elena had been in the area, and their usual first port of call was the top floor of a department store where the restaurant was located. Whenever they could, they chose a seat by the windows that overlooked the Mall.

'You know, Sasha, I hardly know a thing about you,' said Mawusi as she moved her latte from her tray and positioned it in front of her on the table.

Elena had done her best to avoid the conversation that she realised would almost inevitably occur at some point. Mawusi had been kind to her from the moment she had arrived at Cotswold Mews, introducing her not just to the residents, or 'guests', as Maureen liked to call them, but also to the procedures and routines of the place. She had managed to sidestep the issue, but she knew that she could not do it indefinitely. There was no way that she would disclose her real identity and her past, not even to Mawusi, but she had to say something.

'Oh, there's not much to tell,' she began. 'Not much to tell? What a ridiculous thing to say,' she thought. Not only was it stupid; she knew it was also a lie. 'I was brought up mainly by my mother. My father left us and went off with another woman. I've always blamed the alcohol, and I have no doubt that that was a large part of the problem, but deep down I knew he was a selfish man. I can never remember him showing affection to my mother and he was never a real father, whatever that means, to me and my sisters. Without going into a whole lot of detail, Mawusi, I did my best to escape from it all and, well, here I am. This is about as good as my life has ever been. I'm grateful to be over here, to have a job and to have a friend like you,' she said, smiling at the woman opposite, whose face showed that she had asked out of genuine interest rather than because she was overly intrusive. 'I can't say it's a fairy tale, though,' continued Elena.

'Well, it can't be a fairy tale,' interjected Mawusi, 'because there's no handsome prince in your life, is there? Not that I have seen, anyway.'

'There certainly isn't, and I'm pretty sure that there won't ever be,' said Elena.

'"Ever" is a big word,' said Mawusi. 'You never know what may happen in the future. You are a beautiful young woman.'

'Listen, Mawusi, I know what I am talking about and I'd rather not go there,' said Elena, hoping that she had not betrayed too much defensiveness in her reply. 'Anyway, what about you? I do know something already, don't I? You are forty-two and you were born in Accra. You married Kwame while you lived in Ghana and after a while you moved over here. How much of that did I get right?'

'Wow,' exclaimed Mawusi. 'That's spot on. What a memory you have!'

'Not really,' replied Elena. 'There isn't a whole lot of data in there, is there? But the big question is this – are you happy?'

'Well, I've certainly got my handsome prince, but finding a man is far from the antidote to every woman's ills – I think from what you have said that your mother would agree with that.'

'She most certainly would.'

'Yes, I would have to say that I am happy – at least I am now,' continued Mawusi, 'but no one is happy all the time.'

'We can't expect to be,' said Elena.

'I didn't quite mean it like that,' responded her friend. 'There was a whole period of my life when I was desperately unhappy – but that's all changed.'

Elena wondered whether to proceed with this, or to change the subject. There was a strong argument for changing the subject because, if she enquired further, Mawusi may encourage her to be more open and that was the last thing she wanted to do. On the other hand, she was intrigued. One of the things that had attracted her to Mawusi in the first place was not just her kindness but what she could only describe as her sense of 'joy' – there was no other term for it. She had assumed that Mawusi must have always been like that. Perhaps that was how she was wired. Some people were pessimists by nature and other people were optimists. Some folk were introverted and others, extroverted. But now she was hearing that Mawusi had not always been like this. She didn't want to pry into the sadness, but she did want to know what had happened to cause what appeared to be a seismic change. Should she ask, or should she let the matter drop? She made her decision.

'Do you want to tell me what you mean?' asked Elena, apprehensively.

'I can if you want me to,' said Mawusi. 'Although it's not something I often talk about – at least not about the tough years.'

'Did you say "years"?' asked Elena.

'Yes, I most certainly did. My upbringing was a happy one,' began Mawusi. 'My parents weren't rich by any means, but we managed. There was a lot of love in the family. I knew Kwame from our days in school. He was in the class above me and we had the same group of friends. Our parents knew one another too. I suppose it was when we were in our late teens that we knew that we were in love. Both families were in favour of us being married and there was a great celebration when it happened. We do things like that well in Ghana. African culture is different in many ways to the culture of the West. Over here, people choose not to have children and no one questions it. If they want to have children but can't, that attracts nothing but sympathy from most people. It's not the same where I come from. If a couple doesn't produce children after a period of time there can be a question about a man's masculinity or a woman's femininity. Having a family, especially a large family that includes sons, is seen by everyone as something to be very proud of. Both Kwame and I wanted a family, but not just so we could comply with society's expectations; we just wanted kids so much. Kwame would have made an incredible father and I hope I would have been a good mother.'

'I'm sure you would,' said Elena. 'So neither of you were able to have children?'

'Well, yes and no,' responded Mawusi. 'I conceived four times and four times we lost the baby.'

'Oh, Mawusi, I am so sorry,' said Elena. She wanted to hug her but couldn't, being conscious of everyone around.

'Oh, it's OK now. Well, I should say it's as alright as it's ever going to be. I spent years asking myself if I would ever be able to forget. The sense of loss will never be absent, I know, but I've got to the place where I'm at peace about it.'

Elena's stomach tightened. A big part of her, especially the part that had not even begun to deal with her own sense of loss, gnawed away at her. She glanced across the restaurant to where a young woman was rising to leave the table and her little girl, probably about two, she thought, was looking up at her mother expectantly with arms stretched wide, waiting to be picked up. How many times had she witnessed moments like that in the space of a week? It was not as if each one was a huge trauma. It was the sense of incremental attrition – lots of small hurts that, like water wearing away rock, ground her down, lowered her sense of worth and increased the awareness of her perpetual pain. She had lost one child and Mawusi, four – so how was it that her friend had reached a place of peace when, for her at least, peace seemed a distant dream: a million miles away?

'Would you say that your husband is in the same place as you?' asked Elena.

'He is now, but it's been a huge journey for him as well. There were times,' Mawusi went on, 'when I even wondered if our marriage would survive. There were so many tensions around our lives. We were both dealing with disappointment, but I was also struggling with a huge sense of failure. Though everyone – doctors, midwives, family and my husband – tried to assure me it was not my fault, I couldn't bring myself to believe any of them. The bottom line, as far as I was concerned, was, having been pregnant, I had failed to bring a child into the world and present him or her to my husband. I know you will say that so much around those sentiments is cultural baggage, but that's not the point. It's how I felt.'

Elena thought back to the times she had watched news reports over the years of couples who had lost a child through cot death or even abduction and had wondered why, when the story was revisited years later, so many of the parents were no longer together. It seemed to happen so often. She always thought that shared pain would bring families closer, not drive them apart. She needed to understand.

'Well, from where I am sitting, I think you are a hero, Mawusi,' said Elena. 'I know I'm only adding my voice to the multitudes you must have already heard, but of course it wasn't your fault. How could it be? But I'm not sure I understand what you mean about it affecting your relationship with Kwame.'

'I know,' continued Mawusi. 'People often struggle with that. They think that our dealing with the pain would be the common denominator that we would cling to for shared support. Unfortunately, it rarely works like that. There are so many factors involved. I don't want to be too dramatic, but it's like different fast-flowing tributaries joining a river at different places and creating a vortex that, if you are in the middle of it, can very quickly drag you under if you're not careful.

'One problem was that while Kwame was doing all in his power to comfort me, he was not dealing with his own sense of loss. Another was the man–woman thing, in that we heal and grieve in different ways and at different rates.

'It gets very complicated. It only takes one of the many tensions that can enter any marriage, not directly related to loss, to become the catalyst that tips the balance. Add to that the problems of just "doing life" and you have a potentially toxic cocktail.

'They say that when some animals become critically wounded they go and look for solace within a group. Others just slink away to a solitary place to either heal or die. The latter was where we both were. Neither of us knew how it was going to work out. We couldn't see the endgame, if you like. We didn't even know if there *was* an endgame. And then there was the biggest problem of all … There was just no support out there. It wasn't just that no one understood. No one understood that there was anything *to* understand – if you see what I mean.

'If someone breaks a bone, there's a finite time before that bone heals. The problem is that the authorities so often tend to treat child loss during pregnancy, birth or infancy like a physical fracture. No one seems to take on board the potential issues of emotional or relational fracture.'

'Oh,' responded Elena. 'I just had no idea, no idea at all, but what you are saying makes so much sense. It seems a miracle to me that you survived one miscarriage, but *four*, Mawusi! How on earth did you cope?'

'"Miracle" is about the right word, it really is. People always assume that miracles are instant things. I'm sure that they can be, but often miracles are the end results of a process.'

'So what kick-started your process, then?' asked Elena.

As Mawusi did not reply immediately, Elena assumed that she was intruding into a place that her friend was reluctant to go.

'Listen, if it's very personal …' Elena said, hesitantly.

'No, it's not that,' responded her friend, with a shy smile. 'It's just that if I told you, I think you would laugh.'

'Laugh? Hardly, Mawusi. How could you think I would even think of laughing at a story like yours? Come on, I thought we were friends.'

'We are friends, Sasha, but I just think you will find it very odd.'

'Well, in that case, try me,' challenged Elena.

'You've been to our apartment, haven't you?'

'Yes, several times. You know that, so why do you ask?'

'Did you notice anything unusual?'

'No, not that I can think of,' responded Elena, gazing up and to the right, trying to conjure up the scene. 'You have a sofa, two armchairs, a sideboard, a television – things like that.'

'Anything else?' asked Mawusi.

Elena thought again, but couldn't really think of anything that stood out as particularly unusual. Certainly, there were ornaments on the sideboard that were clearly African in origin, and there was that beautifully woven colourful blanket that she always noticed because of its bright Ghanaian colours of gold, red and green.

'The coffee table?' added Mawusi, helpfully.

'Oh, did I forget the coffee table?' asked Elena. 'Yes, of course the coffee table but, forgive me for saying it Mawusi, it is just a coffee table ...' and then she remembered. 'You mean the old book ... the old leather-bound book ... Is that what you meant?'

'You never asked me what I did before I came to work at the care home, did you?' said Mawusi.

'No, I suppose I didn't,' replied Elena, wondering if her friend was using this moment to change the subject, and allowing her to do so if that was what she wanted.

'I worked in a place like this,' said Mawusi, as her eyes left Elena's and swept the room from left to right. 'I worked in a restaurant, a café, in Cheltenham.'

'OK,' said Elena, hesitantly, and totally convinced now that Mawusi had steered her to an entirely different tack. She resolved that she was prepared to go with the flow.

'Anyway,' went on Mawusi. 'It must have been at least ten years ago when I think of it ... I was clearing away the dishes and came across something I assumed was lost property. It was an old book.'

'You mean the one on the coffee table?' asked Elena, with interest.

'The very one,' continued Mawusi. 'Someone had left it behind in the café. We had a clear procedure for lost property, as you might imagine. The most common thing to be left ...'

'I'm guessing umbrellas,' interrupted Elena.

'Exactly,' went on Mawusi. 'Umbrellas, but occasionally it's other things like mobile phones, keys, wallets – you name it. But not often books. Very occasionally if people have brought a paperback, and finished it while they're having their coffee, they might leave it behind on purpose. It's amazing what some customers will do. I think they must see it as an opportunity to empty their pockets of receipts, rail tickets – all manner of things. Men always seemed to be the worst. Anyway, back to the story.

'As I said, I came across this old book. I took it back to the supervisor and asked what I should do. When they saw the state it was in, they came to the same conclusion, that someone had left it behind to be thrown away. When we opened it up and saw it was an old Bible, one of my colleagues suggested we just put it to one side for a day or so just in case someone came for it, and only then would it be put in the bin.

'To be honest, we all forgot about it and so when after a few days no one had claimed it, it was decided to consign it to the rubbish. For some reason, I found myself asking the supervisor if I could take it home. She thought for a moment or two, and then told me she saw no reason why not, as it was only going to be thrown out anyway.

'I showed it to Kwame but he didn't take a great deal of interest and, frankly, neither did I. In fact, it ended up discarded again.'

'Well, you obviously didn't throw it out, because I've seen it,' said Elena.

'No, we didn't throw it out, but we may as well have done. It found its way to the back of a cupboard under the stairs. If you remember, our apartment is on two levels. It remained there forgotten for years.'

'For years?' exclaimed Elena, incredulously.

'Absolutely. It was there but hidden from sight throughout the whole time we were going through the loss of our babies. We never gave it a thought. Why would we? Both sets of our parents back in Ghana belonged to the Church of Pentecost. It's absolutely huge.

They were very committed to it and went twice on a Sunday as well as midweek. Both Kwame's story and mine paralleled in that as soon as we could make our own choices, we announced to our respective parents that such things were not for us. This really upset them, but what could they do? They often tried to get us to attend for special events, but mostly without success.

'Don't get me wrong, Sasha, we both grew up in very loving homes and they were, and are still, wonderful parents. But we had made our choices. The last thing they said to us as we left to come to the UK was that they would pray for us every day. Well, to cut a long story short – I'm not boring you with this, am I, Sasha?'

'No, not at all, please go on. I am intrigued.'

'OK, then,' said Mawusi, reassured. 'When we had lost the fourth child I was beside myself with grief. Kwame was out at work and I was on my own. I couldn't sit, because when I sat I would think, and when I started to think, I would begin to cry. I decided to clean the apartment from top to bottom – not that that was going to take very long – and when I took everything out from under the stairs I came across the old book – or the old Bible, I should say. I had been on my knees rooting through everything that was there. I can remember the moment as if it was yesterday. I had a black plastic bin bag on the floor to my left. I would look at every object. If it was something I could use or wanted to keep, I placed it on my right. If it was a tin of out-of-date paint or an old magazine, I would put it in the bag on my left. I lifted the old book. I wondered for a moment what it was – and then I remembered. I paused for a moment or two as if I was weighing it up. I suppose I was, really. I was weighing up in my mind if it should go to the right or to the left. You know, Sasha, history moves on small hinges. Small decisions can open big doors, or close big doors. I'm ever so glad I made the decision that day that I did. I could never have known how that book would change my life.'

'So you became religious and that solved all your problems, I suppose!' Elena was amazed at the sound of her own, suddenly angry, voice. Why had she responded, not only so emotionally, but so fiercely?

Mawusi looked totally taken aback. Elena knew that she had never seen her react like this before. Perhaps Mawusi was wondering which part of what she had said had detonated the explosion.

'I am sorry, Mawusi, I need to leave now,' said Elena, as she rose from her seat, her breathing heavy. 'Could we please go, if you don't mind?'

'Of course, Sasha,' said Mawusi, embarrassed. 'I'm sorry if ...'

'Please don't say any more. It's OK ... I just want to leave.'

There was no conversation on the drive home. Sometimes Mawusi would glance left, as if questioning if she was free to turn, but Elena knew that what she was really trying to do was to see how her friend was. Elena sat motionless, her head erect and facing towards the front. But her eyes were moist with tears.

Both women were apprehensive when they signed in for work the next day. Elena was the last to arrive. She was not late, but knew she was last because she saw that the cars belonging to the other members of staff were already parked. As she made her way through the front entrance, she was met by a subdued Gemma Belham.

'Is everything alright, Gemma?' asked Elena. 'You look dreadful.'

'Not really, Sasha, but Maureen will explain. She's asked us all to meet in the staffroom as soon as we arrive. The others are already in there, and she asked me to keep an eye out for you. She will explain everything.'

When everyone was seated, Maureen Stibbes began.

'Ladies, the passing of any one of our guests here at Cotswold Mews is always an unhappy occasion, but given that people come to us in their declining years, it is never entirely a surprise. You must all be wondering, therefore, why I have called this meeting. At 4am this morning Maudie Roberts passed away.'

Each of those gathered looked across at one another with glances that expressed a mixture of regret and surprise. The regret was present because they all liked Maudie. The surprise was evinced for two reasons. The first was that, though elderly, Maudie had given no indication of being particularly unwell. The second had to do with why this meeting needed to be called.

'You will all be aware,' Maureen continued, 'that recently Maudie had been unaccountably distressed.'

Everyone nodded.

'Well, it now appears that we know why,' Maureen added, softly. 'After Maudie had died, I asked one of the auxiliaries who was working a late shift to empty the wardrobe and small chest of drawers in her room to pack away her bits and pieces. Now, I know what you will be thinking: wasn't this an example of indecent haste? And if that's the case, I would have to say that normally I would agree with you. But the night shift was very quiet and I just thought it would give the member of staff something to do.

'Anyway, tucked into a corner she found a crumpled white envelope which, on opening, she discovered contained a letter and a small black and white photograph of a child – a little girl. The letter …' Maureen paused and bit her lip. 'The correspondence was a letter of condolence. It appears that several years after her husband was killed, her daughter, the only person she had in the world, also died after a brief illness. When the letter was handed to me, I looked at the date. This week was the sixtieth anniversary of her daughter's death. She had lived more than half a century with all that grief and with no one to share it with, or to console her.'

The room fell silent. Elena glanced briefly across the room towards Mawusi before slowly rising from her chair and leaving the room.

Mawusi had been hurt by the events of the previous day but was more concerned about what had precipitated Sasha's reaction. However, after this morning's event, she had reached the inevitable conclusion that Sasha had her own pain and that it was likely to be connected to both her story and that of Maudie.

She had told Kwame about the incident in the restaurant when they were in bed the previous night. She wanted to know his thoughts about it – particularly about the timing and as to whether she should contact Sasha or not. Her heart wanted to, as she did not like the idea of there being an issue between them. He had said that, whatever had triggered the problem, it might be that Sasha needed to find some space and that she should be the one to bring the matter up, if she wanted to, in the future.

'Perhaps she has suffered loss herself,' Mawusi had suggested to him. 'I can't see why, but judging by her reactions, there must be something connected with the Bible. But I can't understand what.'

Having watched Sasha's reaction to Maureen's account this morning of Maudie's death, Mawusi was rethinking her previous conclusion and returning to the proposition that Sasha had deeply buried emotional wounds of her own. There was nothing for it but to talk to her. But when, where and how?

As it transpired, the matter was taken out of Mawusi's hands. It was at the end of their shift, as she was entering the staff car park and in the process of opening her car door when, from behind, a hand rested lightly on her arm.

'Mawusi, I am ever so sorry,' said Elena. 'I don't know what came over me yesterday. Well, perhaps I do, if I'm honest, but there is no way I should have reacted to you as I did …'

Mawusi turned to her friend, drew her close and hugged her tight.

'Listen, love,' she said. 'There is nothing to worry about. I'm good if you're good. You don't have to apologise.'

'But I do,' insisted Elena. 'I really do.'

'Is there anything *you* need to talk about?'

'Well, perhaps … but I'm not sure …'

'Look Sasha,' continued Mawusi. 'Kwame is on late shift tonight. You can come round now if you want to and we can have dinner together. It won't be anything special, though. I was just going to make something for myself out of the freezer, but it would be easy to make something for two.'

'It's not fufu, is it?' asked Elena, her eyes twinkling and reminding her friend of the night that Kwame and Mawusi had asked her round for a traditional Ghanaian meal. Though she had tried the dish out of politeness, both of them had laughed as she struggled with it.

'No, it won't be fufu, I promise you. It'll be more like cottage pie. You're not going to turn your nose up at that as well, are you?' asked Mawusi, teasingly.

It was not until later that evening, when the plates were being stacked in the dishwasher, that Mawusi brought the issue up.

'Come on, then, Sasha, out with it. Tell me what's going on.'

Mawusi did not know that her friend was trying to negotiate in her mind how much she should reveal.

When Mawusi had invited her to sit, the book, which Elena now knew to be a Bible, seemed to loom out larger before her. On previous occasions she was aware of something lying there on the coffee table. Now it seemed to take on a new identity. It appeared to represent so much that had apparently changed the life of her friend but, on the other hand, it also symbolised things that had been proved to accentuate her own pain. How could one inanimate object mean something so different to two different people?

'As you've probably guessed, I have also suffered the loss of a child, though in very different circumstances to either you or Maudie Roberts. In your case, you and Kwame longed for children and watched as your dream evaporated before your eyes – four times! How anyone deals with the death of hope on four occasions, I do not know. As for Maudie, well, her child was born but cruelly snatched from her. I don't know what is worse, not having a child or having a child that you later lose. It's hard to say. I suppose they are both as bad in their different ways.'

'So, in what way does your story differ?'

'I was raped, Mawusi! I was raped! I was raped by more than one man and the result of that was my pregnancy.'

Mawusi's hands came up to her mouth in horror.

'Oh, my poor, poor dear, no!' she said, in muted exclamation.

'Yes, that is my story, and I was being driven to hospital – just minutes away from giving birth – when I was involved in a car accident. The driver of the other car, a woman, was killed and, as a result of my injuries, the baby inside me died too.'

'And what of the driver of the car you were in? Were they injured as well?'

'No,' responded Elena, shortly. 'The man who was driving survived. I know what you are going to say,' she went on. 'Why would I grieve so much, and why had I not wanted the child inside me to be aborted anyway, given the way it had been conceived? Well, I will tell you. You see, I understand the pro-abortionist argument that a woman has rights over her body. However, I knew that there was a baby inside me, not a foetus, you understand – a baby. Of course a woman has choices, but I happen to believe that both lives matter. There is a universal lobby that speaks up for the woman. But who speaks for the baby? How can it be, in a so-called caring and tolerant society, that today the most dangerous place in the world to be is in a mother's womb? I had experienced probably the worst thing that can ever happen to a woman, but I would never add crime upon crime by willingly putting my baby to death.'

'Does this point of view come from your upbringing, your culture or your church?' asked Mawusi.

'No, not at all,' answered Elena. 'We never discussed that kind of thing.'

'So my speaking about my miscarriages touched a raw nerve. I understand that now, and I'm sorry.'

'No, actually that wasn't really the trigger. There was something else.'

'As you can imagine, I thought constantly about the conversation we had yesterday. I have thought about it over and over. I was so concerned, Sasha, that I may have said something that had offended you.'

'No, please don't think that.'

'Sasha, please let me finish what I was saying. What I did remember was that things went wrong at the point I mentioned the difference this Bible,' Mawusi pointed in its direction as she spoke, 'had made to me. It seemed it was at that point that you reacted. It was something about the Bible. Am I right?'

'Yes,' admitted Elena. 'That was it. I don't know what life was like for you in Accra as you grew up, but for me in my village, it was one crisis after another and, in the gaps between them, there was perpetual tension. My sisters and I watched my mother trying to put food on the table, just to keep body and soul together. I looked on helplessly as my father hovered between fecklessness and violence – mostly directed at my mother. I'm not saying that we were the only people to live like this, as I knew that several of my friends could relate similar stories.'

'I don't want to interrupt you,' said Mawusi, cautiously, 'but what has that got to do with the Bible? Why did the Bible set you off as it did?'

'It wasn't so much the Bible itself,' replied Elena, and this time is was she who pointed towards the book that lay between them. She could see by her friend's expression that Mawusi was at first at a loss to understand what she meant.

'Do you see that cross on the spine of your Bible?' asked Elena. 'There was a gold cross like that on the church in the centre of our village. As a small child I asked my mother what it signified. She told me that Jesus died on the cross because He loved us – though I don't think that she had any idea what that meant then any more than I do now. What I *did* know was that the priest from that church would call at our home from time to time, asking for donations for the repair of one thing or another. Sometimes it was for the restoration of a shrine, or perhaps the restoration of the roof. There was always something, and that something was always about money. It was money that we sorely needed. If I answered the door as a child, he only needed to look past me, down our shabby entrance hall and into the downstairs room to see how little money we had.'

'I'm sorry about that Sasha, I really am,' said Mawusi. 'There is nothing I can really say. People can be insensitive, whoever they are and whatever role they play.'

'Yes, but we're not talking about plumbers and bakers here, we're talking about priests. We are talking about "Jesus loves you". I mean, for heaven's sake! When I heard you tell your story, I was heartbroken,' Elena continued, 'and then when you said you had come to a place of peace, I could not have been more thrilled for you. But when you resurrected those memories in me – well, it was more than I could stand, to be honest.'

'It may not help,' said Mawusi, 'but I have to say, you cannot judge everyone who calls themselves a Christian on the basis of your experience with just one man. There are also ministers, pastors and priests who give their lives to serve the poor. In my country whole congregations, not just clergy, see it as their Christian responsibility to "love their neighbour as themselves". And think of this country, the one we both live in. Where did schools and hospitals originate from? It was not initially government. It wasn't politicians. It was the Church, Sasha.'

'I suppose I'll have to take your word for it,' said Elena. 'I can only speak from my experience and out of the world that I know. It's just that you touched a nerve the other day and, when you did, I flinched. Anyway, Mawusi, let me hear your story. That's only fair. You've listened to mine.'

'There's not really a whole lot to tell, I suppose, other than that I found within that old book a level of comfort that I couldn't have imagined. I don't mean comfort in the sense that we get comfort from music or poetry, or things like that. It was learning about how God sees us.

'I was brought up in church, as I told you, and so was Kwame, but somehow nothing ever seemed to sink in. In some ways my experience paralleled with yours, when I think about it. For you, God was taking your resources, your money. For me, I saw it as God taking my freedom and my independence. However, when Kwame and I later began to read the Bible for ourselves, we came to realise that the cross, rather than being a minus sign, was actually a plus sign. If you think about it, it actually looks like that, doesn't it? The cross, I mean? When you've gone through the kind of loss that you and I have experienced, Sasha, you need a lot of plusses to balance the books. I don't know if that makes sense.'

'But four miscarriages, Mawusi,' said Elena. 'I just can't imagine how you coped.'

'I know,' replied Mawusi. 'It wasn't easy. And even with my new-found faith I found myself stumbling sometimes and questioning God. Kwame was a huge help to me, but I know that he had his dark times too. One of the worst moments was after we had been reading the Bible together.'

'You mean reading the Bible upset you rather than helped you? Is that what you're saying?' asked Elena.

Mawusi's comment had taken her by surprise. She was expecting a fairy-tale account that expressed something like, 'Now I've seen the light, everything in the garden is rosy.' Instead she was hearing about struggles – but she found it was making her friend's story more credible rather than less.

'So why did the Bible affect you in such a negative way?'

'Well, as I said, Kwame and I were reading the Bible together and we came to a part where Jesus talks about faith – which really means "trust in God". We were reading where He said that if we had faith, we could call upon a mountain to remove itself and it would.'

'You are joking, aren't you, Mawusi?' said Elena, incredulously.

'No,' said Mawusi. 'Jesus really did say that. I think He was talking about huge problems – things that could disappear in an instant if we had faith.'

'OK, so why did that distress you, then?' asked Elena.

'It confused us, really, because we certainly didn't see our problems disappear every time we prayed.'

'So how could you reconcile that in your mind?'

'We were going to church by then, and we went to our pastor and told him about our problem. Talking to him seemed a safe place for us. We could share doubts and fears without feeling we had failed or were less than good enough.'

'So, go on. What did he say?'

'He told us that when we pray, God is able to transform things instantly according to our faith – a miracle, if you like. But then he really blew us away by his next statement. It was a question, really. He asked us what we thought took greater faith – having a mountain removed instantly, or being given the strength to climb one. We thought for a while and both came instantly to the same conclusion. It was the second option. He then went on to talk about a man called Daniel, who was thrown in the lions' den. He said God delivered Daniel not by killing the lions, but by protecting him while they continued to growl. Then he talked about friends of Daniel who were thrown into a fiery furnace. He said God did not put the fire out, but ensured that the fire did not harm them.

'We saw what he was saying immediately. The issue was not whether we felt loss, disappointment or pain, but that even in those circumstances, God could ensure that these things didn't consume us, and I have to tell you, Sasha, God has been continually faithful and brought us through every trial that we have ever faced. The losses of our babies were the worst, but there have been other things too.

'You wouldn't know this, of course, but all Ghanaian names have meanings. Mine, "Mawusi", means "In God's hands" – and Sasha, that's how I feel right now.'

October 2007
Murieston, Scotland

'All I am saying is that I'm worried about Jack,' said Beth, as she turned off the radio. Kanye West had been performing 'Stronger', the best-selling track that month, but it was music that was neither to her nor to her sister's taste.

'We've been assured time and time again by the police that that business last summer is over and done with,' responded Sarah, 'and there's not been the slightest hint ...'

'No, I'm not talking about that – well, not that exactly,' continued Beth.

'Well what *do* you mean? Are you concerned about his safety or not?'

'Like you, I agree that no one is coming after him, but it's all this business he's got himself involved with – assisting victims of sex trafficking. Of course, it's not wrong in itself, and it's very laudable and all that, but ...'

'I know what's going through your mind,' interrupted Sarah. 'You're worried that while he's helping people from that background, he is in danger of stirring things up again with the people who were after him.'

'Yes, that's it exactly,' admitted Beth. 'Why can't he just ...'

'... Let sleeping dogs lie?' offered Sarah.

'Precisely. I'm not saying that these people don't need help, but Jack gets himself so emotionally involved.'

'Well, you can understand that,' responded Sarah. 'It was those people who were responsible for Celia's death, and now the business is sold and he doesn't have to do consultancy work in order to provide an income, he's doing what Jack always does –

focusing on something and then throwing all his time and energy into seeing it through.'

'I hope you don't misunderstand me when I say this, but it's more than eighteen months now since Celia died, and as far as I know, Jack hasn't even contemplated the possibility of taking someone out for a date. He's got the charity and he's very involved in the church, of course, but I just want to see him settle down, that's all – find someone, have kids, that kind of thing.'

'Well, he's not going to listen to us, particularly on matters like that,' said Sarah.

'I hope you don't mind me saying things like that, do you?'

'No, of course not. He's my son, but he's your nephew, and we both love him and want the best for him.'

When the phone rang, it was Beth that answered.

'Jack, I can't believe it! We were just talking about you. Where are you?'

'Talking behind my back, were you, Aunt Elizabeth? Shame on you!' said Jack, teasingly. 'I'm about thirty minutes away and was going to drop round, if that's OK. I've got some news to share with you. I thought I'd give you a ring, though, and make sure you were in.'

'Of course it's alright. We'll look forward to seeing you.'

It was almost thirty minutes later, on the dot, that Jack's car drew up. After the initial greetings, and when they were comfortably seated with a cup of tea, Jack updated them with his latest news.

'You both know that I've been involved with a group that helps those who have become victims of people trafficking – especially as it relates to the sex industry?'

Beth risked a quick glance across the room to her sister before replying. 'Yes, Jack, we know about that. In fact, you hardly talk about anything else when we're together.'

'Oh, don't I?' responded Jack. 'I go on a bit much about it, do you think? Sorry if that's the case, it's just that ...'

'It's just that it means a lot to you. We know that,' said his mother. 'It's something that you are spending a lot of time on at the moment, anyway.'

'Well, someone has to, Mum. The people trafficking industry rakes in £120 billion every year – more than £3,000 a second if you look at it like that. The number of people trafficked worldwide is in the region of twenty-four million. Many of these modern-day slaves are in the sex industry and 99 per cent of those are women.'

'That's heartbreaking,' exclaimed Beth. 'It really is. But, I suppose, with numbers like that the authorities are doing their best to put a stop to it. They are, aren't they?'

'The problem is too big. The resources are too small and those who are trying to get a handle on the situation are often fighting with one hand tied behind their back.'

'How do you mean?' asked Sarah.

'Political correctness is one issue, but there are many others,' Jack went on. 'To give you an idea – of all the people who are trafficked, only about 1 per cent ever see their exploiters brought to justice.'

'Anyway, you were going to tell us some news about what you are currently involved in at the moment?' asked Sarah, and this time it was she who glanced across the room to Beth.

'Yes, well, you may remember that we have places across the country where we try to give initial support to the victims of the trade. We are already in London and Birmingham, and this is my bit of news for today – we are going to be opening places in Manchester and Glasgow.'

Had Jack been expecting rapturous applause, or even encouraging affirmation, he would clearly have been disappointed. His 'news' was met with an embarrassed silence.

'Jack,' began his mother. 'You know that Beth said that we were talking about you just before you phoned? Well, we were. And I wonder if you can guess what we were talking about?'

'I haven't a clue, Mum,' said Jack, 'but by the look on both your faces, I guess I'm about to find out.'

'You see, Jack,' Sarah continued, 'we know there is a great need in this area – goodness, the numbers speak for themselves. To get to the point, Beth and I really wonder if this is the best area for you to get involved in – you know, given what has happened … There are so many charitable organisations – worthy causes, if you like –

that you could get involved in. So why does it have to be this? That's all we're saying.'

Jack paused for a few moments before continuing.

'Listen, I know you both have my best interests at heart, but I have to do this, I really do. It's almost as if I don't have an option.'

'We all have options,' interrupted Beth.

'I know we do,' replied Jack, 'but it's as if God has called me to it. Let me tell you a story. After the last war, there was a village in Germany that had not managed to escape bomb damage. The first priority was, of course, homes, schools and hospitals, but in the centre of the village there had been a statue of Christ that was slightly damaged. Although everything else was intact, the two arms were missing. The town council held a meeting about it and it was decided to get a repair estimate from a local stonemason. However, when they realised what it would cost, they agreed it would be far too expensive. Then one member of the group had an idea and when their proposition was voted on, it was unanimously accepted. Instead of spending money on a repair, they would spend a much more modest sum on a plaque.'

'A plaque?' asked Sarah and Beth simultaneously.

'Yes,' replied Jack, 'and it just had seven words on it: "God has no hands but our hands".'

There was silence again in the room and it was eventually broken by Beth.

'OK, Jack, we can see your mind is set on this. We won't try to dissuade you any more, will we, Sarah?'

'No. We'll also do everything in our power to support you.'

'That means a lot to me,' responded Jack. 'By the way, I have some more news for you. I almost forgot.'

The two women held their breath.

'We're bringing on a key member of staff to our Glasgow office. His background is in public relations and he's just the person we need across the charity as a whole. It's Simon Bellenger. Mum, do you remember him?'

Beth looked quizzical, but Sarah lifted her arms in the air and said, 'Really? That's wonderful! I can see how you think he would be ideal. He just the person, but how do you know him, Jack?'

'Well, as you can imagine, the recommendation came from Damian and Sue. So much has been going on recently! I'm not sure if I told you but they are getting involved with the Manchester branch. It's going to be a drop in salary for them, but they are totally committed to the project and feel that it's right.'

'I'm sorry,' said Beth. 'I seem to be the only one out of the loop here. I know of Damian and Sue, of course, but Simon?'

'We met him on the cruise, Beth. He's a brilliant guy and I can see why Jack and Damian would have approached him. It's quite a commitment, him coming to live all the way up here, though, isn't it?'

'Yes, it is,' replied Jack. 'As with Damian, there's going to be quite a shortfall compared with what he's been earning in the past. I've been able to inject capital into the purchase of some of the centres – but salaries roll over year on year and it's less easy to cover those contingencies. Simon has said that house prices are far more reasonable up here than in the south, so that, at least, will be a help.'

'It seems to me,' said Sarah, 'that everyone is getting fully on board.'

'It does, doesn't it?' agreed Jack.

November 2007
Cotswolds

Mawusi had been relieved that the problem that had arisen between her and Sasha had now been resolved. In some ways, the very act of dealing with it had brought them even closer together as friends. She had worried initially that there would be an atmosphere when they were at work and that the times they had spent together when Kwame was on shifts would just taper off until they no longer happened. She so valued Sasha as a friend and was relieved that the matter had been resolved.

She brought to mind some advice her mother had given her back in Accra in her rebellious years: 'Keep short accounts with God and with people.' By which she meant praying for forgiveness from God as soon as possible after any failure, and seeking to repair broken relationships with people as soon as one was able to do so. Since Mawusi and Kwame had become Christians, they had also applied a similar practice in their marriage, taking the advice they found in the fourth chapter of the book of Ephesians – 'do not let the sun go down while you are still angry'. So, on those occasions when they had fallen out during the day, they always made it a goal to put things right with one another before they went to bed.

With this in mind, Mawusi had suggested to Sasha that they do another day at the shops. So, having been to Cribbs Causeway last time, she had suggested that they go north on this occasion, to the Bull Ring centre in Birmingham.

She found parking a nightmare in big cities, so this afternoon they had travelled by train from Cheltenham to New Street station. They meandered around the various sections of the huge complex and were continually amazed at how far it was possible to walk around a place like this.

Both of them had avoided talking about any big issues. No one had decided that that was how it was going to be. It just seemed as though they had come to a mutual conclusion on the matter.

They had not bought much during the day, as that was not really what the trip had been about. Mawusi had bought some special soaps that she liked, and Elena had purchased some cosmetics.

'Fancy a drink before we catch the train back, Sasha?' Mawusi enquired.

'Good idea,' Elena answered. 'There's a Starbucks just a little way along from here – would that be alright?'

When they got to the coffee shop they could see through the window that every seat inside had already been taken. There were also half a dozen tables outside in the Mall area, but it was clear that these were taken too. However, they noticed that there was one table with four seats around it that was occupied by a young woman on her own, who was immersed in her phone.

'Excuse me,' said Mawusi. 'Would it be possible for my friend and I to join you? The place seems pretty full.'

The woman looked up from her phone uninterestedly, as if to indicate that she could not care one way or another, and so the two women decided to take this as a 'yes'.

Mawusi joined the queue of about six people to place their order while Elena occupied a seat at the table.

'Sorry to have intruded into your afternoon,' said Elena, at a loss for something else to say.

Without looking up from her phone, the woman just shrugged her shoulders and in accented English said, 'It's OK, there is room. There is not a problem.'

It was evident that Elena and Mawusi had not been the only people intent on getting a coffee before they caught the train, because a steady stream of people were making their way towards Starbucks. Almost all of them, once they had glanced through the window and seen the place was packed, had veered off in an alternative direction in search of their caffeine hit.

That was all except one large man who, perhaps because he was short-sighted, was pressing his face almost onto the glass window of the shop. Eventually, he too was convinced that there was no point in pursuing his course, and so turned around to leave. However, as he did so, he knocked the chair on which the woman opposite Elena was sitting, causing the phone she was holding to spin out of her hand.

It bounced once on the table and then landed at Elena's feet. Four things took place simultaneously.

The first was that the man apologised profusely. The second was that Elena stretched down to pick up the phone. The third was that the young woman bent down to see where her phone had landed and if it was damaged. The fourth was that the woman let out a cry. When the large man heard that, he concluded the phone had been damaged and, not wanting to get further involved, especially in any suggestion that reparation be made, had hurried off into the swelling crowd.

For one brief moment, the heads of the two women had been beneath the level of the table as they rummaged for the fallen phone. The cry had not been caused by any recognition as their eyes had met. It had occurred because, as Elena had stretched forward to retrieve the phone, she had revealed the arm that bore the crudely formed brand of a serpent inside a pentangle.

In the same second that the young woman's eyes had fixed themselves on the mark, Elena's eyes had done the same. She hurriedly pulled her sleeve down, but it was too late. Elena passed the phone to the woman, who did not even check the screen to see if it was broken. Instead she locked eyes with Elena and, without removing her gaze for an instant, slowly moved up the sleeve of her own jacket to reveal the identical insignia.

It was at that precise moment that Mawusi emerged through the door towards the tables, carrying a tray with two cups of coffee. She was concentrating so hard on not spilling the latte or the cappuccino that she remained totally unaware of the brief exchange that had just occurred between Elena and the other woman. Carefully laying the tray on the table, and acknowledging the young woman with a brief smile, she said to her friend, 'I was going to bring a couple of pastries as well, but you told me yesterday at work that you were cutting down, so I thought I'd better not.'

Both Elena and the woman heard Mawusi's voice in the background, but it was like audible wallpaper to them; they heard the sound and knew it was there, but paid not the slightest attention to it. Their eyes were still locked.

Mawusi emptied the tray of its contents, positioning the coffees in their places. She continued to talk and was still not being heard.

Elena stared at the cappuccino in front of her as if it were an object that had just been teleported from another planet, and then she snapped back into reality. Mawusi was so relieved that she had completed the manoeuvre without calamity that she still remained oblivious to all that had transpired.

'Oh, thank you, Mawusi, that's great,' said Elena, eventually. 'Sorry that you had to queue for so long, though.'

Mawusi considered the other woman at the table to be as disconnected from the two of them as she had been before. She therefore did not notice her reach into her handbag and pull out a pen, though, out of the corner of her eye, she was vaguely aware that the young woman had begun writing something on a scrap of paper. She was very surprised indeed, however, when the woman passed the paper to Sasha, rose from her chair and then left without a word.

'What was all that about?' asked Mawusi, when the woman was out of earshot.

'Oh, nothing,' replied Elena, a shade too quickly. 'She dropped her phone when somebody pushed past her and I managed to save it from breaking, that's all.'

'But what's on the paper that she passed to you?'

'I don't know,' said Elena, as she lifted it closer to examine it. 'It appears to be a mobile number or something.'

'But why would she give you that?' asked Mawusi. 'You saved her phone, not her life. It doesn't make sense.'

'Well, how should I know?' said Elena, with a little more defensiveness than she had meant to express.

Mawusi watched as, instead of screwing the paper up and leaving it on the table, Elena folded it carefully and slipped it into the pocket of her coat.

As soon as Elena arrived home that evening, she threw her coat on the back of her settee, having first retrieved the scrap of paper, and lifted the handset of her landline phone. She had found recently that mobile-to-mobile connections were unpredictable as the signal often showed only one bar at her end when she tried to connect and, occasionally, the signal had been lost altogether. There was no way she needed any technical complications during this next call.

She dialled the number that had been given her and, after about three rings, a hesitant voice in broken English said, 'Hello. Who is speaking, please?'

'It's me,' answered Elena. 'The woman at Starbucks this afternoon.'

'Oh, it's you. I hoped that you would phone, but I did not think that it would be so soon. It's when I saw the … you know, the mark …'

'I know,' said Elena. 'I don't know who was the most surprised, you or me.'

'I was more than surprised. I was alarmed. But why did you phone back so quickly, and what is your name? My name is Aleksandra.'

'My name is Sasha,' said Elena, 'and I phoned back straight away because I was concerned that you might need help.'

'*Me* need help?' said the voice at the other end. 'I gave you my number because I assumed that *you* were the one in need of help.'

There was silence at both ends of the line for a moment or two as both women attempted to reorientate themselves after the mutually wrong assumptions they had made. The hiatus was eventually broken by Elena.

'I honestly don't know whether this is a good idea or not, but would you like to meet somewhere, you know, and talk?'

'I would like that very much,' said Aleksandra. 'Do you live in Birmingham?'

'No, I was just there today, shopping with the friend you saw me with.'

Elena was thinking fast. She didn't know anything about this woman, but obviously she was currently, or had been, in the same predicament as she herself had been. Nevertheless, she didn't want to introduce her into her world. Not at least until she knew a lot more about her and had rallied her own thoughts.

'I live about sixty miles away,' continued Elena. 'Listen, do you have a car?'

As soon as the words had left her lips she realised what a stupid question that was – of course she didn't have a car.

'No,' said Aleksandra. 'That is something I can't afford.'

'OK, I'm sorry,' said Elena. 'I should have guessed that. I guess you do live in the Birmingham area, though. Am I right?'

'Yes, that is right,' responded Aleksandra. 'Not in the city centre, but at a place on the outskirts.'

Elena was surprised, and not a little worried by the term 'at a place', but went on nevertheless. 'I'll tell you what, Aleksandra, why don't we meet at the same time next week at the place we were at today? Would that suit you?'

Aleksandra assured her that it would, and the time was arranged for 2pm.

Elena thought it best not to say anything to Mawusi, even though she considered her to be her best friend. And for her part, Mawusi did not bring up the incident of the note that had been exchanged.

Exactly one week later, Elena arrived at the arranged location in the Bull Ring shopping centre where she had first come across Aleksandra. Even though there was plenty of room inside Starbucks, she decided to occupy the same seat at the table outside. In this way she could look out for the woman as she approached. For the briefest of moments it had crossed her mind that this was all an elaborate trap set by her previous captors. It had just seemed too much of a coincidence. Yet she had dismissed the idea almost as quickly as it had come. Nobody but Mawusi and herself had known the arrangements that day, and they had not been approached by the woman. She had been at the table before they had arrived.

She watched the crowds of shoppers laden with their bags. Some were laughing and joking with friends and others walked alone, sauntering past the stores, window-shopping. Then she saw the woman she had arranged to meet emerging out of the crowd.

When Aleksandra caught Elena's eye, she noticeably quickened her pace as she moved towards her.

Although, looking back, she would not know why she did it, as Aleksandra reached the table, Elena stood up and opened her arms to embrace her. The engagement was cordial and warm but without being effusive.

'I'm glad that we could get to meet,' began Aleksandra, as she took her seat.

'So am I,' said Elena who was still standing, and then added, 'What would you like? I'll get them.'

'Oh, thank you, that's kind of you. Just a black coffee and nothing to eat, if you don't mind,' Aleksandra replied.

There was only one person before Elena in the queue, and within five minutes both women were looking at one another over two cups of black coffee.

'So, which of us is going to go first, then?' asked Elena. She had already settled in her mind a long time before she had got there how much she would divulge, and was very clear about the details she would choose to omit.

'I was just so shocked when I saw your arm,' began Aleksandra, without addressing the question but clearly getting what she wanted to say out of the way. 'I'm sorry that I cried out, but I think that anyone nearby would have thought I was responding to the dropped phone!'

'I'm sure you are right,' replied Elena. 'It seemed that both of us initially assumed that the other needed help. But of course we should have realised that if either of us were still being controlled, the last thing that we would be doing is drinking coffee in such a public place.'

'I know,' said Aleksandra, 'but even up until the time we spoke on the phone, I was concerned you might be in some kind of trouble.'

'Well, I certainly was at one time, as you can imagine, if I'm carrying a mark like this.' Elena touched the sleeve of her coat that covered the place where the branding was. 'I don't know how long you were with them, Aleksandra, but they didn't hold me captive for as long as most. Having said that, the days that I was held were worse than any hell I could have imagined up to that point.'

'So how did you get out? How did you manage to escape?'

Elena was totally convinced that the woman sitting opposite her was genuine. However, there were obligations and promises that she had made. She was not about to break that trust. This was not just because of a desire to comply with the assurances given to others, but because her life could still be in danger if she revealed too much. She was not going to divulge anything about the trial or the fact she was living under an assumed name. The woman across the table believed her to be Sasha, as did Mawusi, for that matter, and that was the way that it was going to stay.

'I didn't escape,' answered Elena. 'Well, not in the conventional way you would use that term. What happened was that I got pregnant.'

'You got pregnant?' said Aleksandra, in surprise. 'I don't want to offend you, Sasha, but that's ridiculous. All of us are put on contraceptives as a matter of course.'

'Yes, I know,' said Elena. 'There are two things about my story that you will find incongruous.'

'Incongruous? What do you mean? I do not know that word.'

'Oh, I'm sorry. It means "hard to understand" ... hard to believe, if you like.'

'Alright, I see. Please go on.'

'It would have happened after the initial gang rape, I suppose.'

Elena looked across the table and, by the way that Aleksandra's eyes didn't even blink, she realised that that part of the story would certainly not need any explanation.

'And now we come to the next part that you will find hard to believe,' Elena continued. 'They let my baby go to full term!'

'You are kidding me!' exclaimed Aleksandra. As she did so, she looked around quickly in case she had spoken too loudly and had drawn the attention of people nearby. However, they were the only ones sitting at the outside tables and none of the shoppers, as they passed, were giving them a second glance.

'That is ridiculous,' said Aleksandra, emphasising every syllable.

'To this day,' said Elena, 'I do not know why. It never happens.'

'Of course it never happens in our business,' began Aleksandra. Elena baulked at the phrase 'our business' but did not interrupt.

'It does not happen,' continued Aleksandra, warming to her theme, 'because pregnant women are useless to the clients and, if they are useless to the clients, they are not making money for the organisation. I know that different groups operate in different ways, but either the kid is terminated straight away or, if the girl has fulfilled her usefulness, she is later found in an alley with a needle in her arm – and the police will jump to the conclusion that either she has given herself an overdose, or the heroine was bad.'

'You don't need to tell me this, Aleksandra,' said Elena, with conviction. 'I know. You and I were in the same boat, remember. All the girls were. As I said, I cannot work it out. There is one thing that came to mind, but it's too horrible to contemplate – and that is that they intended to sell the baby on.'

'Oh no!' exclaimed Aleksandra.

'Well, this particular day I could sense that the baby was coming. I told a man we called "The Handler", and at first he just thought I was making a fuss. But it wasn't long before even he realised that there was an emergency. I was bundled into an SUV and rushed to the nearest hospital. However, on the way our vehicle was involved in an accident. We had taken a corner at speed and found ourselves on the wrong side of the road. We hit a car coming in the opposite direction and there was a horrendous crash.'

Aleksandra's eyes were now like saucers. 'Were the people in the other car hurt?' she asked, looking fearful of the answer.

'There was just one person in the other vehicle, the woman who was driving, and she was killed!'

Aleksandra brought both her hands to her mouth in shock.

'The man who was driving the car I was in ran off,' continued Elena.

'He ran off?' said Aleksandra, emphasising every word.

'He ran off,' confirmed Elena, and then went on with her story. 'The police were quickly on the scene. While some medics were dealing with the woman in the car, I was taken to the hospital. But my baby died.'

'Oh Sasha,' said Aleksandra, genuinely moved. 'I am so very sorry.'

'When the police questioned me, it didn't take them long to realise who I was or, from the sneers on their faces, *what* I was.'

At this remark, Aleksandra's eyes moved from Elena's face on which they had been so strongly fixed, and her head tilted slightly forward, her eyes now resting on the empty coffee cup in front of her.

'Then,' said Elena, 'all hell broke loose. I don't know whether you heard about it, but when a container was opened in Tallinn, several of our girls were found inside. All of them dead. This happened some time before the incident I've just told you about, but the police didn't take long to put two and two together.'

'I certainly know about that, Sasha,' said Aleksandra, 'for it is part of my story, which I will tell you about later – but please go on.'

'Well, there isn't much more to say. The police had had the organisation under surveillance for a long time, and had only held back because they wanted first to expose a number of corrupt police officers. Anyway,' continued Elena, feeling just a little guilty that she was not telling her story in its entirety, 'when I got out of hospital I made my way here to the UK and, because I speak English well, I didn't have too much trouble in getting a job.'

At this, Aleksandra rose from her seat, but Elena's quizzical glance was answered as Aleksandra walked towards the coffee shop door with the words, 'My turn this time, same again?'

Aleksandra began to talk, as they faced one another again with their drinks in their hands. 'Well, I suppose it's not just my turn to get the coffees, but also my turn to tell my story,' she said. 'My story is much shorter than yours but, to some degree, links with much of what you have already told me.

'I'm sure that I came under their control in much the same way that you did. All the girls I met gave accounts that hardly varied except in names, times and locations. I won't go into the details because you, of all people, can imagine them. It was horror upon horror – but enough of that. When the thing with the container happened ...' Aleksandra seemed to fish around in her mind for the right word and then, as she had hooked it, continued, 'Chaos, I think, is the only word to describe what happened next. You don't have real friends where we were, do you? Most of the time, if the girls are not working, they are either dog-tired or spaced out. But there are those that you tend to trust more than others. You might even call them friendships – at least in some sense of the word.

'When many of the key people in the organisation were arrested and taken into custody, the talk was of little else. People who have not been through what we have been through might think that everyone would be happy and elated, but it was not so. Most of us were addicted to drugs. All of us had zero self-esteem and, as hellish as our existence was, we were receiving food and drugs "free". The organisation to us was like scaffolding around derelict buildings that, if removed, would ensure that what had once been *supported* would now most definitely collapse in a heap. To put it another way, we were puppets whose strings were about to be cut.'

Elena's head was nodding as Aleksandra was speaking.

'There were probably only two directions in which things were likely to progress. The first, and what most people thought was the most likely, was that another organisation would move in and take over the operation. The second was that, once assessed by the authorities, the girls would be left to fend for themselves in the best way that they could.'

Elena realised at that moment that she was holding her breath, so intent was she on listening to her new friend's story. Aleksandra seemed to sense this and so moved on to bring her account towards a conclusion.

'You said earlier,' continued Aleksandra, 'that the police had been looking into the case behind the scenes. Something similar was happening to us – though it wasn't the police that were involved.'

Elena's brow creased; she did not know what could possibly be coming next.

'There's a group based in the country I was in,' continued Aleksandra, 'whose sole purpose is to get people like us away from the sex industry. You wouldn't believe how radical and edgy these people are. More than once when I was working, I would be approached by men who I assumed were looking for sex, only to find out that they were trying to discover if we wanted their help to get out. At first I thought they were weird do-gooders or religious cranks, but they were clearly not and they were very persistent. What I thought most about them was that they were really …'

Here Aleksandra stopped, as she again tried to capture the right word.

'It sounds like navy,' she went on.

'Do you mean naïve?' offered Elena.

'Yes, that's the word, naïve,' continued Aleksandra. 'I mean, they were putting their lives at risk if they had been caught. But there was another thing. We didn't know who they were. I mean, we could, how should I say it, be jumping out of the frying pan into the fire. What made me really think that there might be something in this, though, was that there were women about our own age who worked with them. In some ways I think it was harder for them to talk to us than for the men, but the women would ask about our health and if we needed anything – practical things like that.'

Elena was transfixed by Aleksandra's account. She had never heard anything like this in her entire life.

'Anyway, let me get to the end of my story or we will be here forever,' said Aleksandra. 'When the organisation was broken up by the police, these people were there for us. There's so much that I could say, but I must leave it for another time. All I can say is they found money to get some of us out of the country and bring us to England.'

'Now it's my turn to respond in disbelief, Aleksandra,' responded Elena. 'You and I both know that the first thing that the people who controlled us do is confiscate our passports. They know that we are trapped without them.'

'I know that too,' said Aleksandra, 'but whether they got to them somehow, or had an arrangement with the police, I have no idea – but here I am!'

As she said this, she smiled and extended out her arms expansively as if showing off a new outfit to a friend.

'That is such an awesome story,' responded Elena, 'but when you say they brought you to England, what does that actually mean? For example, where do you live?'

'We live in a centre – well, it's a house, really – and it's shared by ten girls who come from a similar background to myself and are about the same age. There are live-in staff who look after the place and they are both male and female. There are volunteers who come in from time to time as well.'

'So we are talking "hostel", then?' suggested Elena, trying to conjure up a picture of the place in her mind.

'Oh goodness, no! I can guess what you are thinking. I suppose it's my fault for not making myself clear. If you're imagining some kind of halfway house for the homeless, you are a million miles away from what this is. OK, we do eat communally. It just works best like that with so many in the house, but we all have our own privacy and independence. And professional counselling is available for everyone who needs it – and we all do – and we are also assessed regarding our skills. This means that they make it possible for us to train or retrain with a view to us moving on to live independently of the centre. You have to understand,' Aleksandra went on, 'we are all at different levels. I have problems that I am working through, but at least I am able to be sitting here with you in the centre of Birmingham. Some of the girls are almost completely shot, not just because of what they have gone through, but because of the length of time they have had to go through it.'

'But how much does all this cost?' asked Elena. 'Where does the money come from? Having people working on location around Europe, bringing people to the UK, maintaining the upkeep of the house – or centre, or whatever it is – the cost must be huge!'

'I suppose it must,' admitted Aleksandra. 'All I know is that it does not cost us anything. It's a charity that exists, like all charities do, I suppose, through private donations. They have centres in other places too.'

'I would truly love to see this for myself,' said Elena. 'Is there any chance that that could happen?'

Aleksandra thought for a moment before replying, but then said, 'Well, I can at least see what I can do. Access to the centre by people from outside is monitored for many reasons, as you might imagine. But I will certainly ask, and I think that there is a very good chance, especially if I share some of your story, should you allow me to. Listen, we both have one another's numbers, so I will be in touch.'

At this, the new friends stood, embraced warmly, and went their separate ways.

Christmas 2007
Cumbernauld, Scotland

As Christmas approached, Albert Porter, now eighty-five, looked back over the past eleven years since he had come to Cumbernauld. What a wonderful time it had proved to be. His godson Phillip and his wife Penny had been like the son and daughter that he and his wife had never had. He remembered the initial fears that he had had about moving into the annex of their house. He had thought long and hard about moving anywhere at his time of life. It was not the issue of moving from England to Scotland that had concerned him, but the thought of leaving his friends and connections. Obviously he would have Phillip and Penny, but they had their own lives to live. Many of the friendships he had made over the years had been those that had been formed when he was a student, or later, at the churches where he had been a minister. How easy would it be to develop new relationships at his age?

In the event, it had not been a problem at all. He had found a church at which to worship, the local Christian fellowship, and he had been immediately made welcome by everyone there. The church did not have a large congregation, perhaps around 100, he thought, but there was a wide range of ages represented and the friendships he made were not limited to those of his own age.

The minister there was approaching retirement age, but the congregation had asked him to remain with them a little longer. He had grown to be respected across a wide spectrum of the church, old and young alike. He had agreed to stay on for a while, but made it clear that he believed it was now time for the fellowship to have a younger person at the helm.

Everything was 'paradise on earth' as far as Albert was concerned, except for just one issue and this was something he would have to talk to Phillip and Penny about. The only thing he had to decide was whether he should mention it before Christmas or after. Having given it some thought, he opted to wait until the celebrations were over. Phillip and Penny would be busy in the run-up to Christmas, and during the day itself and Boxing Day family and friends would be around.

It was Thursday, the day after Boxing Day, and Albert was sitting alone in his lounge and reading his newspaper. Laying down the newspaper on his lap, he said out loud to himself, 'Oh, that's absolutely dreadful!'

'What's absolutely dreadful, Uncle Albert?' asked Penny. She and Phillip had walked into the room at the moment the words had been uttered.

'Oh, hello, Penny, Phillip, I didn't hear you both come in. I must have been talking to myself. Anyway, come in and sit down.'

As they did, Penny asked again, 'So tell us, what's so dreadful?'

'It's what happened in Carnation. I'm just reading about it. How awful!' said Albert, pulling the paper up towards him again and searching for the place where he had just been reading. 'Carnation, a small town in Washington State, in America, not far from Seattle … It appears that a couple murdered the woman's parents and other members of the family. Two of the victims were under seven. That's horrific at any time, but … on Christmas Eve?'

'You're right,' responded Phillip. 'When things happen at Christmas, it's doubly difficult for those who are left, because as the season comes round year after year, it marks the anniversary of the pain at the very time families should be enjoying themselves. You won't have heard about it yet, Uncle, because we've just picked it up on the news, but Benazir Bhutto has just been assassinated – you know, Pakistan's former prime minister? News is still coming in, but it looks as though she was shot.'

'It's all terrible,' added Penny, 'but Uncle Albert, we just dropped by to see how you were. I hope you didn't find the last couple of days too tiring – so many people in and out of the house, and all that kind of thing?'

'No, not at all, Penny, dear,' said Albert. 'I was just so appreciative of how sensitive you were.'

'Sensitive? Uncle, in what way do you mean?'

'Well, making sure that I was included to the degree that I wanted to be but, at the same time, not worrying too much if I slinked back over here from time to time to rest.'

'Well, as long as you enjoyed Christmas, Uncle Albert, that's all we wanted to know,' assured Penny.

There was a pause, and in those few moments Albert noticed a certain glance that took place between the two people he loved most in the world.

'There is something else,' said Phillip, 'that we were hoping to talk to you about, Uncle.'

'Oh, there is, is there?' responded Albert. 'This is not just a social visit, then, I see.'

'Well, we certainly wanted to know how you were,' said Penny, 'but we also wanted to ask you a favour.'

'A favour?' echoed Albert. 'And what would that be, then, I wonder?'

'We wanted to ask you if you would be willing to move into the main house for a couple of weeks, into one of the spare bedrooms,' said Penny. 'I'm not sure exactly how long you have been staying with us, Uncle …'

'I can tell you precisely,' interrupted Albert. 'I was asking myself that very question just a few days ago, and I came to the conclusion it must be eleven years.'

Penny thought for a moment or two and then went on, 'Yes, I'm sure that must be right, Uncle Albert. Well, when you first came, everything was in pristine condition. We wanted it to be like that for you. But you know, during all that time this annex has not been either painted or decorated. So what we are asking is if you would be willing to move into our place, so that the decorators can move in here.'

Now it was Albert who paused and thought. 'This is it,' he said to himself. 'There's no escaping it. I shall have to address the matter here and now.'

'I'm afraid that won't be possible, my dears. In fact, it is entirely out of the question.'

Phillip and Penny were so aghast at this response, something they had clearly not anticipated for a moment, that they both sat back in their seats, stiffening slightly. Albert could read on their faces what they were thinking. Of course, it would be an inconvenience, but surely only the slightest one. They were approaching someone that they loved out of courtesy, to the degree that their question was virtually rhetorical. Never for a second did either of them entertain the possibility that he would say no.

'I'm saying that I will not be moving out of the annex for a few days because I have decided that it's time for me to move out of the annex for good.'

'For good!' Phillip and Penny exclaimed simultaneously.

'What on earth do you mean, Uncle?' asked Phillip.

'You two are the dearest and kindest people in the world. I know I don't need to tell you how much I think of you both. If you were my own children I couldn't love you more. The years here that we have been together have been more wonderful than I could ever have hoped for … but we all know that I don't have many more years ahead of me.'

Phillip and Penny moved their eyes from him, and Albert noticed that their postures that had stiffened a few moments ago had now reverted, not just to their previous position, but almost to a slump.

'But Uncle …' interrupted Penny.

'No, Penny, let me go on,' said Albert. 'All three of us know that I am not talking only about my age, but about my prognosis. I know I can get around fairly well now, but I know better than anyone else the degree to which my condition is advancing. I have already talked this over with my GP and, frankly, I have to tell you that she agrees with me. She said that not only would I need to talk this through with you, but that it will be months rather than years until the time when I will need to have constant medical supervision.'

Albert could see that Phillip and Penny wanted to intervene. They wanted to argue with him. They wanted to tell him that he was wrong and that his decision was premature. But they didn't. He knew that deep down they realised that this conversation would one day take place. They were probably grateful that it was Albert who had initiated it.

'In short, dear ones,' said Albert. 'It is time that I went into some kind of a home.'

'Uncle!' began Penny.

'No, stop, please stop. Don't make this any harder than it already is,' continued Albert. 'We all know that what I am saying is right. All I need now, since we have got this out of the way, is for you to work on my behalf to find the right place. It's obviously not going to happen overnight, I know – you'll need to look at brochures, go online and do preparatory visits and the like … oh, and by the way, please don't drag me round to see them all. I trust you to either make a shortlist, or you can make the choice yourself if you want, but I don't want to get all that involved, if you don't mind. I've always been slightly embarrassed that you have taken the barest minimum from me to cover the costs of my staying here. However, I comforted myself in the knowledge that my will ensures that everything I have is left to you.'

'Uncle!' exclaimed Penny again.

'I'm sorry,' said Albert. 'I really must continue. There will obviously be costs involved in my going into a residential home, but – if I believe what my doctor is telling me, and I have every reason to believe she is telling me the truth – I may only have eighteen months to two years left, and then everything that is mine will be yours. So, now that I have expressed what I've been wanting to say for some time, all I would ask is that you start the process as early as you can in the new year.

'And now,' he laid aside the newspaper that had been on his lap the whole time he had been speaking, 'I think I'm going to a take a little nap.'

January 2008
Cotswolds

Elena heard her phone ring but could not work out where the sound was coming from. She had treated herself to the new mobile, and all the reviews had said that it was the best. If only she could find it! She lifted a cushion from the settee on which she was sitting, saw the phone, snatched it up and pressed the 'call-answer' button.

'Happy New Year, Sasha!' declared the voice on the other end.

Elena paused for a few seconds and then realised who it was.

'Hi, Aleksandra, is that you?'

'Of course it is,' came the reply. 'Can't you recognise my broken English by now?'

'Well, Happy New Year to you too, and how was your Christmas?'

'It was good,' responded Aleksandra in a measured tone. 'I miss my family back home, it's true, but everyone at the centre was in a similar position and we had a pretty good time. This is like a new family for me anyway. In fact, that is one of the reasons I am ringing, apart from wanting to wish you a Happy New Year, of course. Do you remember asking me about the centre and saying that you would like to see it some time?'

'Yes, I did,' replied Elena, 'but if I remember correctly you said that it might not be easy, given the secrecy, or at least the privacy, that's involved.'

'I did say that,' admitted Aleksandra, 'but something has just turned up that you may be interested in. It's not exactly an "open day", but one of the main people from the charity that runs all the centres is travelling down from Scotland, and he is doing a talk for people who may be interested in what the charity is involved in. It is strictly on an invitation-only basis, but I don't think I would have any problem in getting you an invite if you really wanted to come. The object is to attract more donors and sponsors, I believe, and although that's not what you'd be there for, if you are sure you would like to come, I am positive it will be OK.'

'I'd love to visit your place, I really would,' enthused Elena. 'When is it? I would need to check I have a day off.'

'It's next Saturday.'

'*This* weekend?' asked Elena.

'Yes, I know it's only a few days away, and there is no point in me asking them to put anything in the post, so if you can make it I will meet you outside and have the necessary admission card to give you. I'll have to ask first but, unless you hear otherwise from me within the hour, you can be assured everything is fine.'

'You'll need to give me the address and the time,' said Elena. 'I'm really looking forward to it. Did you say it was one of the people who run the charity that will be speaking?'

'Yes, it's someone called Simon Bellenger. I've never met him myself so can't really say any more about him. I'll text you the address and postcode. The time is 2.30 in the afternoon.'

On the following Saturday at 2pm, Elena pulled up at the address Aleksandra had given her. She liked to be early and, anyway, there was always a worry about what parking would be like, especially in a place she had never been to before.

As it happened, parking could not have been easier. As she was stepping out of the car and locking it, she noticed up ahead that Aleksandra was already there and waiting for her. She had a white A5-sized card in her hand, which Elena assumed would be her official invitation.

'Hi, Sasha, I'm over here,' called her friend, obviously pleased to see her and excited that she could show her around the place that she now temporarily considered her home.

They hugged and, as the two of them approached the building, linking arms, Elena took in the surroundings. Had there not been a maroon sign outside with gold lettering, she would have taken the building for a large house built for an Edwardian family 100 years ago. It was evidently well-maintained and had almost a cosy feeling about it. Perhaps the neat and well-tended grounds had given her that impression.

'The Celia Centre,' Elena read out loud. 'In my country, schools and hospitals are named after saints. Was Celia a saint or something?'

Before Aleksandra could answer, three of her friends from the centre, seeing her coming, approached her and wanted to be introduced to the person they knew only as Sasha. Elena had agreed that her story, to the degree that she had shared it with Aleksandra, could be divulged to staff in order for her to obtain the invitation. The residents, including the ones who were now greeting her, were only aware that she shared a similar background to them.

In the entrance hall was a trestle table, a quarter of which was occupied by a stack of coloured brochures, which Elena rightly assumed was for the guests attending. The remainder of the table was given over to rows of name tags laminated in transparent plastic. Elena found hers and looped it around her neck with the supplied ribbon. She also accepted the proffered brochure.

Moving on past the table, they came to a room set out with rows of chairs, which Elena realised was going to be the venue for the meeting. At the back of the room, tea and coffee were being served.

By 2.25pm everyone had taken their place and Elena noticed that every available seat had been occupied. A few minutes later, a woman in her mid-forties left the place where she had been sitting on the front row and approached the microphone.

'Good afternoon,' she began. 'Welcome to the Celia Centre and, for those of you for whom it is a first visit, we offer you a very special welcome. My name is Jennifer Summers and I am the person who has the privilege of leading the team here. When you picked up your name tags, you should also have been given a brochure outlining the aims and objectives of our charity. We trust it will serve as an ongoing reminder of your time with us today.'

Then, looking across to the chair on the front row next to the one she had just vacated, she continued and with a smile said, 'Today we are delighted to have with us a very special guest. Someone who has come all the way from Scotland to be with us. I don't want to take any more time before introducing him to you, so would you please welcome – Mr Simon Bellenger!'

Elena could not have described in advance what she was expecting, but it was certainly not the tall, good-looking, athletically built man who now approached the Perspex lectern.

'Good afternoon, ladies and gentlemen. Thank you for taking the time to be with us today. I know you are all busy people, and lending us part of your weekend must have been something of a sacrifice for you. However, I trust that in the next thirty minutes or so I will be able to share with you something of our passion for this place, and others like it, in and around the country. By the time the day has concluded, I trust you will have considered that your time with us today has been well spent.'

Elena glanced at her watch when she heard the closing words: 'So there we are. These places were our dream and now those dreams have become a reality. Without the dedication of the team here led so wonderfully by Jennifer, we most certainly could not operate. And similarly, without the support of our donors we would not be able to maintain our presence around the UK, let alone consider expanding further. Thank you all so very much for being with us today.'

'That could not have been thirty minutes!' she said to herself. But when she checked the time, she discovered that Simon Bellenger had in fact been on his feet for the best part of three-quarters of an hour.

The speaker resumed his seat to enthusiastic applause. Jennifer Summers, who by now had returned to the microphone, stood for a short while as the applause continued and, with her face towards the speaker, said, 'Thank you so much, Mr Bellenger. I'm sure that from the warmth of that applause you can gauge the degree to which everyone present has appreciated everything that you have shared with us.'

Then, turning to the audience, she continued, 'Thank you, ladies and gentlemen, for being with us, but the afternoon is by no means over. Refreshments will be served for those who wish to stay and chat. In twenty minutes' time I will be conducting a short tour of this facility. Please do not feel you have to rush away. If any of you have any questions, there are staff members – you will recognise them by their badges – who will be on hand to assist you in any way that they can.'

There was a further short burst of applause, followed by the noise of people commencing conversations with those nearby, moving to where a finger buffet was being served, or generally milling around.

'So what did you think of that?' asked Aleksandra.

'Well, he is certainly an amazing speaker. But it was the content of what he said that really gripped me. This obviously is a phenomenal place, and these seem to be wonderful people who are running it.'

As they were talking, Elena could see Jennifer Summers approaching. Elena stopped the conversation and, addressing Aleksandra, said, 'Oh, it seems that you are needed, Aleksandra. Ms Summers wants to speak with you.'

'Hi, Aleksandra,' Jennifer Summers began. 'I believe the afternoon has gone well, don't you think? Actually ...' and here Jennifer Summers gave a quick glance at the name tag that Aleksandra's friend was wearing before she continued, 'It's you, Sasha, that I would like to have a brief word with, if I may.'

Elena faced her, surprised.

'Yes, you!' Jennifer Summers continued, smiling. 'Aleksandra has told me something of your story and, prior to the meeting, I relayed some of it to Mr Bellenger. He's going to be tied up in some conversations for about half an hour, but he asked me to find out if it would be possible for him to meet you before you left. He fully understands that may not be possible, of course, but he did ask me to at least ask you and find out.'

Elena could feel her heart beating so loudly that she imagined that those around her could hear it too. What had she let herself in for? Talking to Aleksandra had been one thing, and she had given her permission to share as little or as much of her history as she wanted to, but a conversation with someone like today's speaker! What would he be asking her, and what might she inadvertently divulge? Of course, she could make the excuse that she had a pressing appointment and had to leave, but she knew that that would be a lie. And anyway, would it not be amazing to meet Mr Bellenger personally?

It was then that she heard herself saying in a voice far calmer than she felt, 'Yes, OK, if you like. That won't be a problem.'

Jennifer Summers smiled and patted her shoulder, while saying, 'That's wonderful, Sasha. I'll let him know. I'm sure he'll be so pleased.'

When she was out of sight, Aleksandra drew her friend around to face her straight on and, with eyes as wide as saucers – just as Elena had remembered them when Aleksandra had first heard her story – said, pronouncing each word with emphasis, 'Mr Simon Bellenger wants to meet you for a chat!'

It was actually a little less than half an hour before Jennifer Summers walked up to Elena with a smiling Simon Bellenger in tow.

'It's Sasha, isn't it?' he asked, looking her directly in the eye and offering his hand. 'It's so wonderful that you are able to spare me some time.'

'Oh it's not a problem, Mr Bellenger, and thank you for your marvellous talk,' Elena replied.

'Please call me Simon. I would be much more comfortable with that. Jennifer here has kindly made her office available, if that's OK. I won't detain you long, but I would love to hear more of your story.'

Jennifer led the way and Elena and Simon followed. Elena noticed that all the doors to the offices had clear glass panels and that Simon had left their door slightly ajar. She realised that everything had been designed with the utmost sensitivity, given the experiences that all the young women who lived here had gone through. When Simon had occupied what would normally have been Jennifer Summers' seat behind a desk, he pointed across the room to an easy chair for Elena to take.

Elena told her story almost exactly as she had relayed it to Aleksandra. When she reviewed the conversation later at home she would remember that for some reason she had omitted just one thing. She had said that she had lost her baby in an accident, but had not made it clear it was a car accident. But, anyway, why would that make any difference?

He listened to her entirely without interruption, and was clearly fascinated.

'You know, Sasha,' he said, once he realised that she had finished all that she wanted to say, 'there are obvious common denominators in all the stories the women in our centres share with us. But at the same time every account is unique. What you have shared is, of course, your story and the account of your pain. We very quickly learned at the beginning of our work – and we are learning all the time – that those staying with us have suffered at various levels of intensity and are recovering at very different rates. That's why we find it so important to customise – tailor-make, if you like – the restoration process. But listen, I've kept you long enough. Before you leave, Sasha, have you got any questions for me?'

Elena thought for a moment before replying.

'I suppose the biggest one is, why you are doing this? What is your motivation? It's obviously not money. You talked in there …' Elena moved her head briefly in the direction of the room they had recently left, 'about the "what" of what you are doing. But you didn't say a great deal about the "why".'

Simon smiled and paused before making a response. 'Well, speaking for myself, and I think I speak for most of those involved from the charity's very earliest days, it arises out of our Christian conviction.'

'Oh, I see,' responded Elena, 'but I didn't pick up, unless I missed something, that you referred to that in your talk.'

'You are absolutely right, and there is a reason for that. Although the majority of our staff are committed Christians, the people we are here to serve come from many diverse backgrounds. Some have faith, or religion, in their past. Some had faith but have lost it because of what they have had to endure. Others never had faith to begin with and have no faith now. We are here to serve everyone – not just people with the same convictions as ourselves.

'There's a story in the Bible of a miracle that Jesus did. He fed more than 5,000 people out of a little boy's lunch. Sasha, He didn't feed them because He wanted to prove anything to them. He fed them just because they were hungry. And I suppose it's the same here. We're not trying to prove anything either. We're just trying to do what Jesus would do if He were physically here today. Does that make any sense to you?'

'I think it does,' replied Elena, pensively. 'I think I understand what you're saying.'

'Would you call yourself a Christian, Sasha?'

'No, I wouldn't,' replied Elena, 'but I've got a friend, Mawusi, a colleague in the care home I work in who is a Christian. She's Ghanaian.'

'And did she grow up in a Christian family in Africa?'

'I think so, but from what she told me, she didn't become a Christian in the sense that I think you mean it, until she came over here. She told me about it once. It was a really weird story.'

'Weird? In what way?' asked Simon, intrigued.

'Well, I feel silly even saying it,' continued Elena apologetically, 'because I don't think you will believe me. It's just that she told me that one day somebody left an old Bible at the place where she was working, and she said that after she had read parts of it, it changed her entire life.'

Elena involuntarily pushed herself back in her chair as the man she had been speaking to rose to his feet in one swift movement. Her eyes flashed towards the door that was still ajar. She looked through its glass pane but was conscious that there was no one in sight.

Simon seemed to realise straight away the effect that he had had on her and immediately apologised.

'I'm sorry, Sasha, what was it you just said?'

'I said that my friend had found a Bible and that what she had read in it had changed her life, Mr Bellenger. I warned you that you would find it hard to believe, so why would you react like that?'

Simon resumed his seat.

'This wasn't in Cheltenham, was it, Sasha?' asked Simon.

'Yes, it was,' replied Elena, surprised, 'but how would you know that? I work near Cheltenham and Mawusi lives in Cheltenham too.'

'Sasha, once again, sorry for startling you, but you see, that is exactly how my Christian journey began. I found an old Bible on a bench in Cheltenham – on the High Street!'

Elena sat transfixed and amazed.

'But it can't have been the same Bible because Mawusi and her husband have their Bible on their coffee table. I see it every time I visit them, and anyway, Mawusi didn't find hers on a bench. Hers had been left at a café where she was working at the time.'

'Sasha, I need to ask you a great favour. Could you let me have the contact details of your friend?'

Elena thought for a moment before saying, 'I'm not sure that I can do that without asking her permission.'

'No, of course not,' interrupted Simon. 'You are absolutely right.' And then, reaching into his jacket for his wallet, he withdrew a card. 'Sasha, would you pass my card on to her – and please tell her why – then, if she wants to get in touch, she can.'

Coming round the desk towards her, Simon extended his hand to Elena for the second time that day; and a startled but thoughtful young woman left the office.

Elena noticed as she headed towards the door that the place that had so recently been buzzing with visitors and staff was now almost entirely empty. The guests had gone and the staff, she assumed, must have retired to their own rooms. The only people that were around were a few volunteers who were clearing the area where refreshments had been provided, or tidying the chairs in the hall where the meeting had taken place. She looked around for Aleksandra but could not see her. Then she noticed one of the young women who had been introduced to her when she had first come in.

'You haven't seen Aleksandra, have you?' Elena enquired.

'Oh, it's you, Sasha. I'm glad to have caught you. Aleksandra asked me to look out for you and apologise for the fact that she had to leave. She said she would give you a ring later this evening.'

Elena thanked her and left the building in the direction of her car.

As promised, Aleksandra phoned later that evening, just after Elena had finished her supper.

'So, what was all that about?' Aleksandra enthused. 'You got to see the gorgeous Simon. How long were you with him? What did he ask you about?'

'Hang on,' said Elena. 'One question at a time. Obviously I was as surprised as you that he wanted to talk to me. He mainly wanted to hear my story based on stuff that you must have told Jennifer Summers about me.'

'You didn't mind, did you, Sasha?' Aleksandra asked, with just a little hesitation in her voice.

'No, not at all,' responded Elena. 'I realised that in order to secure an invite you would have to say something. He just wanted me to unpack it a bit more, that's all.'

Elena thought she would leave out the bit about the Bible. She wasn't a Christian and she didn't think Aleksandra was either, so she didn't think that she would find that part of the account of any particular interest. She did, however, make a mental note to pass on the message from Mr Bellenger to Mawusi first thing on Monday morning.

'But you do agree that he is good-looking, don't you? I mean ...'

'Listen, Aleksandra, we've talked about this sort of thing before when you've asked me about dating. I don't see men in that way any more. I'm just not interested in relationships after everything that I've been through. I admire the fact that you are more resilient than me and that's great, but at this point in my life I don't want to know. Besides, even if I were interested, what decent man would want to have anything to do with me anyway?'

'Well, I'm not going to get into all of that on the phone, Sasha. I've said how you need to start working through things. That's one of the great benefits of being at our place. They encourage you to process it. So, what did you think of the centre, anyway?'

'I thought it was amazing, but I didn't realise it was a Christian place.'

'Christian?' replied Aleksandra. 'So, what's wrong with that?'

'There's nothing wrong with it,' said Elena, somewhat defensively. 'All I'm saying is that I didn't realise it, that's all. I wasn't saying any more than that. There's no need to be prickly, Aleksandra.'

'Me, prickly? You are joking?' responded Aleksandra. 'It seems you are prickly – about religion?'

'No!' retorted Elena – and then her mind flashed back to the incident when she had been with Mawusi and the conversation about the Bible.

'So are you a Christian, then?' asked Elena.

'No, not really I suppose. I mean, I didn't even realise that all the centres were started because of the convictions that people like Simon Bellenger and Jennifer Summers had. I had been there for a couple of weeks before I found out. But, if I'm honest, I have been thinking more about it recently. I often think that some of them have a strength I don't have.'

'Oh, come on, Aleksandra,' said Elena. 'It's not only Christians that want to see a better world. Lots of people who profess no faith at all want to do their bit for others. Christians haven't got a monopoly on compassion, you know.'

'I know that,' replied Aleksandra, 'but I'm still increasingly drawn to it anyway. But look, it seems that we have got into an argument somehow, and all I did was to phone you to see how you enjoyed today.'

'I know,' said Elena. 'I'm sure that the fault is entirely mine, and I'm sorry.'

'Are we good, then?' asked Aleksandra.

'Of course we are,' said Elena, warmly. 'Look, I'll speak to you soon, and enjoy the rest of your night.'

As Elena drove to work on the following Monday morning, she thought it might be a good idea to pass on Simon's card to Mawusi straight away, just in case she forgot. She caught up with her later that day and, as anticipated, Mawusi almost responded in the same way that Simon had done.

'What is it with these Christians?' she thought. 'I mean, it's a coincidence, for God's sake, these things happen all the time – why should people make such a fuss? It was hardly divine intervention.' And then she reflected on the irony of her using the phrase 'for God's sake' in such a context.

When she had spoken to Mawusi, she had been very careful not to talk about the centre, in the same way that she had never mentioned Aleksandra to her. The last thing she wanted was to divulge her past to anyone who did not need to know. She had given the impression, without lying about it, that she had 'bumped into someone when she had been in Birmingham' and Mawusi had not questioned her further.

'Anyway, I've got some news for you too,' Mawusi said, once the story of Saturday had been related and the card passed over. 'Now, you've got to keep this to yourself,' Mawusi continued, with a conspiratorial smile.

'You're not leaving?' exclaimed Elena, pleased for her friend but wondering at the same time what else it could be, when there were no vacancies that she knew of at Cotswold Mews.

'Now listen, you have to keep this to yourself, at least for a while. Do you promise?' Mawusi asked.

'Of course I will, but you've got to explain what you're talking about!'

'Maureen Stibbes is leaving!'

'Leaving! What do you mean, leaving?'

'She's taking early retirement.'

'Oh dear, she's not ill or something, is she?' asked Elena enquiringly.

'No, nothing like that,' said Mawusi. 'I don't know exactly, but I think she may have come into some inheritance, something like that. Anyway, I am very pleased for her. She brought me into her office and said that this would be happening in about three months' time – she has to give quite a bit of notice, you see – and she said that she saw me as her successor!'

'Wow, that's amazing, Mawusi. I'm so happy for you.'

'Thank you, Sasha, I knew you would be. She said to me, "Mawusi, you have been on staff at Cotswold Mews longer than anyone else, but that fact has a downside as well as being positive." Of course, I didn't realise what she meant, and then she told me. "The group that all our homes in the UK belong to like to think that there is a consistency throughout the organisation. However, it's almost inevitable that there are some nuances – things that are done differently at different locations."'

'I don't see how that has any bearing on you, though, Mawusi,' said Elena, puzzled.

'I think the idea is that she wants me to spend some time at other locations. It seems that we will be a bit understaffed here for a little while, but Maureen says it shouldn't be too much of a problem and perhaps some staff will appreciate the overtime.'

'Well, I know I would,' responded Elena, half laughing.

'From what I understand,' Mawusi continued, 'the first place they are going to send me to is Scotland.'

January 2008
Glengarrick House, Scotland

'This is certainly some place,' said Damian to Jack, as he and the rest of the guests walked with their overnight cases from the stylish reception area where they had just secured their keys en route to their rooms.

'I know,' said Jack, 'and I wanted us all to be together for a relaxed twenty-four-hour stay so that we could review where we are and think a little about the way ahead.' Then, looking at his watch and addressing the small group, he added, 'I'll tell you what, why don't we get settled in our rooms and then meet in the lounge I've reserved at ...' Looking at his watch again, he said, '... eleven o'clock? We can start by reviewing the meetings we conducted across the country – and then that should take us up to lunch.'

At the appointed time, everyone was refreshed and ready to start. Jack looked across at those assembled. He was really appreciative of all that they had accomplished in the relatively short time the charity had been established. Damian and Sue were there, as was Simon.

'I'm not sure why you have included us,' said Sarah, who was sitting next to her sister on a comfortable sofa. 'We're not exactly hands-on, are we?'

'Mum,' Jack responded. 'We had to have you both here. We know you're not involved in the day-to-day running of what we do, but your encouragement and support has been amazing over these past few months. I don't want to embarrass you both in front of everyone, but the amount of capital that you have injected has been, I would have to say, beyond generous.'

Beth moved her hand in front of her as if batting away a fly.

'Compared to what all of you have done, and continue to do, it's the least we could do,' she said, dismissing the accolade.

'As we are all aware,' Jack continued, 'the last few days have been occupied by some of us here speaking at our centres, and I thought that we might start by sharing how things had gone. Damian, you and Sue were speaking at a hotel in Manchester with a view to eliciting support for a centre there. Sue, can you tell us your perception of how the day went?'

'It went very well indeed, I think,' said Sue, looking across to Damian. 'Numbers were much as we expected and, judging by the questions that were asked afterwards, I would say that we had generated quite a lot of interest. Would that be your view, Damian?'

'Absolutely, there were representatives from the social services, community groups, church leaders and also people from the business sector.'

'One of them, a woman,' continued Sue, 'indicated to me privately that she was impressed by what we were endeavouring to do, and implied that she would be putting some resources at our disposal, were we to go ahead.'

Everybody seemed to see this as a very positive report.

'Sue, you have been especially busy,' said Jack. 'You went on to do the London event on your own a few days later. How did that go?'

'It was very different, of course,' responded Sue, 'because we are already established there, but nevertheless, it was very positive.'

'I think that much the same could be said for my time in Glasgow,' said Jack. 'It all appears to have been very encouraging. I hesitate to say that we are "on a roll", but there certainly seems to be a very evident momentum. Did you find that in Birmingham too, Simon?'

'Precisely so. I think I was well received. The staff there are doing a great job, and I was very impressed by Jennifer Summers, who is the team leader, as you know. However, it's what happened after the session had finished that really blew me away.'

Everyone had been listening with interest to all the reports, but at this statement those gathered appeared, just ever so slightly, to lean forward to better understand what Simon was saying.

'Blew you away?' asked Sarah. 'How do you mean?'

'Well, before the session had begun Jennifer mentioned to me a young woman called Sasha.'

'I don't recognise that name,' said Sue. 'Because of my role, I'm familiar with the names of most of the residents at the centres.'

'No, she's not one of our girls, but rather a friend of one of the residents. From what I could make out, they had met socially, and it transpires that this Sasha has a background in the trafficking industry – as a victim, of course. She had asked if she could come and hear what we did at the Celia Centre, and that's why she was there. I was intrigued even by the little that Jennifer had told me, and asked if she would arrange for Sasha to meet me before I left. Frankly, it was the kind of tragic story we hear all the time and, on top of everything, she had had an accident and lost a baby.'

'What kind of accident?' asked Beth.

'I don't know,' replied Simon. 'She didn't say.'

'And having a baby doesn't fit the normal template either,' commented Sue.

'I know,' said Simon, 'but let me get to the hub of the thing. At the end of the conversation I asked if she had any questions about what we were doing, and she asked about our motivation – why we did what we did. I told her that many of us operated out of our beliefs as Christians. She seemed surprised at that. I then asked if she was a Christian and she said that she wasn't, but that her friend was – a work colleague, I believe.'

'What does this woman do now?' asked Damian.

'I think she said she worked in a care home of some sort,' responded Simon. 'Anyway, to cut a long story short, she brought up how her friend had become a Christian – and *you are never going to believe this* – she found an old Bible that had been left behind at a café in Cheltenham!'

'You are kidding us!' exclaimed Jack.

'No, I am not,' confirmed Simon. 'You remember on the cruise when I told you how I found a Bible on a bench?' he said, addressing Damian, Sue and Sarah.

'Of course we do!' responded Damian. 'It was one of the first things that we told Jack about when we got home because we knew that Celia had come to faith in exactly the same way. So what did you say when she told you?'

'I told her, of course, that I had become a Christian in the very same way.'

'Did you tell her about Celia?' asked Jack.

'No, I didn't. I was so taken aback I think.'

'So, what did you do then?' asked Sarah.

'I left her my card and asked her to pass it to her colleague, with a view to her friend getting in touch with me.'

At that moment Simon's phone rang. His immediate reaction was to move to close it down, but when Jack saw him about to do that, he said, 'Take it, Simon. We're about finished here now, and lunch will be soon.'

Simon pressed to take the call and heard a voice on the other end say, 'Is that Mr Bellenger? This is Mawusi.'

'I'm sorry,' Simon began. 'I don't think I know …'

'Sasha?' the voice added.

'Oh, Mawusi!' exclaimed Simon, turning and indicating by a wave of his hand to those who were rising to leave the lounge that they should pause and listen to the conversation. 'Mawusi! Thanks for calling … we were just talking about you.'

'About me?' responded Mawusi, surprised.

Simon noticed everyone in the room slowly retaking their seats and doing their best to listen in to one end of a conversation.

'Yes, about you,' continued Simon. 'But to be more precise, about how you found a Bible that led you to become a Christian. I am assuming that Sasha told you about me. Is that right?'

'Well, she told me she had met someone who had had a similar experience to mine, but she didn't tell me anything about you,' Mawusi replied. 'She said that you seemed very surprised!'

'Indeed I was,' answered Simon, 'but now I am going to surprise you.'

'Is that so?'

'In the very room I am in just now are some friends of mine, and the wife of one of those friends came to faith by finding a Bible too!'

'No! I can hardly believe it,' responded Mawusi. 'And did she find it in Cheltenham, just as I did?'

'In Cheltenham,' affirmed Simon. 'I found mine on a bench in the pedestrianised area of the High Street, and his wife found hers on a bench in Imperial Gardens.'

'Oh, I know where that is,' responded Mawusi. 'I've passed it many times on the way to the shops in the Montpellier district. How extraordinary!'

'Would you like to speak to the man whose wife I am referring to?'

'Yes, I would,' replied Mawusi.

'Hi, Mawusi, my name is Jack Troughton. It's nice to talk to you. Because of my wife's faith, I have become a Christian too! I am sure you must be as amazed by all this as we are.'

'Totally amazed,' said Mawusi. 'I think the term is "gobsmacked". How could such a thing be? I think the three of us must get together sometime to talk about this – me, Mr Bellenger and your wife.'

'Well, I'm afraid,' said Jack, after a pause, 'my wife is no longer with us. She passed away.'

'Oh, I am so sorry … I didn't know …' stammered Mawusi.

'Of course you didn't. How could you have known? What I would like you to do, though, is to leave your number with Mr Bellenger and perhaps we could get together at some point, as you suggest. We share an extraordinary story.'

'I would be very happy to do that,' responded Mawusi, 'but before you go, could I ask you something?'

'Of course,' said Jack. 'Please go on.'

'Thank you,' said Mawusi. 'Well, in the back of our Bible – I say "our" because my husband, Kwame, became a Christian at the same time as me – there was a strange message. I haven't looked at it for some time because I dismissed it as meaningless. I just wondered if your wife's Bible contained something similar, or if Mr Bellenger's did.'

'Hang on a minute, I think my wife did say something about that. Let me think … what was it? Something about a concierge showing someone to an entrance and the entrance leading to God. I don't think the word was concierge, but I get the feeling it had something to do with a hotel. I thought "hotel" because my wife found the Bible near a hotel. Anyway, that can't be right because they don't have a concierge, well, not one on the door anyway. And then there was some code too, if I remember. Is that in yours?'

'Yes,' replied Mawusi. 'A capital letter J followed by a short series of numbers. It really would be remarkable if that was in all three of the Bibles as well.'

'Yes, it would,' agreed Jack, 'but listen, here I am chatting away on your phone bill and probably detaining you too. Thank you so much for getting back to us and be sure to leave some contact details with Mr Bellenger.'

The mobile was passed back to Simon, who also thanked the caller and took down the details that he had been given.

They sat for a few moments in amazed silence before moving off for lunch.

March 2008
Cumbernauld, Scotland

'You'll need to put your scarf on today, Uncle,' said Penny. 'It's very chilly out there this morning.'

She and her husband had spent the last few weeks looking at possible residential homes that lay within a twenty-mile radius – and there had been a great number of them. Apart from the obvious criteria that anyone would consider for someone they cared about so much, there was the matter of accessibility. They were determined to visit as regularly as they possibly could and, given the parameters that they had set, a forty-mile round trip seemed doable. They had filtered out several that they had come across because of poor online reviews, and some that had looked like possibilities had not fulfilled the promise presented by the publicity once they had visited them in person. In the end, they had narrowed it down to three likely places. Albert had already visited two of them and, although on the face of it there was little to object to, none of them had had a 'wow factor' about them that made them feel in any way special.

If Caledonian Mews, the one they were visiting today, did not fit the bill, then they would simply continue their search. All that mattered to them was that Albert would be happy. His general health had deteriorated within the past few weeks, although his memory and coordination remained unchanged.

They were met as they entered the two wide glass doors by a cheerful lady in a pastel pink uniform.

'Hello, you must be Mr Porter,' she said, addressing Albert with a smile. 'We've been looking forward to meeting you.' And then, looking across to Phillip and Penny on either side of him, she added, 'And that means you must be …'

The woman looked confused for a moment. Were these his children? Or were they son and wife or daughter and husband? She should have checked. All she had been told was to go and meet a Mr Porter at reception.

Seeing the slight confusion on the woman's face, it was Penny who intervened.

'Mr Porter is our uncle. Thank you for taking the trouble to come to meet us.'

'Oh, no problem at all, love,' said the member of staff. 'Just follow me and I'll take you through. Have you come far? Can I get you a tea or coffee or something?'

'No, we haven't come too far, and no, I think we are fine regarding tea or coffee,' responded Phillip.

'Well, as long as you are sure. Mrs Addo will be with you in a moment and I will call you through in just a little while.'

'Thank you, that's very kind of you,' answered Penny.

'So, if you make yourselves comfortable,' the woman continued, 'I'll be back shortly.'

Penny and Phillip helped Albert onto a chair, avoiding the sofa and easy chair in the room that they knew would be too low for him. Once he was settled, they then found a place for themselves.

'Looks nice enough from the outside, Uncle Albert. What do you think?' asked Phillip. 'The flower borders have been kept nice and I think that's always a good sign. The reviews are all good too, from what we can make out.'

'Looks fine and dandy to me,' replied Albert. Deep down all he wanted to do was get the whole thing sorted – to get settled.

'You can come through now,' said the woman who had first met them.

When they were ushered into the room, they could see that three seats had already been arranged in front of a desk at which a woman, whom they presumed to be of African descent, was seated. However, rather than remaining at her desk, she came round to their side and, extending her hand, greeted each of them warmly. Then, instead of returning to her seat behind the desk, she went over to a corner of the room and brought a chair so she could join them. If asked later, they would not have been able to express why, but they felt immediately put at ease by this gesture.

'Well, now, let me welcome you personally, although I assume that Mrs Campbell has already done that – the lady that met you at the door. My name is Mrs Addo – Mawusi Addo – and I am the one who will be chatting over things with you today. I should at first let you know that this is not the place where I normally work. I am on the staff of a home within the same group, near Cheltenham. I'm just here temporarily.'

Phillip, Penny and Albert nodded to indicate that they understood, and Mawusi continued.

'Basically, my role today is to take you on a tour of the place, but we won't be doing that until I have answered any questions that you may have. And I want to say at the outset that you are free to ask me anything, however trivial it might seem. It's often the little things that make the difference between a place being right for our guests, or unsuitable. I know you will have read the brochure about us, but there is nothing like seeing a place for yourself, is there? Also, when we have done the tour, we'll come back here before you go, just in case any questions may have arisen as we went round that still need clarification.'

'That's thoughtful of you,' said Penny.

'Thank you. The last thing we want is that on the way home, you say to one another, "Do you know, I wish that we had asked …" Before I hand over to you for questions,' said Mawusi, as she opened the file on her desk, 'can I just check over the preliminary paperwork that you have sent us? Obviously, the main application will come later, in the event that Mr Porter decides to become a guest here, but I just need to check that I've got all that I need in terms of personal details and medical history and things like that. I notice here, Mr Porter, that although you have been retired for some time, for most of your life you were a minister of religion, is that correct?'

'Yes, indeed,' answered Albert.

Everyone realised that this was the first time that he had spoken. 'Virtually all my working life, actually.'

'Should I address you as Mr Porter or Reverend Porter? Which would you prefer?'

'Oh, Albert will be fine. I am quite happy with that.'

'I am a Christian too, Albert,' said Mawusi, smiling across at him, 'and I notice that although you have lived in Scotland for almost twelve years now, you actually lived not too far from where I currently live in Cheltenham. Have I got that right as well?'

'You have indeed,' responded Albert.

It was so nice to have someone addressing questions to him directly. He had noticed as he had grown older that so many people talked to people of his age through anyone who happened to be with him. It was the old 'Does he take sugar?' syndrome. He warmed to the fact that this lady did not assume that because his body was frail, his mind was somehow frail too.

Phillip, Penny and Albert all had questions and, over the best part of an hour, Mawusi answered them comprehensively, concisely and with patience. In fact, there was more than one occasion when Albert asked the same question that he had asked only minutes earlier, but no one felt the need to point that out to him.

When everyone was satisfied that everything that they could think of had been covered, Mawusi pointed to the door, indicating that it was now time to take the tour.

'Just before we set off,' said Mawusi, 'let me outline where we will be going. As you will have seen from the outside, Caledonian Mews is a two-storey property. On the ground floor, where we will go first, is the reception area that you will have seen, the communal lounge and the eating area, together with a small number of offices that our staff use. I would also like you to see the grounds; they are beautiful in the summer, but it's a bit cold out there today. I don't think,' she added, smiling, 'that you want too much of a hike today, do you, Albert?'

Albert smiled gratefully in response to the rhetorical question.

'On the second floor are the bedrooms and they differ in size. Some are for couples. We have a number of husbands and wives among our guests. And some, of course, are for single occupancy. These occupy most of the bedroom areas. Oh, and one more thing – you'll be pleased to know that there is a lift to the second floor!'

The tour was completed within the hour and, as arranged, everyone met back in the office occupied by Mawusi. There had been no more questions on either side, and so all that was left was for Mawusi to bring the interview to a close.

'So where do we go from here? I can say right away that for our part, Albert, you are just the kind of guest that we love to have here, and we would be thrilled if you were to make this your new home. However, I know that we've given you a lot to think about, and so, what happens now is that we would like you to give the matter some further consideration – and you must take as long as you think you need – and then get back to us. How does that sound to you?'

'It sounds good,' answered Albert.

'Yes, Mrs Addo,' added Penny. 'We certainly will get back to you, and thank you so much for the time that you've given us.'

'Exactly so,' said Phillip. 'We obviously need to talk everything through with our uncle here, but I don't think it will take us too long to at least come to a decision one way or another. How would it sound if we pencilled in a date for two weeks' time? If for any reason we decide not to proceed, then we will let you know straight away. If, however, we feel that it is right to proceed, at least we will have a date in the diary.'

'That sounds absolutely perfect as far as I'm concerned,' answered Mawusi and, addressing Albert, she added, 'Albert, we would love to have you here with us so much that if you would like to come and stay with us for a couple of days, to try us out, I would love you to do so, and there would be no charge to you at all for that.'

Albert expressed his appreciation and, with handshakes all round, three people left Caledonian Mews believing that their time there had been well spent.

'So what did you think, Uncle Albert?' asked Phillip, once they had settled him back in the annex. 'How did it compare with what you've already seen?'

'I think it would be just right,' Albert answered.

'Are you absolutely sure?' said Phillip. 'How about taking Mrs Addo up on her offer to stay there for a couple of days?'

'I don't think so,' Albert replied. 'I think I can judge a good place when I see it. I'll be happy to move in as soon as you are ready to arrange it.'

'Really, Uncle?' added Penny. 'It's a very big decision, you know.'

'I do know, but I am totally sure,' replied Albert. 'You two really have to stop worrying about me!'

'I don't think that will ever happen,' said Penny, hugging him. 'We love you too much.'

The date for making a decision had been set for the middle of the month. Phillip had phoned Mawusi a few days earlier to confirm that Albert would like a place there. She had expressed great delight in hearing the news.

'You realise that he doesn't have to come to the next meeting unless he wants to,' she had said. 'I see from the paperwork in the file that he has given you the power of attorney, so you have all the authority you need to act on his behalf, if that is what you prefer.'

Phillip had answered that he realised that, but added that his uncle had said that he wanted to come nevertheless.

Mawusi had replied that she would love to see him, and now the day had arrived.

There was almost thirty minutes before the meeting and so Mawusi lifted the file from the admissions folder to refresh her memory on the salient facts and, as she did so, she stared at the name on the front of it with absolute amazement.

'It couldn't be. No, it couldn't be,' she kept repeating to herself. 'Surely not!'

It had been the label on the file that had stopped her in her tracks.

She looked at her watch and realised she now had just twenty minutes. She picked up the phone and dialled her home number.

'Come on, come on,' she said to the mouthpiece. 'Please be in!'

On the second ring a voice said, 'Hello, Kwame Addo.'

'Kwame, thank goodness you're there. Is the Bible on the coffee table where it normally is?'

'Of course it is,' replied Kwame. 'We rarely move it except to read it. You know that. Mawusi, are you alright? You sound in a terrible state.'

'I'm fine,' responded Mawusi. 'It's just that I need you to do something for me right away, if you would.'

'Of course,' said Kwame. 'What do you want?'

'I want you to bring the Bible to the phone and turn to the back pages. Not to the text, but to the white sheets at the back.'

There was a brief pause before Kwame got back.

'OK, I've got them. What now?'

'Can you find the strange cryptic sentence that has puzzled us for so long?'

'Yes,' said Kwame. 'I've got it here.'

'What does it say then? Read it out to me,' said Mawusi impatiently, looking at her watch.

Kwame read it out: 'A porter points to the entrance that leads the way to God.'

'That's what I thought it said,' responded Mawusi, looking at the name on the file that read 'A Porter'. 'It wasn't a concierge like Jack Troughton had thought. It was a porter.'

'What on earth are you talking about, Mawusi?' asked Kwame. 'And anyway, who is Jack Troughton?'

'I'll tell you tomorrow when I get home,' said Mawusi, glancing at her watch again. There were ten minutes to go.

'Now I need to you to turn to John's Gospel and read out chapter 10, verse 9.'

There was another pause, followed this time by a rustling sound and then Kwame read the following:

> I am the door: by me if any man enter in, he shall be
> saved, and shall go in and out, and find pasture.

'I don't believe it!' exclaimed Mawusi. I know what John 14:6 says, but read it anyway so I can be sure.'

Kwame read it out of the old King James Bible:

> Jesus saith unto him, I am the way, the truth, and the life:
> no man cometh unto the Father, but by me.

'Kwame, we've solved it! We've worked out the clue,' said Mawusi, 'but what is more, I think I have found the person who planted the Bibles.'

'You've what?' asked Kwame.

There was a knock at the door.

'Look, I have to go now,' said Mawusi. 'I'll tell you tomorrow.'

'Oh I'm sorry, Mrs Addo. I didn't realise you were on the phone. Shall I come back later?' said the person who had knocked.

'No, it's perfectly alright, Mrs Campbell. I've finished now anyway,' said Mawusi. 'Please bring in our friends.'

When Phillip, Penny and Albert came into the room, they occupied the same seats that they had taken two weeks earlier. Mawusi did not come around the desk to join them this time.

'Well, it's lovely to see you all again, and especially you, Albert,' Mawusi began. 'I'm so delighted that you will be joining us here at Caledonian Mews. I say "us" but, of course, as I may have mentioned to you last time, I am only here temporarily. In fact, today is my last day. However, before you leave I will be introducing you to Mrs Julia MacKenzie, who is the main person in charge here, and for whom I have been standing in for a while. She is so looking forward to meeting you and I know that you will love her. I plan to be visiting this location a number of times over the coming year, though, and you can be sure I will always be dropping by to see you.'

Mawusi looked across at this dear old man, who she thought appeared even more frail than he did on the previous occasion that she had seen him. Could this really be the person who was responsible for such a massive change in her and Kwame's lives? Perhaps she had got it wrong. She had unravelled the clue at the back of the Bible, but that didn't mean that this was the very person she had wanted to meet but had concluded it would be impossible to. Should she ask, or should she not?

It did not take very long to complete the necessary formalities and, when these had been concluded, she phoned though to see if Julia MacKenzie was free. A couple of minutes later she had joined them in the room, and everyone seemed to get on very well. The whole admission process had gone smoothly from start to finish. It was the first time she had done one of these on her own, and she could see the wisdom that Maureen Stibbes had had in suggesting that she get some experience outside her normal comfort zone.

As they made their way across the corridor to the front doors, and had watched Julia MacKenzie veering off in the direction of the office she occupied, Mawusi made her decision.

'I wonder if I might ask you a question, Albert?' she began, hesitantly.

She could see that Albert, Penny and Phillip were all thinking the same thing at the same time: was there a snag, something that had been overlooked? Was there going to be a problem, when everything had seemed to go so well?

They had paused in their journey towards the entrance and seemed a little concerned when Mawusi indicated they might occupy some chairs that had been placed in the vicinity of the reception desk.

Everyone sat down and waited for her to continue.

'Albert, this may sound a very silly question but, about twelve years ago, did you leave some Bibles around various locations in the Cheltenham area?'

There was a long silence. Penny looked confused, and it was clear that she had thought it a very odd question indeed. Phillip seemed puzzled, but not confused. Albert was sitting very still, but his breathing had become noticeably more rapid. He steadied himself and, rather than addressing Mawusi, spoke to Phillip.

'Phillip, do you remember the day when you came to help me clear out my house in preparation for coming to your home? I think you were to go on to Oxford.' And then turning to Mawusi, he said, 'You see, my short-term memory continually fails me, but my long-term memory is as sharp as a pin.'

He then turned back to Phillip, in anticipation of his reply.

'Of course I do,' responded Phillip.

'And do you remember clearing out the loft and coming across a box in which Annie, my beloved hoarder, had stored some Bibles?'

'I do indeed, now you mention it,' confirmed Phillip. 'In fact, if I'm right, you were in something of a quandary, Uncle, as to what you should do with them, if I remember.'

'That's right, Phillip, I was indeed. And that is the reason why, later in the day, I transferred them to a carrier bag and took them with me into Cheltenham. However, before I did so, I prayed over the small stack that had been my companions throughout my ministry and asked God to use them – should it be His will to do so.'

Mawusi left her seat, squatted down in front of the old man and took his two hands in hers. Looking into his eyes, she said, 'Albert, I was one of the people who picked up one of your Bibles and as a result of that I became a Christian and, not only that, my husband did too.'

Albert's mouth opened in surprise and his eyes grew slowly more moist.

'Is that right, Mrs Addo? Oh, that is such wonderful news. Just to think, so many years later, I would get to meet you. What a wonderful answer to prayer, and what news for someone like me at my time of life to hear.'

'And that's not all, Albert,' continued Mawusi. 'By the way, please call me Mawusi, as I think we are going to be great friends from now on. I have even better news for you than that.'

Phillip and Penny sat silent in stunned amazement. Mawusi was sensitive in regard to the shock this might prove to be for Albert, and so waited a moment or two before continuing.

'Albert, you are going to find it hard to believe this, but by an amazing set of circumstances, I have come into contact with someone else who picked up one of your Bibles, and he became a Christian as well.'

Albert pulled himself back in his chair, stunned and visibly moved by what he was hearing.

'And there is even more,' went on Mawusi.

'Not more than this,' gasped Albert. 'Already this is far beyond anything I could have imagined or hoped for. What more than this could there possibly be?'

'Well,' said Mawusi softly, and still clasping his hands tightly, 'through this man I know of a third person who picked up another of your Bibles, I think it was in Imperial Gardens …'

Albert was nodding as she spoke.

'She became a Christian, but sadly died. Unfortunately, I don't know the details. Anyway, before she passed away she led the man who was to be her husband to the Lord. What I am saying, Albert, is that I know of at least five people who have come to faith as a result of what you did that day.'

Mawusi released her grasp on Albert's hands, rose to her feet, and stepped back. The old man's head was bowed and he was quietly sobbing. No one sought to interrupt him. Phillip and Penny simply sat on either side of him, a hand laid on each shoulder. Mawusi looked on silently, considering this a holy moment.

After a short while, when Albert had had a chance to compose himself, he slowly stood to his feet and approached Mawusi with open arms. Mawusi stepped forward and warmly embraced the frail old man. Phillip and Penny thanked her for what she had said, and the joy and happiness she had brought to Albert by sharing such news. Then, promising to keep in touch, the three of them waved goodbye and headed in the direction of the car park.

Mawusi went back to her office and couldn't wait to phone Simon and tell him the story. He listened to the account in an amazement bordering on disbelief. He asked Mawusi to hold the phone for a moment and, when she did, she wondered if there was something wrong with the line as he had been away for so long. But eventually Simon came back.

'Mawusi, I'm sorry to have kept you waiting so long. It's just that I've got Jack in the room with me and I was telling him what you have just told me. As you can imagine, he's as staggered and overjoyed as I am. The reason I kept you waiting is that we were talking … and I know that this is a long shot and you must say no if this can't be done … but how far do you live from the M5? I'll tell you why – Jack and I are travelling south to an appointment this Saturday and wondered if we could break the journey and get to meet you and your husband.'

'Well, let me think,' pondered Mawusi. 'I'm in Scotland at the moment.'

'Oh, I'm sorry,' responded Simon. 'That won't work, then.'

'No, it's OK, we can make it happen. I travel home tomorrow and I can phone Kwame to make sure that he is free. We're just three miles from junction 10, so finding us won't be a problem for you. It would be absolutely wonderful if we could all meet. What time were you thinking of?'

There was another pause, and Mawusi assumed he was consulting Jack.

'Would 2.30 work for you? I'm afraid we won't be able to stay long – two hours max. We'll be driving on to an appointment.'

'2.30 would be good,' replied Mawusi. 'I'll phone Kwame and, unless you hear back from me by return, the date will be fixed.'

'That's awesome,' replied Simon. 'Jack and I can't wait to meet you.'

On her first day back at Cotswold Mews, Mawusi's first port of call was to update Maureen on her time away – something that was to take up most of the morning. This meant that she didn't get to see Sasha until the lunch break and, as they met, Elena enfolded her in a huge hug.

'I missed you, stranger. How was Scotland?'

'I've missed you too, missed you loads, and I've got so much to tell you,' responded Mawusi.

'Well, I know you are busy today, but we've both got the weekend off. How about we meet for lunch somewhere? I know you and Kwame will be at church on Sunday, so how about we meet Saturday – go shopping or something?'

Mawusi thought for a moment and then said, 'Saturday isn't going to be easy, we've got some people coming round, but listen … I'm just thinking, they won't be with us until half past two. You could come for lunch if you like, or late morning, and we'll have plenty of time together. If you wanted to go shopping, though, I'm afraid that wouldn't work.'

'No, that will be fine,' said Elena. 'I can make it for lunch if that's OK – the main thing is catching up. Not a lot has happened with me, but I can't wait to hear how you got on in Scotland. I'm keen to hear if their place is much different from ours as well.'

'That's settled, then,' confirmed Mawusi.

The day arrived and, once the two women had settled down with a coffee, it was Elena who spoke first.

'How did it all go? I bet Kwame missed you.'

'I missed him too,' said Mawusi. 'He's popped out for a while leaving us to talk, I suppose, but he'll be back later when the people come.'

'Do I know them?' asked Elena.

'You know one of them for sure. You were the connection. You don't know his friend, though.'

'You've lost me now,' said Elena. 'What on earth are you talking about?'

'One of them is Simon – you know, the man whose card you gave me. The man who became a Christian, like Kwame and I did, because I found a Bible in Cheltenham. The guy who will be with him – you won't believe this – is his friend whose wife also found a Bible! I know, it's crazy, isn't it? What are the chances?'

'What are the chances?' responded Elena. 'It's ridiculous. That can't be true!'

'It is true, honestly, but that's not the end of it,' said Mawusi. 'You know I said that when I was in Scotland I was dealing with stuff that I didn't deal with here?'

Elena nodded.

'Well, wait for this, I was handling admissions and I met this prospective resident, Sasha … he turned out to be the very person who left all the Bibles that we found!'

'I don't believe it! All this is too much of a coincidence. You read about this kind of thing in novels, but not in the real world!'

'Well, all I am telling you is that it is absolutely true. I'm as amazed as you are. What's more, I'm not sure if I told you about the cryptic sentence at the back of the Bible?'

With this, Mawusi reached across the coffee table, picked up the book and turned to the back pages. 'Look at this!' said Mawusi, pointing to the place.

Elena read: '"A porter points to the entrance that leads the way to God J109–146" … It doesn't make sense.'

'Well, I worked it out,' said Mawusi. 'I had been thinking of a porter being someone who works in a hotel or at a railway station, though you don't see many of them these days, do you?'

'That's what a porter is, though, isn't it?'

'That's what I thought, until I looked at the name on the file of a retired minister that I was interviewing for Caledonian Mews and saw that his name was Albert Porter – *A Porter*. Do you see?'

Elena looked unconvinced.

'When I realised he was a minister, I looked at the numbers. 109 didn't mean anything but when I saw 146, something clicked. I remember learning John 14:6 at Sunday school back in Accra, and of course with the capital J in front of it, I thought this could be the answer. I phoned Kwame and he confirmed that they both referred to passages from John's Gospel – a book in the New Testament.'

'But what do they mean?' asked Elena, still puzzled.

'Look,' continued Mawusi. 'We have already established that *A Porter* is the name of a man.'

'Well, *you* have,' interrupted Elena.

'Be patient,' insisted Mawusi. 'Let me read out the whole thing so you can see what I mean. Let's start with John 10 verse 9 and then read on to John 14 verse 6: " I am the door: by me if any man enter in, he shall be saved, and shall go in and out, and find pasture … Jesus saith unto him, I am the way, the truth, and the life: no man cometh unto the Father, but by me" … Now look at the clue again: "A porter points to the entrance that leads the way to God".'

'Wow,' exclaimed Elena. 'That really is amazing. So did you actually ask the man if he was the person who had planted the Bibles?'

'Yes, I did,' said Mawusi, 'and he confirmed that it was him. It was a very moving experience for us all, I can tell you.'

'And did you tell him about Simon?' asked Elena.

'Naturally, he was in tears by the end of it all, and so was I. I know you said it's all too much of a coincidence, but he didn't think so and, frankly, neither do I. I know this won't convince you, Sasha, but he told me that before he placed the Bibles around the town he prayed over them, and that's why all of these things happened as they did. A few moments ago it was you who used the word "planted", and you could not have chosen a better word. Those Bibles really were seeds and, the way I look at it, Albert Porter had watered them with his prayers, and we are the harvest.'

The two of them chatted on, mostly about the rest of Mawusi's time in Scotland, and then, as they were finishing lunch, they heard a sound at the front door. Both Mawusi and Elena looked at their watches. It was almost 2pm, and instinctively Elena got up to leave.

'This will be Kwame coming back,' said Mawusi. 'Look, Sasha, you need to at least say hello to Simon. It would almost be rude if you didn't, especially if I told him that you were here and had left.'

'But why would you have to tell him?' asked Elena. 'Why would he have to know?'

'He wouldn't I suppose, but why not just wait? It'll only be half an hour.'

Elena hugged Kwame as he entered the room.

'I bet you missed her while she was away,' Elena said, looking across at Mawusi.

'I most certainly did,' said Kwame, 'but we've made up for it.'

'Hey, too much information,' responded Elena, laughing.

The banter was then cut short by the ringing of the doorbell.

Mawusi looked at her watch.

'They must have arrived early, but it doesn't matter. As least you are going to get to say hi to Simon before you go, Sasha,' said Mawusi, with a smile.

Mawusi went to answer the door. Elena could hear a man's voice saying to Mawusi that it was good to meet her at last, followed by Mawusi responding with, 'I thought you said there were two of you,' and the man going on to tell her that his friend was just checking that he had locked the car.

As the tall, handsome man entered the room, he went up to the person he assumed would be Mawusi's husband and said, 'Hi, I'm Simon and I guess you must be Kwame. I've been so looking forward to meeting you. Thank you for making it possible at such short notice for us to catch up today.'

It was only then that he noticed Elena.

'Sasha, what a lovely surprise! I didn't expect to be seeing you today. How are you doing?'

'I'm good, but I'm not staying, I'm afraid. I was visiting Mawusi and she mentioned earlier that you would be coming, so I thought I would just say hello before I got on my way.'

At this they heard the front door, which had been left ajar, being closed and so they realised that Simon's friend had now arrived.

When the second man entered the room he moved first towards the person who, from the description he had of her from Simon, he believed to be Mawusi. He shook her hand and was just about to grip the hand of her husband, when everyone in the room heard a voice exclaim, 'Jack!'

For a moment, everyone, including Jack, stood in stunned silence. He had not expected to meet anyone in the room that he already knew, and then it was he who called out an involuntary, 'Elena!'

There was a confused silence.

Jack realised that he had addressed the woman he had not seen for more than two years by her real name. He had no idea what her cover name was, but presumably everyone in the room did. What damage had been done? There was no way to assess it – not at that moment anyway.

Simon wondered how on earth Jack had been able to recognise a woman he had only met himself a short time ago.

Mawusi and Kwame were stunned that this stranger, who they had never previously met, not only knew Sasha but was also referring to her with an entirely different name.

Elena was trying to think fast, but her brain buzzed like an overheated engine. The more she tried to process, the less progress she was able to make. Eventually, she came to the conclusion that as she was at the hub of this current confusion, she should be the one to provide some attempt at an explanation.

'Mawusi, Kwame, is it OK if we all sit down?' she began. 'There are some things that I need to explain.'

Mawusi nodded, her face mixed with confusion and apprehension at what might be coming next.

'I had no idea that this afternoon would turn out as it has,' Elena said, 'although, if I'm honest, I realised that something like this was bound to happen one day. I trust everyone in this room. I trust Jack because I know him – or at least I know his background, and that is good enough for me. I trust Simon because he is Jack's friend. I trust you and Kwame,' Elena addressed Mawusi, 'because you are my best friends. There is no easy way to begin to explain … well, not easy for me anyway, but I am going to do all that I can to put you in the picture.'

'A few years ago I was abducted into the people trafficking world with the idea that I would be forced to work in the sex industry.'

Mawusi's hands sprung to her mouth with a mixture of shock, pity and sympathy.

'Very early on I became pregnant, and on the way to the hospital I was involved in a traffic accident. It was the driver of the vehicle that I was in who was at fault. The driver of the other vehicle was Jack's wife, and tragically she died instantly as a result of the collision.'

All heads turned towards Jack.

'The baby I was carrying died as a result and, as I was a key witness, not just to the traffic accident but also to the operations of the organisation that controlled me, I was placed under a police guard at the hospital. When I was discharged I was put on a witness protection programme. I was supplied with a new name and, of course, new papers, and moved to the UK. The authorities, both in Estonia and over here, worked in tandem and so, for that reason, my residence is legal. Nothing about all this compromises you, Mawusi, or the people we work for. The cover name I was given was Sasha, but my real name, as you now know, is Elena.'

There was a short silence before Jack spoke.

'That was incredibly brave of you, Elena,' and then addressing everyone else, he continued, 'I'm sure that you all realise how sensitive this is. Because of Elena's testimony at the trial, virtually everyone connected with the organisation was arrested, charged and subsequently imprisoned – most of them for a very long time indeed. There is very little threat now to Elena, but part of the arrangement she had with the authorities was that she would not reveal her true identity. You have now been brought into this most important of all confidences. I am confident, however, that we can contain all this between ourselves.'

Elena's heart warmed to Jack as he spoke. He had evoked feelings in her that she had not experienced towards a man for a very long time. She could not remember any time in her life when someone had affirmed her to the degree that he had just done. Her father certainly never did, and her abusers had made it their constant goal to make her feel totally worthless. It might have taken courage to do what she did, and yes it had, but Jack had mentioned nothing of his part in it all. She had no idea what had happened to him since Tallinn, but she certainly knew what had happened there and his involvement in the prosecution; at no little risk to himself.

'What a week this has been,' said Mawusi. 'The revelation about the Bibles was one of the most joyous feelings I have experienced in my life. Listening to you right now – I don't know whether to call you Sasha or Elena – has been one of the saddest stories I have heard. I want you to know we love you all the more for sharing it,' and, turning to her husband for his assent, added, 'Isn't that right, Kwame?'

'It most certainly is,' came the immediate response.

Elena knew Kwame to be a quiet, humble and self-possessed man. He seemed a man of few words, so anything he might say now, when she had made herself so vulnerable and transparent, she knew she would particularly treasure.

'You know how much you mean to Mawusi,' Kwame began. 'I think she sees you more as a sister than a friend. We can't begin to imagine the pain you have been through, but one thing is certain, you need to know that we will always be there for you. Of course we'll keep what we have learned today between ourselves. Don't think for one moment that what we have learned today has put a wedge between us. On the contrary, I can assure you it has brought us much closer.'

The conversation lasted for some time before Elena explained that she really would need to leave. She said her goodbyes, accompanied by hugs and handshakes, and headed out of the room and along the hall. As she reached the door, she turned around to see that Jack had followed her out.

'You handled that amazingly well, Elena,' he said to her. 'I'm sorry that I used your name … '

'Please don't think about it,' Elena assured him. 'I'm almost relieved that it came out as it did, especially as far as Mawusi is concerned. I always felt that in some way I was deceiving her by not revealing who I really was. The thing that I will remember most about what happened in there is not the fact that I had to tell my story; it was the lack of condemnation and judgement I felt, and the presence of so much … acceptance and *love*.'

She hesitated. 'Because of my past, I've had real struggles thinking about God. But I'm wondering if you Christians just might have something after all.'

'I'm glad to hear that,' replied Jack, 'but listen, I hope this won't be the last time that we will see one another. I would like to keep in touch.'

'I would like that too,' responded Elena, warmly.

They exchanged telephone numbers and Elena continued to the door.

June 2008
Cumbernauld, Scotland

A lot of things happened in the months following the revelations in Kwame and Mawusi's home.

The charity continued to grow and develop, and Sarah and Beth had become increasingly involved in it. They had talked about, and sometimes worried about, the priority it had taken in Jack's life. But now they felt almost as committed to it as were Jack, Simon, Damian and Sue.

Aleksandra had developed to the stage where the team in Birmingham were talking about employing her part-time on staff, with a view to her becoming full-time if that was what she felt she wanted to do with her future.

Maureen Stibbes had taken early retirement, and Mawusi had taken over her role and was extremely happy in her job.

Jack and Elena had met on several occasions for dinner. Jack found that many of their conversations revolved around issues of spirituality, and they gave him flashbacks to those that he had had with Celia early in their relationship – though now he was taking with Elena the position that Celia had once taken with him.

Elena would not admit it to Jack yet but, in her heart of hearts, she knew that she was coming very close to committing her life to Christ. She worried, though, that if she did, this might accelerate the likelihood of her committing her life to Jack and she did not know if she was ready for that yet. She was intelligent enough, however, to realise that these were two entirely different issues, and was determined to take just one step at a time.

For Jack's part, his emotions were mixed. He was aware of his growing affection for Elena, but at the same he wondered if he was being disloyal to Celia's memory by allowing the relationship to progress further.

Albert had settled well into Caledonian Mews. He got on well with the staff and they all seemed to think the world of him. The other guests, or inmates, as he liked to jokingly refer to them, were fine too. He wasn't able to attend his church any more but got regular visits from his friends in the congregation. The minister had retired, and he had heard that a young pastor had been inducted, but he was yet to meet him.

On Thursday 19th June at 8am, Phillip was stacking the dishwasher when he was interrupted by the ringing of the home telephone. Looking at the clock on the wall, and wondering who could be phoning so early, he lifted the receiver to hear the voice of Julia MacKenzie on the line, asking if it was Phillip she was speaking to.

'Yes, Mrs MacKenzie, are you phoning about Albert?'

'I'm afraid I am, Phillip. He has had a very difficult night and the doctor has been called. I'm sorry to phone you so early, but …'

'Don't worry about that. We appreciate you getting in touch. How serious is it?'

'We won't know for sure until the doctor has had a look at him but, in my experience, I would have to say that the next twenty-four hours will be critical. He has been asking for you and has been talking about the church a good deal. It might be an idea to contact the priest or vicar or whatever …'

'We refer to him as a pastor. He's only just arrived and I don't think he has even met Uncle Albert yet, but I'll contact him and I have no doubt that he'll be along. It's his first appointment since leaving theological college, I believe, and he's new to everything.'

'Well, that's alright, then. I'll leave all that with you,' continued Julia MacKenzie. 'I imagine you will be dropping by …'

'Indeed,' replied Phillip. 'Penny and I should be there within the hour.'

Before replacing the receiver in the handset, Phillip dialled the number of the new minister who, hearing the news, assured him that he would get to Caledonian Mews that morning.

Phillip and Penny entered their uncle's room to find him in bed, his face parchment-white. Julia MacKenzie had come out of her office when she saw them arrive at the reception desk and informed them that the doctor had only just left. He too had formed the view that his patient would not have long to live.

'Uncle Albert,' said Penny gently, 'I'm here with Phillip. We hear you had a bad night.'

Albert opened his eyes and, as if reorientating himself in a place with which he was not familiar, scanned the room without moving his head for the source of the sound. When his eyes had focused on the two people who meant the most to him in the world, his dry lips moved into the approximation of a smile.

'Phillip and Penny,' he said, weakly. 'Thank you for coming in to see me. Isn't it strange? I've only been here such a short while and now I've been taken bad.'

Penny reached across to his bedside table and took hold of a tumbler of diluted orange juice that was there. She slowly moved it across towards Albert and offered it to his lips. He managed just a couple of sips and blinked his eyes, as if to indicate that he had had sufficient, but that he was grateful for the thought.

Phillip and Penny were struggling for what to say next. They didn't want to sound trite and certainly didn't want to trot out the kind of clichés that people always seemed to use at times like this. They loved and respected Albert far too much for that.

'That was amazing about the Bibles, wasn't it?' said Phillip, in an attempt to broach a subject that he knew would brighten him.

Albert appeared to pause a moment while he processed the question and then, seemingly having done so, moved his head forward in assent.

'The only problem was,' he responded in a faint voice, 'though it was so gratifying to hear about the three Bibles that were found, I left four, you know.'

'Well, you should be grateful for that at least,' said Phillip. 'Out of those three, if I remember rightly what Mrs Addo said, at least five people became Christians as a result.'

A smile creased Albert's face. 'Yes, that's wonderful, isn't it? What a thing to happen at the end of my ministry, and I certainly thank God for allowing me to be used in such a way.'

Just then, Phillip and Penny turned as they heard behind them the sound of the bedroom door being opened. It was Mrs MacKenzie and she was accompanied by a young man in his thirties.

'This is Pastor Saunders from the church,' she said by way of introduction.

The minister made his way in and, approaching Phillip and Penny with an outstretched hand, turned his head back in the direction of the door and said, 'Thank you, Mrs MacKenzie, I appreciate your help in conducting me to the room.' Then turning back to face Phillip and Penny, he said, 'Hello, I am Stephen Saunders, very pleased to meet you – and please do call me Stephen.'

Having greeted him, Penny bent down to Albert and said, 'Uncle, the new pastor has come to see you. Isn't that wonderful?'

Albert looked across and focused on the new visitor.

'Oh, how so very kind of you to come and visit me. You must be so busy after only so recently moving in.'

'Please don't mention it, Reverend Porter. Here I am just starting out in ministry and one of the first people I get to visit is someone who was a pastor before I was even born. It's a privilege for me to meet you, sir.'

'Well, first of all … I'm sorry, Stephen, I'm finding it hard to speak properly today … no more of the "Reverend", just call me Albert, everybody else does. Of course, I will want you to pray for me before you go but, to save me talking, why don't you tell me something about yourself and I'll just listen?'

'Alright, then … Albert,' Stephen began. 'I was born and brought up in a small village called Dinnington, not far from Sheffield. I don't come from a Christian family and never entered a church except when my parents took me to a wedding. Dinnington was a mining village many years ago, but there are no mines there now. When I left school I trained to become a mechanic and, when I qualified, worked for a car dealership in that role. I don't know what more to say, really, except that when I was nineteen I met the wonderful woman who is now my wife. We have two small children and well … here we are!'

'But if your background was not Christian and you trained as a mechanic,' enquired Penny with a quizzical look, 'how is that you are now a minister?'

'Oh, that's a long story and probably not for now,' said Stephen, looking across at Albert. It was obvious to all that, though hanging on every word, Albert was visibly tiring.

'Mrs MacKenzie suggested that I shouldn't be too long,' continued Stephen, looking knowingly at the couple next to him. 'Perhaps it would be good if I just prayed.'

'That fine,' responded Phillip, realising that Stephen was trying to be sensitive to the situation and knowing that he wanted him and Penny to have the maximum time together with their uncle. 'But at least finish the story for us before you do.'

The pastor looked across to Albert to ensure that he also wanted him to continue, and was met with a confirmatory smile.

'It all began on our honeymoon, actually. We were staying at a big hotel in the Cotswolds. It's in a picturesque village called Broadway. Sally, that's my wife, was in a nearby shop and I was sitting waiting for her at bench by a monument they call Broadway Cross. I looked across to my left and I saw an old Bible laying on the bench beside me ...'

The story was interrupted by a long sigh. They all looked towards the bed.

Albert had passed peacefully away.